Sleepless nights . . .

Jason woke in the middle of the night, drenched in sweat and filled with terror. The sound that had awakened him, the sound of his own scream, seemed to echo through the room. Beside him, Arethia was stroking his forehead, mumbling soft reassurances as she held him close.

It was the same dream, the one that had plagued him for days now, ever since his return from the raid into Kansas. He held a gun in his hand, one that he did not wish either to hold or to fire. But his finger was tightening on the trigger. Some power had claimed control of his hand, forcing him to squeeze the trigger, to squeeze and squeeze and squeeze . . . And the face below him, the face filled with fear and desperation, was his own.

BORDERLAND

BORDERLAND

GREG HUNT

PaperJacks LTD.

TORONTO   NEW YORK

AN ORIGINAL

PaperJacks

BORDERLAND

PaperJacks LTD

330 STEELCASE RD. E., MARKHAM, ONT. L3R 2M1
210 FIFTH AVE., NEW YORK, N.Y. 10010

First edition published December 1987

CDN. ISBN 0-7701-0828-8
US. ISBN 0-7701-0752-4
Copyright © 1987 by Greg Hunt
All rights reserved
Printed in the USA

To Daniel F. Hunt
I hope, at least in part, I'm living your dream.

March 1854

A barn owl called out in alarm as it swooped low through the trees. The heavy flapping of its wings shocked Jason Hartman suddenly awake. He dodged reflexly, and his hand dropped down to the grip of the cap-and-ball pistol he wore at his side, his heart thudding wildly the instant that it took to establish where he was and what had startled him awake.

"Just an old hoot owl, Ned," he said softly, as if his horse also needed a dose of reassurance.

It was the kind of pitch-black night that prompted a man to conjure up all sorts of things, as if danger lurked everywhere. No sensible man would attempt this, Jason thought, but he rode on, so tired now that it didn't seem to matter anymore whether he stopped to camp or simply slept in the saddle.

The road he was following, which was actually more of a trail than a real road, snaked through an oak forest. Only the instincts of his horse kept them headed in the right direction, and only his belief that there had to be something ahead, a settlement or a farm or even a roadside cabin, kept him going.

He had considered stopping for the night when a farmer outside Buckner offered to let him sleep in his barn. But since Independence was just a few miles away, he had decided to press on. What he had not figured on was how much the thickly forested hills and valleys would slow his progress or how treacherous the riding would be once darkness fell.

Even after the noise of the owl had faded, Jason couldn't rid himself of the edginess he now felt. The clop of Ned's hoofs and even the rhythmic creaking of his saddle seemed to herald his presence, and his skin tingled more from alerted senses than from the late-March chill, which seeped through his thick woolen shirt and heavy trousers.

He didn't know whether to trust the sense of danger he suddenly felt or to dismiss it as the aftereffect of being jolted awake. Although this part of western Missouri was fairly well settled now, he knew better than to believe that a man riding alone in the night on an isolated road was truly safe. And the thought of the seventeen hundred dollars in gold that he carried made him even more apprehensive.

It was times like this, when he was tired and hungry and assailed by loneliness because of his long separation from Arethia and the children, that he experienced the most serious doubts about his mission. A voice deep within him would argue that he should have been content with the small farm they had in western Virginia and that only an idiot would give it all up and strike out across the country on a fool's errand such as this one.

The gold, buried deep in the pack tied across the back of his saddle, had come from the sale of their farm, and it represented virtually every cent they had in the world. If anything happened to him, as well it might in a frontier region like this, not only would his family be deprived of a breadwinner, but they would also be homeless and destitute in an impoverished area where few people could afford the luxury of charity.

But they had agreed that it was a necessary risk, he reasoned. Arethia had been a full partner in all the decisions — selling the farm, moving to Missouri, Jason going on ahead and putting down some roots before the rest of them followed.

William's letters had helped, of course. His brother's reports of cheap, fertile land, of good markets for corn and beef and pork, of seemingly unlimited opportunities along the frontier, had been a strong catalyst in helping him decide to let go of the old and reach out for the new.

Deep in his heart, Jason still felt that he was doing the right thing, for his and Arethia's sake, and for the members of the next generation of the Hartman family, who should have the chance to grow up in a place where their opportunities in life were not limited by a split-rail fence that surrounded forty acres of stony, unproductive soil. But still there were times — when he thought about jostling one of the kids on his knee or rolling over in the night and feeling Arethia's body, warm and still, beside him — that he still wished he had never climbed on Ned's back and started the trip westward six weeks before.

The road crossed a small creek, then rose to follow the spine of a bush-covered ridge for a few hundred yards before descending again. Ahead loomed more woods, and suddenly Jason dreaded the idea of riding into them. He knew he had to stop soon. Both he and the horse were exhausted, and his apprehensions would only grow as his fatigue increased. He decided he would turn and ride into the brush, far enough to get him clear of the road, and sleep on the ground as he had done so many times during his journey. He was close to the end now, so close that the need to have the trip ended almost overwhelmed him — but then again, Independence would still be there in the morning.

Later Jason couldn't recall whether he spotted the small fire before or after he heard the voices of the men who stood around it. What he did remember was that he had reined in his horse abruptly.

The men appeared to be making no effort to conceal their presence, which seemed to indicate that they were not out to waylay strangers. They could be hunters, but about the only game men hunted in the middle of the night was coon, and he had not heard the bellow of coon dogs, as he surely would have. Or they could be travelers, just like him. But if so, why were they still awake?

He decided finally that there was no good reason to try and satisfy his curiosity about these strangers. They hadn't yet detected his presence, so the smartest plan would be to ride back a safe distance and get off the road for the rest of the night. He reached down and stroked the side of Ned's nose to keep him calm as he pulled on the reins to turn the horse around.

"No use turnin' back," a gruff voice said from the darkness, "Kansas ain't thataway."

Jason froze. Instinct told him not to go for the pistol. Judging by the commanding tone of the man's voice, he was certain to be armed, and Jason knew he made a target too big to miss. The brush at the side of the road rustled, and a dark shape moved into the open.

"Step down careful, unless you like the feel of double-ought buckshot splatterin' into your hide," the man said. Then he called out excitedly, "We got us another one, Judge!"

The talk around the fire stopped, and several men hurried up the road toward Jason and his captor, one of them carrying a lantern. As they neared, Jason could see by the nervous flicker of lamplight that all of them were armed with rifles and shotguns.

"I told you to get down, you bastard," the man beside Jason growled. He was so close now that Jason could make out the shape of the double-barreled shotgun he carried. Jason dropped Ned's reins and cautiously swung his leg over the saddle, being careful to keep both hands in plain sight as he slid to the ground. After he had been disarmed, the men examined him as if he were some rare breed of dangerous animal that they had just had the good fortune to corner and capture.

Taking his hat off, Jason ran his hand through his thick brown hair and waited. He couldn't imagine that he would appear to them to be anything more than what he was — a farmer, a man whose flop hat, faded garments, and scarred work boots said all there was to say about the simple country life he led. He stood just under six feet, with broad shoulders and thick, muscular arms that made him look powerful. Under other circumstances these men might have immediately noticed the open, good-natured expression that was common to his tanned, bearded features, but tonight that look was absent, replaced by a guarded, apprehensive scowl.

Jason, who remained quiet as his captors looked him over, studied the men around him. Most of them were dressed in simple work clothes much like Jason's own. The most noticeable exception was a tall, dignified man in his early forties wearing an expensive, if somewhat dusty, black suit and vest. He wore twin pearl-handled revolvers in holsters under his open jacket and carried a beautifully tooled shotgun that was as much a work of art as a lethal weapon. Jason guessed that this man was the 'judge.'

"We got a friend of yours over at the fire," one of

the other men said finally, "but don't be too surprised if he don't act glad to see you." Jason heard some of the others chuckle.

"I don't know what you want with me," Jason answered, "but it's not likely you have anybody I know over there. I'm not from around these parts." He was beginning to understand that he'd been mistaken for someone else and that if he didn't get the matter cleared up soon, he might be in for some serious trouble. He was about to try to explain who he was and what he was doing here when he noticed that one of the men already had a strap loose on the pack where his money was stashed and was at work on the second.

"Hey! Leave that alone!" Jason yelled and lunged forward.

Pain exploded inside his head as the steel butt plate of a shotgun collided with his temple. Reality swirled away in a blinding flash of white-hot agony as he slumped heavily to the ground.

He was vaguely aware of voices and movement around him. Consciousness was returning slowly, like water seeping through the base of a dam. It was accompanied by a pain in his head as sharp as any Jason had ever felt. He tried to move, only to find that his hands and feet were tightly bound. His mouth was stuffed with a foul-tasting piece of cloth, which was secured by a rag tied around his head.

". . . mercy on this pore, misguided sinner, as well as on these here brave men who is jus' doin' what they have ta . . ."

The voice was close. Jason fluttered his eyes open for a moment before the pain inside his head demanded that he close them again. A lean, bearded man was kneeling at his side. Something swung slowly in the shadows behind him. Others were moving about nearby.

". . . prob'ly got it at the Farley place. Folks always said Ol' Man Farley kept money hid about . . . "

". . . kin use his own horse to do it with . . ."

". . . an' iffen you see fit, Lawd, to turn him into fuel for the devil's infernal furnaces . . ."

". . . plumb wore out, an' a full day's work still to be done time I get home . . ."

". . . just leave 'em here after, I s'pose, like a warning to all the rest . . ."

". . . not much else to speak of, except the gold . . ."

". . . yore holy will be done. Amen. Okay, boys, he's had all the prayin' over he deserves, an' it looks like he's comin' around. String 'im up!"

Stunned by the announcement of his fate, Jason struggled clumsily and uselessly against his bonds, gagging on the wad of cloth as he tried desperately to find some way to communicate to these men what a terrible mistake they were making. Images flashed through his throbbing head — his wife's face, his children huddled by a muddy roadside waving forlornly as he rode away, a gaunt scarecrow in worn broadcloth invoking God's mercy on his soul, an apparition floating four feet above the ground, swinging slowly in the nighttime breeze . . .

Suddenly hands gripped his arms and raised him to his feet. He struggled again, but his limbs seemed to have very little strength in them, and after a fist landed in his midsection, he was unable to fight back at all.

Ned was standing a few feet away, and a hangman's noose dangled three feet above his saddle. Just beyond the horse, swinging by a second rope tied to the same limb, hung the limp form of a dead man, the "friend" his captors had mentioned earlier.

Jason's churning stomach produced a bitter clot of vomit that lodged in the back of his throat as he looked at the dead man's face and the bulging eyes, which seemed to Jason to stare in wonderment at this proof of its own mortality. I'll look just like that, Jason thought. In another minute, that will be my face.

They heaved Jason across the horse's back, then took one of his legs and moved it around until he was slumped in the saddle. Ned sidestepped nervously and had to be calmed and coaxed back under the noose. Too stunned and weak even to sit up, Jason tried to fall off, but his captors would not permit it. One of them stepped up in the stirrup beside him and began fitting the rope around his neck as two others held him upright.

He felt the coarse hemp bite into his neck as the thick knot was pulled tight. The stark, undeniable realization that he was about to die filled him more with wonder than terror, and all his senses began to come alive, as if to soak up a last draft of this world before he was dispatched to another. The faces of the men gathered around him came into sharp focus; their eyes filled with hatred, determination, and an impatience to be finished with this business. The smell of pine needles, wood smoke, and leather mingled in his nostrils. The saddle creaked as the man with his foot in the stirrup shifted his weight, and Ned huffed in irritation over the added burden.

Jason turned his head and looked at the man, whose face was inches from his own. It was an ordinary enough face, the kind you saw all your life and never took any notice of, but Jason studied it closely; it was the last face he would ever see.

"Shouldn't we take this gag out, Judge?" the man said, reaching uncertainly for the rag.

"If you do, he'll just go out blubberin' like the other one did," one of the men complained. "This is a hard 'nough business already without havin' to hear that again."

But a deep voice filled with authority said, "A man deserves to have his last say. It only seems fitting, even if all he wants to do is bawl or damn us for doing this to him. Take it off, Jonah." No one argued.

With the rag gone, Jason's mouth was as dry as dust and his throat was so tight that he wasn't sure he could get any words out. But finally he managed to rasp, "I don't know who you are or why you're doing this, but if there's an ounce of Christian feelings in any one of you, you'll at least get word to my brother William Hartman that I'm dead so he can let my family know."

For an instant no one spoke. The moment of stillness was so complete that when the fire popped and threw a spark across the clearing, the man beside Jason actually flinched with surprise. When Ned fidgeted and took a small step sideways, several hands flashed out quickly to grab the reins and hold him in place.

"Goddamn it, Jonah! Don't just hang there like a side of beef!" the judge barked. "Take that noose off and get him down!"

The steaming coffee was generously laced with corn liquor. It slid down Jason's throat like liquid fire, warming and relaxing him, easing the pain in his head and slowly banishing the shaking that had begun soon after they removed the noose and lowered him to the ground.

William, the brother whose name and reputation had saved his life a bare instant before the quirt struck Ned's flank and the rope snapped Jason's neck, was now stooped near the fire a few feet away, dividing his time between solicitous glances in Jason's direction and quiet conversation with the judge, who, it turned out, was named Thomas Jefferson Younger.

They were letting him alone, allowing him to grow accustomed to the fact that he was still of this world and wasn't likely to leave it for some time yet.

William and half a dozen other men had reached the roadside camp only a short time after Jason was released. He would not have been there in time to save his brother's life had Jason not been allowed to utter that last, desperate appeal, but the timing was such that, Jason decided morbidly, he might have been able to witness the final twitch and shudder.

Most of the other men stood in groups of two and three at the fringes of the firelight. Jason could feel their eyes on him, but was still too numb to respond to them in any way.

Finally, Jason slugged down the remainder of the dark liquid and set the cup on the ground in front of him. Then he looked up, and his gaze met William's squarely. It had been six years, maybe seven, since they laid eyes on one another.

"Better?" William asked gently.

"Some," Jason said slowly. "At least, the shakes are over, but my head still hurts like hell." He raised his hand to the hasty bandage someone had made for him by ripping up his only spare shirt and tying it around his head. The blood had soaked through, but the flow had finally stopped.

"It's been a bad night all around, little brother," William told him soberly, "a night none of us are apt to forget for a long time to come."

"I can't argue with that."

"But this isn't all of it," William said. "What happened here, what almost happened to you, is just a part of all that's gone on tonight."

His brother continued. "Earlier tonight, about four hours ago, a band of men attacked the home of one our neighbors, the Farleys." William paused. "They gunned Paul Farley down in his front yard, and near as we can tell, they burned the house down on his wife, Liza. Then they gathered up all the Farley niggers, torched the rest of the buildings, and headed west, toward Kansas.

"I live closest to the Farley place, so I was the first to spread the alarm, and within less than an hour we had the men you see here assembled and were on the trail of the bastards."

"Who were these men, William?" Jason asked.

"The same bastards that have been stirring up trouble in these parts for the past six months," his brother growled. "They're abolitionist trash from over on the Kansas side."

"But they didn't get away with it this time," Judge Younger broke in. "We got three of them, including that bastard over there." Then, as Jason's glance roamed to the dead man, whose body still swung from the tree limb nearby, the judge seemed to read his thoughts and added, "We were sure about him. He had Paul Farley's rifle strapped across the back of his saddle when we caught up with him."

"The raiders split up after they left the Farley place," William said, "so we split our group up as well. The judge led one group south, and I took another one west. The men my group was after were driving the Farleys' livestock with them, so we didn't have much trouble catching up with them. We came onto them just as they were starting to cross the river. We shot two of them dead, but the others got away from us in the darkness."

"I don't suppose we would have caught any of the second bunch," Younger added, "but when this fellow's horse went lame, he didn't have sense enough to get off the road and hide. Then when you showed up, we figured you were a friend of his that had come back to look for him."

"You figured," Jason said dully, looking hard at Younger.

"None of us are particularly proud of this night's work," William said quickly. "We're not gunfighters and trained killers. We're farmers and shopkeepers and tradesmen. But when our homes and families and friends are attacked and the little bit of law that's scattered around can't do us any good, what else can we do but strike back?"

Jason didn't feel that William's explanation was adequate as an excuse for his near execution, but he was just too tired and battered to make an issue of it now. As it was, he was struggling just to keep his eyes open.

Seeing that his brother was about to collapse, William

said, "I think tomorrow might be a better time to talk more about this. My place is only about an hour's ride from here. Do you think you can make it that far, Jason?"

"I can make it," Jason said, forcing his leaden limbs to perform once more as he rose to his feet. As if his movement were a signal, suddenly everyone began preparing to leave. There was a brief discussion about whether the corpse of the dead abolitionist should be left hanging where it was, but finally a couple of men cut the body down and tied it across a horse.

Someone had stacked Jason's gear near where Ned was tethered. Before strapping the pack on, he loosened the straps and reached inside to where his seventeen hundred dollars had been, but the pouch filled with gold coins was gone.

"William!" he called out sharply, loud enough to catch everyone's attention. "Some bastard's stolen my money!"

Every man there stopped what he was doing and looked over at him, but for a moment no one spoke. Jason turned so his back was to the dark woods and his gaze could rake the party of men before him.

"Big brother, your friends might have to string me up yet for what I plan to do if I don't get that gold back pretty quick," Jason snarled. They had returned his pistol to him earlier, and he was in no mood to let it sit idle in its holster again if its services were needed. That money was his family's future.

"Uh, Reverend Septin," Judge Younger said finally, "I believe you were holding the gold for safekeeping, weren't you?"

Jason's eyes met those of the preacher who had, less than an hour before, so glibly offered his soul as kindling for the devil's furnaces. Septin was a tall, gangling man of about thirty-five, with skinny arms and legs that stuck out like broomsticks from the sleeves and cuffs of his disheveled brown suit. His head sat atop an overly long neck, like a gourd on a fence post, and the pale flesh of his bearded face was stretched taut across his rawboned features. His hair looked as if it had recently been cropped with a dull skinning knife, and his eyes protruded from his skull with unnerving intensity.

Without a word, Jason held his hand out, and the expression on his face made it clear that his threat included men of the cloth. Septin fumbled in the pocket of his frayed suit coat and produced the pouch. Even now his hesitancy to part with that much money was so obvious that it fanned Jason's anger anew.

"It was in my mind to give it to the Widder Farley iffen the Lawd seed fit to spare her from that fire," the preacher stammered as he handed the pouch over. "An' after all that happened, I clean forgot to give it back."

"Well, I'm sorry for the lady," Jason said sternly, "but this money is going to put a roof over the heads of my wife and family, and I won't let anything or anybody stand in the way of that."

William Hartman started the buggy team out of the oak grove in front of the small country church and pointed them down the road toward his farm. Jason settled back on the seat beside him, glad to finally be out from under the unabashed, slack-jawed scrutiny of the assembled country folk who were destined to be his new neighbors.

Now, two days after the long night of violence, the community had gathered for the funeral of Paul and Liza Farley. Boone Septin had presided over the affair, dispatching the aged couple to the next world with an abundance of morose oratory and a flood of furious condemnations for the cowardly curs who had stolen their lives from them. To Jason, who had good reason to hold the backwoods parson in low esteem, it seemed that Septin had worked the congregation like a sideshow barker, but he also had to afford the man a grudging degree of respect for his ability to bring a tear to the driest eye and yank emotions from the sternest heart.

All who filed out of the church that morning to walk the short distance to the nearby graveyard did so with the feeling, at least for the time being, that dear Paul and Liza must have been the finest, kindest, most loving man and woman ever to live in the state of Missouri and that the men who struck them down must be creatures more closely akin to Eden's serpent than to human beings.

But the conversations that had taken place after the funeral had been more telling.

Back in Virginia, Jason had been aware of the growing tensions along the Kansas-Missouri border over the subject of slavery. Even now debate was raging in the Congress over the Kansas-Nebraska Act, which would permit the residents of Kansas territory to determine whether they wished to enter the Union as a slave state or a free one, and the newspapers carried frequent accounts of the growing push by both factions to pack the territory with their own supporters before the bill passed and voting time arrived.

But somehow, before coming here, Jason had believed that because he owned no slaves and had little real interest in the slavery question, he could keep himself apart from the trouble. Although he had grown up in a slave state, he had no real interest in who lived in Kansas or whether or not they permitted the South's peculiar institution to exist within its borders.

He was moving to Missouri, not Kansas, and whatever he accomplished and accumulated in his new home would be the result of his own labors. Let others, like his brother, dream of empires built on the hard work of gangs of sweating blacks if they chose to do so. He would be content to house and clothe and feed his family decently and to raise his children into honest, hard-working, God-fearing men and women.

But Jason was learning fast that any man who chose to remain neutral would be eyed with increasing disapproval and distrust by those slaveholding Missourians who viewed the possibility of a free Kansas as a definite threat to their safety and the security of their property, human and otherwise.

In the snatches of conversation Jason was privy to, he heard the words *sound on the goose* used repeatedly. During the long day before, William had explained that the phrase indicated a man who supported slavery and, by inference, a man who knew he might have to fight to support slavery.

Being sound on the goose, William implied in none-too-subtle terms, spelled acceptance to a newcomer like Jason who planned to establish himself here in west-central Missouri. And being otherwise could, under the right conditions, stir up more trouble than any sensible man would want to take on.

Jason had said little in response to his brother's warnings, but William's words had done little to change his mind. Why should it? Jason thought, with a surge of defiance. Why should he suddenly become so eager to take up arms and defend the rights of these people to own their slaves when only two days before they themselves had come within a breath of hanging him, almost offhandedly, because he had been caught on the wrong road at the wrong time?

It wasn't his business, Jason decided, and already he was beginning to anticipate the time when he could settle on his own place and shut himself off, as thoroughly as might be possible under the present circumstances, from this business of slavery and all the scheming and intrigue that invariably accompanied it.

But after the funeral the brothers managed to avoid discussing local politics. Instead, they discussed the richness and productivity of the land and all the opportunities available to any man willing to dedicate himself to growing and prospering here along the frontier.

William's own achievements were evidence enough of what could be done. He had come to this area only five years before, after fighting in the Mexican War with a tough, gallant band of local volunteers called Doniphan's Raiders. Starting out with a forty-acre farm and a single slave, both heavily mortgaged, he had since increased his holding to six hundred acres and a dozen stout black field hands.

Of course, Jason had no illusions that he could do as well in the same amount of time, but he was certain nonetheless that his family's lot would drastically improve once they were all settled here.

When they reached the turnoff to William's farm, he drove on past instead of turning in.

"As long as we're out and about," William suggested, "I thought I'd show you a piece of property which might be suitable for you and Arethia."

Jason was all for that. The previous day he and William had discussed what might be available for the down-payment money Jason could provide. The one big advantage that Jason would have in acquiring available acreage, William explained, was that at this particular time a few families were beginning to move out of the area. Some were leaving to try their hand in Kansas, and a sprinkling of others ("panicky sheep," William had called them) were being frightened off by the threat of violence over the slavery issue. But circumstances made the time right for buying good land at reasonable prices.

It all sounded very promising, and now that they were actually going out to look at property, Jason felt his enthusiasm surging. Whatever doubts he might have had about the prospects in Missouri faded as he gazed at the broad fields, ready for planting, which stretched away on both sides of the wagon road.

After going another mile on the main road, William turned left onto a narrower lane that led through a patch of woods before emerging into open country once more.

"I've got a place in mind which would be perfect for you," William told him, "and it's just come available."

"Is this part of it?" Jason asked, indicating the freshly turned fields on both sides of the road.

"Yes, it it," William replied. "It surveyed out at one hundred forty acres. Eighty are cleared, and as you can see, most of that is already broken and ready for spring planting. The rest is in virgin timber."

"I like what I see, but I can't afford that much land, William," Jason protested. "Don't forget, the seventeen hundred dollars I brought with me can't all go for land. Some of it has to get my family through the next few months, until the first crop comes in."

"It might not cost you as much as you think, little brother," William said. "You see, there's no house or out-buildings on the place. We'd have to build those before your family gets here." A sly grin spread across his face, causing Jason to wonder what his brother had yet to explain to him.

"But still, at any fair market price —" Jason began.

At last, William played his trump card. "If you want the farm, it's yours, Jason," he announced grandly. "Today. Right now. I can guarantee it, because you'll be buying it from me!"

Jason was struck dumb by the announcement. Until this very moment, William had given him no indication that he had any land for sale or that whatever Jason might be able to buy would be in such good condition. As far as the house was concerned, there was no major problem. If the land had timber, as William had said it did, he could build a place himself.

This farm was his for the taking! Today! Right now!

"I don't know what to say, William," Jason stammered. "If you . . . I mean, how . . ."

"We'll get into the details later," William told him magnanimously. "There's no problem with that, I assure you. So for now just take it all in."

Jason did just that. He asked William to stop the wagon, then climbed down and walked a few feet into a field.

The loose, dark soil gave beneath his footsteps, and there was no sign of grass or weeds. It must have been plowed very recently. He picked up a bit of dirt and put it in his mouth, tasting and testing it as his father had taught him to do.

It was good land, rich and fertile, and at that moment he was more than ready to supply whatever amount of hard work and careful attention it might require to produce bountiful, and profitable, crops for years to come.

When he returned to the wagon and climbed up on the seat, his brother could tell by the broad smile on his face how pleased Jason was.

As he popped the reins lightly across the backs of the horses, William said, "You know, little brother, there's a big difference, a basic difference, between you and me. I farm for profit. The only reason I do it is because it's the best way I know to make money."

"Well, I don't exactly have any strong objections to making money either, William," Jason protested lightly.

"I know, but at the heart of things, you do it because you love it. You're just like our old man in that way. It's in your blood. Seeing you out there rolling that dirt around in your mouth like it was a spoonful of honey, I could tell. That's what he'd do too, right off."

Jason chuckled.

They rode on in silence for a little while, then Jason turned to his brother and announced, "Well, William, I'm sure you realize that I want the place, so let's talk details now."

"I guess it's time," William agreed. "Last fall the man who owned this place broke a hip at harvest time, and he sent word to me that he needed some help getting his crop of corn and tobacco in, or it would end up rotting in the fields. At the time my slaves were busy with my own crop, and I couldn't spare any of them, so the best I could do was hire a crew and get them over here to bring the crop in. He already owed me four hundred dollars from the previous spring, and paying for his harvesting ran the debt up even more. I knew he was no great hand at managing money, and by that time I was beginning to get pretty nervous about my unsecured investment.

"So what I did," William went on, "was to take a legal mortgage on his land and set him up on a schedule where he could pay the debt out over a three-year period. And in the deal I also got first right of refusal at three-quarters of market value in case he decided to sell."

It was beginning to sound like the kind of bargain William would strike, Jason thought wryly. But it all sounded fair as well, and William's original motive had been a good one — to help a friend.

"So he ended up selling the place to you?" Jason asked. They were approaching a high row of hedges, which somebody had apparently planted as a windbreak.

"Not exactly," William said.

"You mean you had to foreclose?"

"Not that either," William said hesitantly.

The story's conclusion greeted Jason abruptly as William brought the wagon around the end of the hedgerow.

The wagon track led straight toward a mound of cinders and blackened foundation stones. Some distance farther away was a second, larger pile of ashes, which Jason did not need to be told had once been a barn.

"Damn it, William," Jason said, exploding. "Don't tell me this is their place! The Farleys' place!"

"It is," William replied calmly.

"And you brought me out here to sell it to me on the same day that they were buried? You cold son of a bitch!"

"Why don't you just get a hold of yourself," William said irritably, "and think about the situation a minute before you run off at the mouth any more." He stopped the team and set the brake against the metal-rimmed front wheel, then turned and looked at his brother intently.

"It might be cold," William continued, "or it might just be practical. Would it have been more tactful if I'd waited until tomorrow, or a week or a month from now? The reason I didn't tell you earlier whose farm this was is because I knew you would do just what you're doing right now. You'd blow up before you thought the whole thing through."

Jason's anger was subsiding, but he was left with a foul residue of disgust, both for his brother and for himself. "But they were your friends," he argued.

"They were my friends, but now they're dead," William said, "and their farm's not going to do anybody any good sitting fallow while we go through a period of mourning. You're a farmer, Jason, born and bred, and you know that now, right away, is the time for planting if this farm is to produce a decent crop this year."

Jason couldn't argue with that. The time for the last of the late-winter frosts was past, and the first spring rains would be starting soon. Most of the other farmers in the area probably had some of their seed in the ground already.

"I had an honest, legal arrangement with Paul and Liza," William continued. "They had no children, and it was in the mortgage agreement that if both of them died, their land would go to me because of the money I loaned them. I'd tear the mortgage up this minute if that could bring them back, but it wouldn't. They're dead, Jason. My friends are dead and beyond caring what happens to the land they owned. But that same land could spell a whole new life for you."

Although Jason couldn't rid himself of the disgust he still felt, he also couldn't argue with his brother's reasoning. He still wanted to own this farm, still needed to own it for the sake of his family's future, and at that instant he realized that any further protests he offered would simply be for the sake of his own conscience. In the end he would still end up buying the land from his brother.

"I've been thinking about this all day, Jason," William

told him. As he spoke, he stepped down from the wagon box, and in a moment Jason joined him on the ground. "I could have found another farm for you. I still can if you want me to after you hear me out, but I don't think you will. This is the best place for you and your family. It's where you should be."

As they started walking slowly toward the wreckage that had been the Farleys' home, Jason tried not to think of what had taken place here less than forty-eight hours earlier.

"Without any buildings, the land would be worth about five thousand dollars," William continued, "but I only have around six hundred in it. I'll be willing to take that amount as a down payment, and since the rest will be clear, unearned profit for me, I'll let you share the windfall by carrying a five percent note for twenty-two hundred dollars over twenty years. Every fall, after harvest, you will owe me about one hundred seventy-five dollars and you will have the option of paying me in full at any time. Chances are, after three or four good years, you'll have the whole amount paid off."

It was an incredible bargain, of that Jason had no doubt. And how would he feel a year from now, he wondered, if he let such a deal go by because of some vague feelings of guilt about two people he had never even met?

William went on hammering away at him with point after irrefutable point. "After the down payment you'll still have eleven hundred dollars left for seed, supplies, and maybe even some lumber. If you need it, I'll also be glad to loan you whatever you need in the way of livestock and implements until you can get everything you need on your own."

They had reached the edge of the heap of ashes that was all that was left of the life's work of the dead couple. Jason stirred the pile around with his foot and turned over an ancient tea kettle, half melted and blackened with soot.

"You wouldn't have to put the house here," William

said gently, "although it would be the best spot. There's a well already dug, and that row of hedges would do a lot to block the north wind in winter."

Jason turned to face his brother, meeting his gaze squarely. "There's no way I can say no, is there?" he said.

"There's no need of it, Jason. I knew Paul Farley well, probably even better than I know you, and I'm sure he would have liked the idea of a family like yours carrying on with what he started here."

That helped. Jason knew that it was only a rationale, but still, it helped.

He turned back to survey the scattered debris that lay before him. Although the fire had damaged the six stone piers that had supported the house, he could probably use a lot of the same stone . . .

2

Tyson and Mollie Hartman stopped their mounts at the top of a low hill and stared in awe at the broad expanse of the Mississippi River below them.

"Oh, Ty! Just look at it! Isn't it wonderful?" Mollie exclaimed. She turned her head to look at the place where the mile-wide ribbon of churning water came into sight around a high bluff, then followed its course with her eyes to the point, far to the south, where it disappeared around a series of gentle hills. "I knew it was going to be big, but I never imagined it would be . . . well, like this."

"It's big all right," Tyson told his sister. "But I'll enjoy the sight a lot more once we're looking at it from the other side." Always the practical one, Tyson was already considering the difficult job they had ahead of them — maneuvering two heavy wagons loaded with furniture and household goods to the west side of the river. To him, the Mississippi was a formidable obstacle.

"But look, there's plenty of boats down there," Mollie said to her brother, "and the men who operate them surely have made the crossing hundreds of times." She pointed to the small settlement of shacks and shanties that was located on the near side of the river just above the high-water line. Beyond the buildings, down a fifty-yard expanse of sloping, muddy levee, was a row of about fifteen boats and rafts of various sizes, which were tied to heavy timbers sunk deep in the river bank.

It was ten in the morning now, and they had been on the road for nearly four hours. About thirty minutes earlier Mollie and her brother had decided to ride ahead of their party and find out how much farther it was to the Mississippi. Their sister-in-law, Arethia, and her five children were now probably no more than a mile or two behind, their pace much slower because of the two wagons.

Despite the optimism she expressed, Mollie could not help but recall the tragic tale they had heard from a man who was headed back east to the Carolinas. Only a few weeks before, he had lost his brother-in-law and a cousin to the dark waters when the raft they were on broke up in the unpredictable currents. Everything he owned had been sucked into the muddy depths of the Mississippi, and when Mollie's party met him one evening along the roadside, he was headed home in defeat, his dreams of fortune and adventure in the West shattered.

But that would not happen to them, Mollie assured herself. For one thing, the man had tried to cross in May, when the river was swollen with the spring runoff, and it was late summer now. And besides, he had also admitted to having tried to save some money by negotiating a bargain rate with the owner of one of the smallest rafts, which was little more than a mass of logs lashed together with ropes and outfitted with a tiller and oars. Mollie was determined to hire one of the best boats available, even if it cost twice as much.

"Listen, Ty. Why don't you ride back and lead the

others in while I go down and try to line up some transportation for us?" Mollie suggested to her brother. "The place is small, and you shouldn't have any trouble finding me when you get back. Just look for Stony," she added, referring to the dun-colored gelding she rode, "and I should be somewhere close by."

"All right, but you be careful down there, Sis," Ty said, reaching out to place a hand lightly on her forearm. "Remember what that man said about how rough these boat people can get."

"I remember." Mollie shrugged. "But I'll be all right. Tell Arethia to wait just beyond the outskirts of the settlement. They're less likely to be bothered there, and the children won't have to be exposed to whatever wickedness goes on down there."

Tyson agreed, then wheeled his horse around and rode off.

It came as no surprise to Mollie that her twenty-one-year-old brother accepted her instructions so easily even though she was a year his junior and a female as well. On the difficult journey from Virginia, Mollie had more and more assumed the position of leader as the miles rolled away behind them. Arethia was simply too busy keeping track of her five active children to take on the myriad other duties, and Tyson had no apparent desire to be in charge of anyone or anything.

But that was not to say that her brother was particularly indecisive or timid. He could be a rock when strength was needed, and the few times when they had faced real danger, he had proven himself to be a competent protector.

Tyson was just different. People had been saying that about him for most of his life. At an early age he had shown himself to be practically useless around the farm, and from the time he reached his teens, he had spent much of his time with his Cherokee friends in their isolated Smoky Mountain settlements. At times, in fact, he seemed more Indian than white, and he clearly was far more comfortable wandering the remote mountain valleys and trails than he was dealing with his own race in their settlements and towns.

Mollie remained on the hilltop a few moments after her brother had gone, still absorbed in the broad panorama before her. In the distance, on the opposite side of the river, she could see a cluster of buildings on the river bank that she knew to be St. Louis. They had also been warned about that place, not only by fellow travelers but by her brother Jason in his letters home. He had cautioned them that it was neither a fit nor a safe place for women and children, and they did not plan to tarry even one night within its boundaries. Whatever supplies they needed would be purchased by Tyson after the rest of the party had passed safely through the city to the open country beyond.

A warm summer breeze tickled Mollie's face, and impulsively she reached up and removed the wide-brimmed straw hat that she used to keep the sun out of her eyes and her hair out of the way on the trail. Her blond hair cascaded down her back, falling in natural waves that shimmered in the morning sunlight.

On the trip she had taken to wearing heavy trousers, a loose-fitting cotton shirt, and worn riding boots. Such an outfit was more comfortable during the long days in the saddle, and it also served to conceal the shapely curves of her young body from any rough customers, of which they'd seen a fair share on this journey. But Mollie was looking forward to reaching Independence, where she could, after two long months, finally go back to dressing, and feeling, like a woman again.

But not yet, she reminded herself. After another minute she reached back and carefully rolled her hair into a loose bun, then put her hat back on and pulled it low over her eyes. These Western men seemed particularly attracted to the sight of that much blond hair, and she had no desire to deal with the distractions it could cause when she reached the waterfront settlement below.

In another few hours, if things go well, Mollie thought, we'll be in St. Louis, with our last major obstacle behind us.

St. Louis!

The thought brought to mind more than just the image of a bustling, rough-and-tumble Western city that was a supply and trading center for much of the limitless frontier regions beyond it.

It was also the place where Kurt Rakestraw had mailed his last letter to her before losing himself somewhere in that expanse of wilderness that stretched from the Missouri State line all the way to California. Although she had never been in St. Louis, she could almost picture him strolling through the streets of the city with that easy, confident gait, his tasseled buckskin clothes drawing curious glances from men and his quick smile and rugged good looks drawing even more glances from women.

Had only six months passed since they'd been together? It seemed like years since she had felt his strong arms around her and listened to him trying to explain that no matter how much he loved her, he could not stand to settle down to the quiet farming life even if it meant that they would be together forever. That life was fine for others, he'd told her, but it would kill him to be locked into such an existence. Something that went to the very heart of who he was would wither and die, and then he would be of no use to either of them.

Then and now Mollie understood what he was saying and recognized it as the truth. To take a man who, at twenty-five, had crossed the continent on foot and on horseback, who had trapped with Jim Bridger and fought the Mexicans with Kit Carson, and imprison that man on a forty-acre hillside farm for the rest of his life, even for the sake of love, would certainly be tantamount to killing him spiritually if not physically.

But despite all that, losing Kurt had wreaked such devastation on Mollie Hartman that for a time she wondered if she would be able to, or would ever want to, go on with life. Even now she could not completely rid herself of an instinctive sense of betrayal which his departure had stirred in her. For the few, brief winter months that Kurt had spent with his brother in Virginia, she had surrendered herself utterly to him, mind and body, and losing him had affected her as deeply as anything she'd ever experienced in her life.

But she was better now. She had come to realize that her life could still be full and happy without Kurt in it. But she knew she would never fully recover from the loss, and she had also made a solemn vow to herself that never again would she let any man affect her so. She would love again, but never would she lose herself to love as she had that one thrilling time.

The small, nameless settlement on the east bank of the Mississippi consisted of two ragged rows of ramshackle buildings and hovels that faced each other across a rutted, dusty road. The place was fairly active at this time of day, and as she rode along, Mollie's watchful glance took in the locals. Buckskin-clad frontiersmen rubbed shoulders in the street with burly, bearded boatmen, some half-drunk despite the early hour. A few Indians were in evidence, along with an occasional black-clad Chinaman.

Here and there were heavy wagons similar to those in Mollie's party whose owners were buying supplies or negotiating passage across the river. Through an open window in one shack Mollie glimpsed a half-dressed woman plying a client with drinks and attention, and in another dimly lit building that she took to be a tavern she saw a row of dour-faced men leaning on a long plank bar. And mixed in with all the other types of establishments, she noted, was a scattering of stores, boardinghouses, eating places, and rude huts.

Mollie rode straight through the settlement, not stopping until she reached the edge of the levee. There she paused to survey the rafts and boats tied up below, judging which ones looked solid and trustworthy and which ones she would not want to risk her life and the lives of her family on. With an uneasy feeling, she realized that most of the boats fell into the second category.

As she watched, a twenty-foot raft loaded with two big covered wagons, more than a dozen head of livestock, and nearly as many people shoved off from the bank. On either side, three men with long oars propelled the raft toward the center of the river while another manned the long tiller.

The raft tilted precariously as the current caught it, but the crew managed to keep it upright. With the oarsmen pumping away as if their lives depended on it, which indeed they might, the homemade craft settled into a long, angling course that was determined half by the rowing of the men and half by the force of the river.

Mollie turned her attention back to the riverfront and spotted a building that sat off to the side but closer to the water than the others. It looked promising, she decided, and she turned Stony toward it.

As Mollie dismounted and looped the dun's reins over a nearby rail, she could hear loud voices from within. She stepped up to the open door and peered inside, letting her eyes adjust to the dimmer light. From somewhere inside, a voice said, "Come on in, little lady." Mollie took a tentative step inside, but remained near the door.

"I'm not sure if I'm in the right place," she said. "I'm looking for a boat to carry two wagons and eight people across the river." Now she could make out the forms of five men sitting on an assortment of rickety chairs and upturned crates. One of the men balanced a greasy whiskey bottle on his knee, his fingers grasping the neck.

"You come to the right place, a'right, girlie," the man with the bottle said. "Any of us'd be glad to give you a dandy ride." He snickered, then glanced around at his companions, who grinned in agreement.

"We want to be across the Mississippi and through St. Louis before dark," Mollie said, ignoring the remark, "which means we would have to start as soon as possible."

"Wal, it don't take all that long to make the crossin',"

the man told her. "There ain't no big hurry. You want a nip of firewater?"

"No, thank you," Molly said stiffly, "and I'd appreciate it if you wouldn't drink any more if I'm going to entrust my family's safety to you."

"We're jus' relaxin', girlie. You oughta pull up a seat and relax a little with us." The man stood up and took a step forward, offering the bottle to her again, but she refused to take it. "We could prob'ly even work out a special rate for you if you'd just give us a chance to get better acquainted with you." Even from several feet away she could smell his breath, which mingled unpleasantly with the stench of his unwashed body and clothes.

"Hell, we might even end up payin' you 'fore the whole thing's over," a man who sat by the door proposed.

Mollie refused to let them see that their suggestions had any effect on her. She had learned that being timid or showing fear with men like these could be dangerous.

"I can see that I've come to the wrong place for what I want," she said icily. "What I was hoping to find was some man who had the ability to think with what was on top of his shoulders instead of what he carried around in his britches."

As she watched the good humor melt slowly from the whiskey-reddened eyes of the man standing in front of her, she knew better than to linger. But as she turned to leave, the man by the door raised a leg and placed it across the doorway.

"Wait jus' a goddamn minute," the man with the bottle said, grabbing her by the arm and spinning her around roughly. "You think you can jus' stroll in here an' talk me down in front of the boys an' then jus' stroll back out?"

"I didn't intend to insult anybody," Mollie said, trying with less and less success to control her voice. "I didn't come here to start trouble. All I want to do is arrange passage for my family."

"Wal, you're fixin' to pay for somethin', girlie," the man growled, "but it might not be for a trip acrost the Mis'sippi!" He reached up and took her by the scruff of the neck as if she were an errant child, then handed the bottle to one of the men beside him.

Panicking, Mollie glanced around at the faces of the other men, but read no sympathy in any of them. Apparently they were just going to sit there and let this brute do whatever he wanted to her. But it wouldn't happen without a fight, she determined, as her captor reached out with his free hand toward her breast.

Mollie lashed out at him, not clawing or slapping with her hands as most women might, but swinging with her fist as her father had taught her to do. Her blow landed on his left cheek, but it carried only enough force to enrage him further. He grabbed her wrist, then twisted and squeezed with force enough to bring her to her knees in front of him. Her hat fell off, and her long hair spilled down over her shoulders.

"Jus' look at this here yaller hair, boys," the man exclaimed, grabbing himself a handful. "I allus did like these here yaller-haired whores the best of all."

Dizzy with pain and fear, Mollie finally succumbed to terror. She opened her mouth and screamed at the top of her lungs.

But the man only laughed. He yanked her hair so that she was forced to look up at him. "Go ahead and squawl all you want, girlie. It ain't gonna help you none 'cause the only law to speak of in these here parts is way over yonder in St. Louie. Scream your fool head off if you think you can roust them from this far away."

Mollie was vaguely aware of a brief scuffle behind her, but she was being held so tightly she could not turn her head to see what was going on. An instant later a fist shot out, as if from nowhere, and landed with a sharp crack in the middle of her assailant's face. The man staggered back several feet and tumbled over his chair. The chair splintered into kindling, and once the man hit the floor, he didn't move again.

Dazed as she was, all that registered in Mollie's mind for the first few seconds was that nobody was hurting her anymore.

Then she heard a deep, angry voice exclaim, "What the hell do you men think you're doing here?" Mollie turned to look at the legs of the man who seemed to have come to her rescue, then raised her eyes to get a look at his face. From that angle, he looked at least ten feet tall.

"Mudcat was only funnin' with the girl 'cause she sassed him, Hank," one of the men responded rather sheepishly.

"I guess I can understand ol' Mudcat Sam doing something stupid and mean like this," the tall man said. "But what got into the rest of you to let him get away with it? You, Pete! Didn't it ever come into your head to try to stop him from hurting her?"

"I woulda, Hank, 'fore things went too far."

One of the men had gone over to stare at the downed man, more in curiosity than in alarm. "Reckon you kilt him, Hank? It don't seem like he's breathin' none a'tall."

"I hope to hell I did," the tall man said, his voice sharp. "Seems like the man who ridded the world of a piece of trash like that ought to get a medal or something. And as for the rest of you, I'd advise you to be out of my sight by the time I walk out of this shack unless you want a dose of the same."

As the other men scrambled to beat one another out the door, the tall man reached down and, with surprising gentleness, helped Mollie to her feet.

"Dang it, miss, I'm just sorry as can be that this happened to you," he told her sincerely.

Mollie's head was beginning to clear, and she was even able to muster a semblance of a smile for her rescuer.

Although he was not as tall as he had originally seemed, the man before her stood well over six feet, with broad shoulders that sorely taxed the seams of the fresh white shirt he wore. His trousers, which were made of a soft brown material, had a crisp crease down the front, and the cuffs were tucked neatly into the tops of one of the fanciest pairs of tooled-leather boots Mollie had ever seen.

"I'm just glad you came along when you did," Mollie replied. "I'd hate to guess what that rat had in mind for me."

"It's a good thing you screamed when you did. I just happened to be walking down the levee. I wouldn't have known anything was going on if you hadn't cut loose like that."

"Well, I want you to know how grateful I am, Mr.——"

"My name's Hank Dalton, miss." The man extended his hand to her and smiled broadly beneath his thick brown mustache. His tanned face was so handsome and his smile was so warm and open that Mollie couldn't help but return the smile.

"And I'm Mollie Hartman."

"Well, I guess I don't need to tell you, Miss Hartman, that you picked a pretty rough place to be wandering around alone. Men like Mudcat Sam over there aren't exactly the exception to the rule in these parts."

As if in response to his name, a sound gurgled from the man's bloody lips. Mollie couldn't decide whether or not she was relieved that he was alive.

"Come on, let's get out of here," Dalton said, turning toward the door.

"And him?" Mollie asked, tilting her head toward the man on the floor.

"Either he'll come around by and by, or he won't," Dalton replied indifferently, not even bothering to glance at the man he might have killed. Then he followed Mollie out into the bright sunlight.

Mollie went to the rail and loosened Stony's reins. "I have to admit that I was warned about this place," she said. "A number of people told us that it was dangerous on both sides of the river. But the rest of my party was supposed to come along soon, so I thought I would be all right on my own for a little while."

"So you're traveling west," Dalton commented.

"To Independence," Mollie confirmed. "As a matter of fact, I stopped at this shack to inquire about getting our two wagons ferried across the river."

"Well, if it's a ride across the river that you're looking for," Dalton said easily, "then you're in the right hands, Miss Hartman. You're looking at the owner and captain of the *Jessica T*, which just happens to be the best and fastest and prettiest ferry boat to be found anywhere between Cairo and Memphis." Then he added with a bright, mischievous grin, "And because we're already acquainted and I like you just fine, I won't even try to charge you twice the going rate like I might if you were any other greenhorn just in from the East."

"That is mighty kind of you, Mr. Dalton," Mollie laughed.

Her new friend led her down the levee to what was, indeed, the best-looking boat in the line. She tied Stony to the thick rope that secured the *Jessica T* to the bank, then followed Dalton up the gangplank and onto the boat. As they crossed the deck toward a small structure, she noted with satisfaction that there was more than enough room for both their wagons and teams. It was exactly the kind of boat she had hoped to find.

When they reached the pilothouse, which also served as Dalton's residence, he poured cups of thick, dark coffee, then laced his own liberally with whiskey from a heavy stone jug.

After a healthy slug of the potent brew, Dalton said, "My usual rate is two dollars per wagon, and ten cents extra for each head of livestock. Then on top of that, you'll have to pay fifty cents a head to the six oarsmen I'll need to line up for the crossing."

Mollie did some quick calculations and was taken aback

by the $7.80 price tag for the crossing. Previously they had never paid more than two dollars total to cross any stream or river.

Although she said nothing, Dalton seemed to sense her surprise. "I can honestly say, Miss Hartman, that that's the best fare you'll find on any decent craft here on the Mississippi. It's a big river, you know, the biggest on the continent, and there's many that will tell you from experience that to try to save a dollar or two by crossing on an unsound raft or boat could very well be a tragic economy."

"I've heard as much, Mr. Dalton," Mollie told him. "I'll pay your price . . . gladly."

Mollie stood on the levee, watching closely as the crew of men worked to move the two big wagons onto the deck of the *Jessica T.* The horses were so unnerved by the prospect of being led onto the rolling deck that they were deemed useless; the men were left to haul the wagons up the narrow planks from the levee by brute strength alone. But Hank Dalton had rounded up an able crew of six husky men, and within about twenty minutes both wagons were safely on board and lashed securely to the heavy iron rings on the deck. Then, one by one, the horses were led on.

During the loading Mollie's sister-in-law, Arethia, had stayed well back, skillfully corralling her brood and keeping them out of the way of the men. When she finally relaxed her hold on them, the children scampered up the planks onto the *Jessica T.* Arethia stopped beside Mollie to gaze at the laden ferry and the churning river beyond.

"I'll sure feel a lot better when we have this behind us," Arethia admitted. "After we've put the Mississippi behind us, it will feel almost like we're there."

"I know what you mean," Mollie smiled. "But don't forget, there's still the Missouri to be faced, over near Boonville."

"Yes, but Jason said in his letter that it's nothing compared to the Mississippi," Arethia said.

"Well, I don't think we have much to worry about with the Mississippi. I trust this man, Arethia," Mollie said, indicating Dalton. "He knows his business, and there's no doubt in my mind that he'll get us safely to the other side."

Before this trip the two women hadn't been that close, though they liked each other well enough. But during the journey a stong bond of friendship had developed that both found gratifying. Despite the seven-year difference in their ages, Arethia had no difficulty accepting Mollie's decisions and leadership, while Mollie had a deep respect for her sister-in-law's untiring patience and dedication to her family.

Such a long separation from her husband, fraught with uncertainties as it was, had to be difficult for Arethia, but Mollie could not recall hearing her brother's pretty young wife complain even once. And during this trip she had, perhaps, worked more tirelessly than any of the others, driving a wagon all day, and then shouldering most of the cooking and camp-tending chores at night.

The children had helped a lot though. John, the oldest, had driven the second wagon much of the way, and the younger ones, Ruth, Daniel, Benjamin, and Cassie, had done their share by gathering wood, carrying water, and performing numerous other chores.

All in all, Mollie considered, they had been remarkably lucky up until now, and she could only hope that their good luck would continue until the end of the trail. She had yet to tell Arethia and Tyson about her confrontation with the drunken man, figuring there was no use talking about it now when everybody had so many other things on their minds.

As near as Mollie could tell, everything was in readiness for the crossing when Hank Dalton came back down the plank and started toward them. Mollie had introduced him to Arethia earlier, and now he gave her a smile and a polite nod.

"I just need to go up to Tom Badger's store to see if there is any mail to go across," he announced, "and then we'll be ready to go. The best place to see everything that's going on will be up front along the rail, and you must caution the little ones to stay away from the wagons during the crossing in case one of them decides to shift on us."

"I was surprised at how easily you handled the loading, Captain Dalton," Arethia remarked.

"Well, ma'am," Dalton grinned, "we have done this kind of thing a couple of times before. To tell the truth, your wagons were fairly easy to handle compared with some of the freight wagons which come through here."

He started up the levee to get the mail he had mentioned but then, glancing past the two women, stopped abruptly.

"Uh, oh!" he muttered quietly.

The women turned and saw three men coming toward them. They were still a hundred feet away, but Mollie easily spotted the battered face of Mudcat Sam. He was clutching an ax handle in his right hand and marching forward in a determined, if somewhat irregular, stride.

"Who are they?" Arethia asked in alarm.

"Some men I had a little trouble with before you came," Mollie said. "Mr. Dalton took care of it for me though, and I thought the matter was settled."

"I guess it's not," Hank Dalton said quietly. "You two get on board the *Jessica T* and stay there. There's only three of them, so it shouldn't take but a minute to handle this."

It was no time to argue, Mollie realized. She started immediately toward the plank, with Arethia only a pace behind.

Dalton waited calmly for the three to reach him. On

the deck, Mollie was too far away to hear what was being said, but she could see that the exchange was not a pleasant one, given the men's gestures.

It was Mudcat Sam who made the first move. Stepping back half a pace to give himself room, he swung the ax handle wide in a blow that was intended to connect with Hank Dalton's skull. Dalton was too fast for him though, and after diverting the blow with his left forearm, he brought his right fist up to the point of Sam's chin, which sent the man staggering back.

Meanwhile Sam's companions, who had managed to get on either side of Dalton, moved in now, their fists swinging. Both were of formidable size, but even together they were not able to drive Dalton back so much as a step. Ignoring one of them for a moment, he turned on the other like a whirlwind, pummeling his head and body with a series of well-placed punches.

"Look!" Arethia said suddenly, pointing off to the left. Mollie glanced around and spotted her brother, who had just become aware of the fight and was running to Dalton's assistance.

For a moment, however, it looked as if the tall captain would need no help. After stunning two of the men, he was now devoting his full attention to the third. The man managed to protect himself from the force of Dalton's first blow, but a second, landing just behind his left ear, turned his legs to jelly. He sagged, eyes rolling, then slumped to the ground.

For a moment it seemed as if the fight were over. But then Mudcat Sam, who lay behind Dalton, stood up. He had lost the ax handle, but in the next second Mollie saw to her horror that he now held a long knife. His hand drew back, and Mollie's heart sank as she realized that there was no way to warn Dalton in time to save him from being stabbed.

But suddenly a shot rang out, and in the same instant Mudcat Sam's head did a crazy little jerk to the side.

His body remained erect for a moment longer, his arm still poised with the knife raised, then he pitched forward and landed face down in the gravel of the levee.

No one seemed to know what had happened. Then slowly everyone became aware of Tyson, who had stopped a full thirty feet away, holding a still-smoking pistol in his hand. Mollie watched in amazement as he started calmly forward toward the man he had just killed.

Needless to say, the fight had gone out of both of Dalton's other opponents. They were standing side by side with the man they had been attacking only moments before, staring down, as Dalton was, at the corpse of Mudcat Sam.

Mollie moved to run down to her brother, but Arethia grabbed her arm. "You'd better stay here and let Captain Dalton handle this," she advised. "There's nothing you can do, and there could be more trouble yet to come."

"I guess you're right," Mollie sighed. A minute later Arethia's five children reached them, drawn from the front of the boat by the gunshot.

The four men stood over the body for a moment, and it was clear from Hank Dalton's gestures that he was just about mad enough to add to the death toll if anybody gave him any more trouble. Finally Mudcat Sam's two companions picked up the dead man by his arms and legs and trudged up the levee. Then Dalton and Tyson turned and started back toward the boat.

As they neared the plank, Hank Dalton called to the two women, "Your brother saved my life."

"We saw it all," Mollie replied.

"I was almost too late," Tyson said, looking stunned by what he had done. "I was over by the water looking at a fish, and it was a minute before I realized what was going on. When I saw that fellow draw his knife, I knew there was no way I would get there in time."

"You did just right, son," Dalton said, "and I'm beholden to you."

"What will happen now?" Arethia asked.

"I guess old Mudcat's buddies will bury him," Dalton answered, "that is, if they don't stop for a bottle first and get too drunk to dig a grave."

"But will Tyson be arrested? Won't the law want to look into what happened here?"

"When we get across the river, I'll tell the police in St. Louis what happened," Dalton said. "But they're not likely to be too interested, because they're in Missouri and this is Illinois. And as far as the Illinois law is concerned, it might be a week or more before they even hear about this. Where will you folks be a week from now?"

"Far from here, that I can guarantee," Mollie said quickly.

"All right, then, let's get under way," Dalton said. He started forward to issue orders to his crew, then paused and turned back to add, "You know, a few days from now, if somebody asks me who you folks were or who it was that shot that damned Mudcat and saved my life, chances are I won't even be able to remember your names!"

"But it'll be fine if you happen to remember that we're on our way to Sioux City." Molly smiled broadly.

"Sioux City?" Dalton grinned. "Sure, that's an easy enough place to remember in case anybody asks."

3

Jason groaned as they lifted the notched ten-foot log up and slipped it into place along the back wall of what would soon be his new livestock shed. His arms and shoulders ached from the strain of the long day's work, but he was proud of what he and his helper, Hannibal, had accomplished since morning. Working from a stack of logs that they had spent three days cutting, trimming, and dragging out of the woods, they had nearly completed all four walls of the shed in just over ten hours.

Knowing that his livestock would need protection from the severe Missouri winters to come, Jason considered the shed to be nearly as imporant as the five-room frame house he had spent most of the summer working on. There would be stalls for the horses and cows and a small room to one side for the hay and feed he had yet to stockpile before the cold weather arrived. Next summer, if all went well, he planned to raise a proper barn and perhaps add on a feed lot for the beef cattle he hoped to purchase in the spring.

"We need a res', Mist' Jason," Hannibal said wearily as soon as the log had been fitted into place. "Dis here sun an' hard work tires a man a'plenty."

Jason nodded, knowing that the slave had made the suggestion for Jason's benefit more than his own. Wiping the sweat from his eyes with the sleeve of his shirt, he turned and started toward the bucket of water that sat on the ground nearby. Hannibal followed, remaining a respectful step behind out of habit and waiting until Jason had drunk his fill before reaching for the second gourd dipper.

It was late August now, and even Jason was amazed at how much he had been able to accomplish in six short months. The crop had been his first priority when he bought the farm, and much of his first two months had been spent planting and tending the fields of corn, beans, wheat, and hay. Then he had turned his attention to the house and had erected an adequate five-room home on the site where the Farleys' place had stood.

In addition to these two major undertakings, he had planted and tended a thriving one-acre garden patch so his family would have plenty of food to eat when they arrived and enough to preserve for the winter. He had made a start on an orchard by setting out twenty apple, twenty peach, and a dozen plum seedlings. He had mended the split-rail fences around all his crop land and had erected a particularly sturdy fence around a parcel of woodland to serve as a pen for the four hogs he had purchased. Rainy days had been spent making furniture, and he had succeeded in putting together crude beds for the entire family, a long dining table, and eight sturdy chairs. Those items combined with the mattresses and a few other pieces of furniture that Arethia was bringing with her would give them everything they needed to set up their new household.

Jason never lost sight of the fact that he would not have been able to accomplish nearly as much without the labor of the slave his brother William had lent him. Hannibal had been with him from the start and had worked as hard as Jason to make the place livable. The towering black man, with a chest like a hogshead and arms like stout oak limbs, had done much of the work in the fields and had assisted with the heaviest labor in the construction of the house and livestock shed.

At the start, Jason had been reluctant to accept William's offer to lend him the slave, but finally his reluctance had taken second place to the sense of urgency he felt to get the place in shape before his family arrived in the fall. Now, with the summer months waning and his family already on the road west, Jason had to concede, if only to himself, that alone he couldn't possibly have accomplished everything that needed to be done.

But beyond the considerable feats of labor that Hannibal performed, Jason had also come to appreciate his companionship during the long, hard months of toil. Though they often had little to say to each other for hours at a time beyond the details of the work at hand, an easy sort of camaraderie had developed between the two men. With the ways of servitude deeply ingrained, and recognizing the fact of his own superior size and power, Hannibal was quick to take on the hardest tasks, to lift the heavy end, and to tend to the final few details of a project after Jason had quit for the day.

Jason's efforts to truly get to know Hannibal, to learn what he thought and how he felt about certain aspects of his life, however, were not very successful. Jason did learn that Hannibal had been raised on a large plantation in Louisiana and, while still in his teens, had been brought north to Missouri by a slave trader and sold to William. But when Jason tried to find out how Hannibal felt about being a slave, the man withdrew into an impenetrable shell. Life was better here than in Louisiana, Hannibal said, because William rarely beat his slaves, the cabins in the slave quarters were tight and warm in winter, and they ate better — William gave them allotments of beef or pork every week and they were able to have their own vegetable plots. Beyond that, he never risked making any comment on how he felt about being owned by another man.

Remarkably enough, Jason discovered that the fact that he was keeping and working a slave, though not his own, made him socially acceptable to his neighbors. In an area where the lines were so quickly being drawn over the South's peculiar institution, it was assumed that he must be sound on the goose because he was accepting his brother's benevolence and was using a black man's labor to establish his home and farm.

Jason was content to let people believe that about him, though he refrained from entering into discussions of the slavery issue and never attended any of the meetings that were held with regularity throughout the summer to consider the Kansas problem. He did begin to make a few acquaintances, mostly by attending church and going with William to the occasional social functions that were held in the community, and his initial opinion of the locals eventually began to mellow. They were just like people anywhere, he decided. When their homes, their families, and their way of life were threatened, they reacted quickly and instinctively, and a few mistakes were bound to be made once in a while. Though he had come close to dying at their hands, no true harm had been done to him. He was still alive and doing better than he ever dared hope.

Now, as the afternoon sun dipped into the elm trees that formed the western boundary of his land, Jason tried to imagine what it would be like once his family arrived. He felt a knot in his throat as he pictured the kids playing barefoot in the yard and Arethia standing in the kitchen doorway, watching them, smiling that special, contented smile, which always warmed Jason when he saw it spread across her face. It seemed as if he had been away from them for centuries.

He began to wonder, as he had countless times since the day of their departure from Virginia, how far along the road to Missouri his family was and if everything was going well with them. It was hard to suppress his fears for their safety, but they would be all right, he assured himself. His brother Tyson, though odd and introverted, was as skilled as his Cherokee friends and teachers with a gun and a knife, and both his wife and his sister Mollie were hardy country women who could prove formidable if threatened.

While he rested, a small white terrier emerged from the crawl space under the new house and approached Jason, tail wagging in anticipation of the petting he hoped to receive. The dog, which William had told him answered to the name Matthew, had belonged to the Farleys. He'd showed up the second day after Jason took over the farm, forlorn and half starved after spending several days in the woods, and had eventually adjusted to the new order of things and accepted Jason as his new owner. Matthew would make a good dog for the kids, Jason thought as he patted the animal absently.

Jason and Hannibal began discussing how much higher the log walls should be built and how they should be tied together. Hannibal explained a method they had used when they erected two additional slave cabins on William's land. It involved tying the tops of the walls together with notched logs so that each wall would lend strength and support to the others, and Jason finally agreed that it was the best solution.

Just as they were about to return to their work, Matthew's ears perked up and a low growl stirred in his throat. A moment later he trotted away toward the road, barking excitedly, and Jason glanced up to see William approaching them on horseback. Matthew met him at the edge of the property and escorted him in.

Jason was surprised to see his brother because William had been over the day before and had said he planned to ride to Independence today to receive a shipment of farm implements. Usually when he made such trips he stayed at least one night, sometimes two, taking care of business and catching up on the current news and gossip in the cafés and saloons.

"You're back early," Jason commented as his brother brought his horse to a halt and dismounted. "I didn't expect to see you for another day or so, and probably not till church on Sunday."

"I cut the trip short for your sake, little brother," William said as he handed the reins to Hannibal. "I didn't think you would want me to waste any extra time in Independence when I had this letter in my pocket." He produced an envelope and handed it to Jason.

Immediately recognizing Arethia's sweeping handwriting, Jason accepted the envelope and opened it eagerly. The letter inside, which was fairly short, had been posted in St. Louis only seven days before. Jason's eyes swept down the page, eagerly devouring the news of his family.

In it, Arethia explained that she had decided to write because the mail to Independence would undoubtedly travel faster than they could. They had crossed the Mississippi without mishap, she wrote, and from information gained from fellow travelers, expected to be on the road about another ten to twelve days before they reached Independence.

"We had some trouble involving your brother Tyson on the Illinois side of the river," Arethia wrote, "but everyone is all right, so there is no need for you to worry. I would explain the whole affair in full here, but your brother is leaving soon to purchase supplies, and I want to give this to him to mail. We can tell you and William all about it when we get there."

Jason looked up and said excitedly, "They're past St. Louis and doing fine! If Arethia's calculations are correct, they should be here in just four or five more days! It's hard to believe. After all this time, I'm finally about to have my family with me again!"

"That is good news," William agreed. "When I picked the letter up, I was hoping it would be something of the sort." He let his brother enjoy the news for a moment longer, then took a second envelope from his pocket. "There was another letter waiting in Independence as well," he said. "This one is from our sister Sarah to both of us."

"Is everything all right?" Jason asked quickly. "Is it news about Daddy?"

"Don't worry. It's not bad news," William said, "or at least it's not the kind of bad news you might expect. Here, I'll let you read it for yourself."

Inside the envelope were several sheets of light paper filled with his sister's graceful handwriting. After a brief greeting, Sarah launched straight into the important news, which had to do with one of the rare letters she had recently received from their brother Charles, in Pennsylvania.

It seemed that Mollie, Tyson, and Jason's family weren't the only ones who were making a trip westward that summer. In his letter, Charles had explained that he had decided to sell his farm and store and to move to Kansas Territory under the auspices of the New England Emigrant Aid Society.

Charles's involvement with the underground railroad had been the subject of quiet rumor within the family for some time now, but it was the sort of scandal that was seldom mentioned and *never* in the presence of anybody outside the Hartman clan.

"I thought Daddy was going to have a stroke when he read the letter," Sarah wrote. "I've never seen him so mad, and it was all I could do to keep him from saddling his horse and starting for Pennsylvania. But finally I was able to convince him that the trip would be useless because Charles would already be gone when he got there.

"I know enough about the situation there to realize that this announcement will be of great concern to both of you, especially because of Charles's former involvements here in the East and the well-publicized intentions of the group which is sponsoring his relocation," the letter continued. "My constant prayer is simply that the trouble in Kansas will not become as serious as many are predicting and that disagreements over the subject of slavery will not pit brother against brother. I can imagine nothing more tragic."

Jason returned the letter to its envelope and handed it back to William.

"It's just like Charles to do something like this," William commented, making no effort to mask his scorn and disgust. "From the day he was born, he never did have the sense that God gave a goose. But this tops any damned fool thing Charles ever did or even thought about doing!"

"Well, maybe it won't be as much of a problem as you think," Jason said quickly. "I'm sure a lot of the settlers that are moving to Kansas haven't come here with murder and mayhem on their minds. Charles is a family man with a wife and nine children to consider. Surely he wouldn't do anything that would place them in jeopardy."

"I wouldn't count on that," William scoffed. "After all, he got them mixed up in that damned underground railroad, didn't he? Take my word for it, Jason, that brother of ours is just about as crazy as they come. You know he tried to kill me with a meat ax in a fight over a brace of mules."

Jason nodded. The fight, which took place when Jason was about seven years old, had achieved legendary status in the family. It was said that the fight was the reason that Charles had moved to Pennsylvania nearly twenty years before and had since severed almost all connections with his family in Virginia. Sarah was the only one who still heard from him, albeit rarely.

"Listen, William. I think we can turn this into a good opportunity if we handle it right," Jason said. "If we can establish contact with Charles after he gets to Kansas, we might be able to patch up some of the problems that have kept him a stranger to the family for so long and to open some lines of communication between the abolitionists in Kansas and the slaveholders here in Missouri."

"You're out of your goddamned mind, Jason," William stated flatly. "I don't want anybody hereabouts to even know we've got a nigger-loving brother in Kansas, let alone that we might be trying to communicate with him. As far as I'm concerned, he's one of *them*. If he stirs up any trouble on this side of the line, he'll get the same treatment as the rest of that rabble get!"

Jason started to respond to his brother's sharp words, but he thought better of it and said nothing. Despite the well-intended prayers of people like his sister, Jason thought, men like their brother William had long since lost interest in seeking any peaceful solutions to the growing problems along the Kansas-Missouri border.

Suddenly, William acknowledged the presence of Hannibal, who had remained a respectful distance away, still holding the reins of William's horse in his hand.

"Hannibal," William said sharply, "come over here to me, boy."

Hannibal approached the two brothers. Although he towered over both men by a good three inches, his steps were quick and his nervousness about his master's foul mood was apparent.

"I'm sure you heard what we were talking about, Hannibal," William said. "I want you to know that this is the personal business of Jason and me and that it's not to be mentioned to anybody. Do you understand that, boy?"

"Yassuh," Hannibal mumbled, studying his toes.

"I treat you good, Hannibal," William continued. "You eat well, you work reasonable hours, and you've never once felt the sting of the whip in the three years I've owned you. But I swear to God, all that will change the day I find out you've mentioned anything you heard here to any other human being, white or black."

"I keep my mouf shut 'bout it, suh," Hannibal said. "I swear I will."

"Enough said then," William said crisply. "Now give me those reins and go on back to work."

With obvious relief, Hannibal went to the stack of logs he and Jason had stockpiled for the shed and, taking up an ax, began to notch the end of one of them.

"Eventually it will still get out about Charles," Jason told his brother. "With as much family as we're about to have in this community, somebody is bound to talk about his moving to Kansas. And even if we swore everybody to secrecy, there's no way to keep Charles from telling the people he knows about us being over here."

"You may be right," William sighed, "but it's still not something I'd like printed in the papers or shouted from the rooftops. I'm ashamed of Charles for the things he's done, and you should be too."

"Well, I'll tell you, William," Jason said, unable to keep quiet any longer. "Out of respect for you and for my own best interests, I've kept my opinions to myself ever since I've been here. But I still feel as if I have no stake in this slavery business, and to my way of thinking, the fact that I now have a brother in Kansas and one in Missouri only reinforces my determination to remain neutral in the matter. I was a litle boy when Charles left to live in Pennsylvania, and I guess I just don't know enough about him to hate him."

As he spoke, Jason watched the anger flare in his brother's face and then disappear, as if it had been brought under control. But what was most surprising to Jason was the realization that he really didn't care if William exploded. The possibility no longer frightened him. He had done a good job of keeping his opinions to himself until now, but he still believed that no man, not even a brother to whom he owed so much, had the right to draw him into the middle of a fight in which he had no vested interest.

William's gaze drifted away from Jason's face to the house that his brother had spent most of the summer working on and then to the shed where Hannibal was taking a measurement for the log he was working on.

"You've got the place looking good, little brother," William said at last. "I'm proud of what you've accomplished and proud that I've been able to help you make a start here in Missouri. It's been my dream ever since I moved here to see my family leave those farmed-out hills of Virginia and resettle here, where their hard work would bring them the kind of prosperity they deserve." He paused and slowly his eyes came back to bore into Jason's with frightening intensity. "But as much as I love you, and as much as I want you here, I'm warning you that you'll rue the day that you cross me on this slavery issue or shame me in front of the good people who live in this community. And mark my words on this as well, Jason. The day will come when you'll have to choose a side, whether you want to or not."

"That very well may be," Jason replied, returning his brother's fierce stare. "But today is not that day!"

The night was still except for a slight breeze from the west, which drifted with silken fingers over the porch where Jason sat. Somewhere in the yard a katydid chirruped its shrill, solitary song, and farther away, in the band of tall shrubs that bordered the road, a mockingbird demonstrated its repertoire. At Jason's feet, Matthew stirred slightly, scratched lethargically, and settled down once more.

Jason was alone now. Hannibal had returned to William's farm two days before. Behind him a single lamp burned in a front window of the house, casting just enough light onto the porch to highlight the delicate swirls of smoke that rose from his pipe.

The memory of the sharp words he and his brother had exchanged lay heavily on his heart, but at this moment even that burst of anger could not taint the peace and contentment he felt.

I just don't understand why any man would want or need much more than this, Jason thought. A home, a piece of land, and soon a family to share it with.

Realizing that his pipe had gone out, Jason struck a match and puffed the bowl of tobacco back to life. Matthew opened one eye to investigate the flame, then closed it again, as if the effort hadn't been worth it.

After supper was finished and the dishes were cleared, Jason had intended to spend an hour or so reading his Bible, but the evening had been so pretty that he ended up here on the porch instead. There was something special and enriching about ending a day like this after so many hours of toil. He could remember many such evenings in Virginia, often with Arethia settling quietly into a seat beside him after the children were put to bed. It wasn't one of those experiences that logged itself in a man's mind, but certainly it was as close as most men ever came in this life to knowing complete peace of mind.

Matthew stirred again, then raised his head and pricked up his ears as he stared into the darkness toward the road. Noticing the animal's reaction, Jason took the pipe from his mouth and peered into the night.

It was a minute more before he began to hear the sound that had caught the dog's attention. The intermittent squeak was very faint at first but grew louder with each passing second. It was a sound that Jason had heard countless times before — the sound of a wagon axle in need of greasing.

They're here, Jason thought with a sudden rush of joy. My family is here!

He jumped to his feet and raced into the darkness, the excited dog yapping close behind.

They were here at last!

4

April 1855

Anson Younger claimed his first kiss from Mollie Hartman in a small, secluded roadside grove about a quarter mile west of the New Salem Church. Earlier in the evening they had attended Sunday-evening worship services at the church, and Mollie had accepted Anson's offer of a ride home.

She had expected something like this, of course, and was not at all surprised when her escort turned his buggy off the road and into the darkened grove. But she wasn't worried. Anson, despite his youthful ardor, was manageable, and Mollie felt no concern that the situation might get out of hand.

Actually, Mollie liked Anson quite a bit and enjoyed the playful necking as much as he did. When a moment later he leaned over for a second kiss she threaded her fingers into his thick, dark hair and responded warmly to him.

"Whew!" Anson exclaimed when their lips parted at last. "I've imagined kissing you, but I didn't expect it to be like this. How did you ever learn to kiss like that?"

"I might as well confess, you're not exactly the first boy I've kissed, Anson," Mollie teased. "Nor even the second or the third."

"Well, if the count's too high, I don't want to know about it," Anson grinned.

"Don't worry, there haven't been all that many, and few indeed who kissed as well as you do."

During the eight months since her arrival in Missouri, Anson was the first young man that Mollie had felt any attraction to, and she was pleased when he began to show that he was drawn to her. Compared with Kurt Rakestraw, he was, of course, just a boy, but he was bright and handsome, and his quick wit and devilish nature provided her with a sorely needed diversion from the tiresome sameness of country life. The two of them had spent several evenings together at various church and social functions, but tonight was the first occasion Anson had arranged to be alone with her.

When Anson drew her to him again, Mollie could tell by his quickening heartbeat that his ardor was growing, and it was no great surprise to her that she was beginning to feel the same. His body was firm and strong, and it stirred an exciting sensation deep within her.

When Mollie first felt Anson's hand envelope her breast, she felt no strong inclination to make him take it away. It felt good, reminding her as it did of all the pleasure her body was capable of delivering in the hands of the right man.

She began to feel the first stirrings of doubt when his fingers tentatively started to work at the buttons on the front of her blouse. Three of them were already opened before she reached up and gently drew his hand away.

"I don't think this is what I want to happen tonight, Anson," Mollie said gently.

"All right, if you say so," Anson replied easily, not seeming to be at all offended. He gave her another light, affectionate kiss, then added, "You know, it's almost a duty for a fellow to see how far he can go, but I'm not all that sure it's what I want to happen tonight either. I like you a lot, Mollie, but if you let me get away with too much, I'm not sure how I would feel about you afterward."

"Because you'd wonder how many others had found my virtue equally as easy to compromise?" Mollie suggested.

"I guess so. I guess that's it."

Mollie chuckled. Sometimes pleasing a man meant displeasing him, and rejecting him often proved the surest way to gain his respect and inspire even more vigorous pursuit.

With the moment of passion past, Mollie and Anson remained in the grove awhile longer and talked. They discussed the growing problems in the area over the issue of slavery, and like many of the other young men in the community, Anson seemed to see in the situation lots of possibilities for adventure.

He told Mollie about a secret foray he and his cousin Cole had made only a couple of months before to the abolitionist stronghold of Lawrence, in Kansas Territory, and spoke with relish about the problems they ran into there when they were recognized in a saloon as being the nephews of Judge Thomas Younger, the notorious slavery advocate from Missouri.

"It was touch and go for us, with near a dozen abolitionist bastards ready to lay hands on us. For a while there, I thought we might have to shoot our way out of town," Anson boasted. "They kept saying our uncle must have sent us over as spies, and nobody would believe it when we explained that we just came to look the town over out of curiosity. But finally one of their leaders, a fellow named Charles Robinson, came in and calmed things down enough that we were able to get on our horses and ride out."

"Why did you go, Anson?" Mollie asked. "Surely you must have realized it would be dangerous for you over there."

"It's like I said," Anson explained. "We went just to see it. But once we were spotted, we were determined that we wouldn't stoop to denying who we were to any damned Yankee abolitionists. My family doesn't own any slaves, nor does Cole's, but a couple of our uncles, including Uncle Thomas, do, and we Youngers are a clan that sticks together. Anyone who does a wrong to one of us does it to all."

"I wish I could have gone with you," Mollie blurted out, realizing, after the first moment of disapproval, how much she envied Anson his freedom to take off on such adventures.

"Why in the world would you want to do something like that?" Anson asked, amazed.

"Maybe for the same reason you did," she replied tartly. "To see it, and to be doing something different and interesting for a change. My God! I get so bored with this farming life that sometimes I think I'll go crazy if I have to shell another pea or hoe another weed. Couldn't you take me with you sometime?"

"Sure, I could, Mollie. And when we started home, all three of your brothers would be waiting at the state line to blow my head off for doing something so stupid!"

Mollie knew better than to argue. Young men of Anson and Cole Younger's age could come up with any number of excuses for disappearing for two or three days at a time, but what acceptable reason could she provide for being away from home so long, and what would the consequences be if her brothers did find out that she had gone over into "enemy territory" with the young men of the community? No good could come of it, either for her or for those who dared to take her along.

They talked for a few minutes more before Anson checked his pocket watch and realized how long they had been sitting there.

"I guess you should take me home now," Mollie said reluctantly. "With all this meanness going on around here, Jason and Arethia will start to worry if I stay out much longer. And besides, we have a long day ahead of us tomorrow. Jason finished plowing the garden patch Saturday afternoon, and Arethia and I need to get some seed in the ground before the next good rain."

Anson loosened the reins from the brake and slapped them lightly on the back of his patient buggy horse.

They had moved through the grove to within twenty feet of the road when Anson pulled suddenly on the reins and called quietly to the horse to stop.

"What is it?" Mollie whispered.

"Listen for a minute," Anson whispered back. "I thought I heard something on the road."

Mollie heard it now. It was the quiet clip-clop of a horse approaching from the east.

"It sounds like just one animal, so there's probably no danger, but I'd rather wait here and let whoever it is pass," said Anson in a low voice.

Mollie agreed. Raiders from Kansas were still crossing into Missouri occasionally to work their mischief. But even if the person approaching was a friend, it would do her reputation no good to be seen coming out of the woods this late at night with a young man.

As the horse drew near, Mollie saw in the pale moonlight that it was pulling a light buggy similar to the one she and Anson were in. For a time it appeared as if whoever it was might move on past without ever realizing they were there, but then Anson's horse caught the scent of the other horse and whinnied a greeting.

The buggy came to a stop, and a voice called out,

"Who is it? I see you over yonder in the trees, so you'd just as well come on out."

The was no mistaking that voice, Mollie thought with alarm. It was the preacher, Boone Septin, who had led the church service that she and Anson had attended that very evening. Of all the people she would not have wanted to find her here, surely Septin topped the list!

"I guess we've been caught in the act," Anson told Mollie with a quiet chuckle of resignation. "I thought the Reverend was going to preach forever tonight, but I bet that's nothing to the sermon he'll deliver when he sees who we are."

"Well, it looks like there's no avoiding it," Mollie sighed, "so I guess we might as well get it over with. Let's go."

Anson drove to the edge of the road and stepped down from the buggy. "It's Anson Younger, Parson. I'm sorry if you were startled."

"What in blazes were you doin' out there in the trees, boy?" Septin asked. Then, staring into the shadows formed by the canopy of Anson's buggy, he added, "Who's that you've got in there with you?"

"It's Mollie Hartman," Mollie replied.

There was a moment of silence as Septin got down from his buggy and approached Anson.

"I see. I see!" Septin looked first at Anson, then up at Mollie.

"You don't see anything," Mollie told him defiantly. "We've just been talking. We haven't done anything wrong."

"Step down here, girl," Septin commanded. "I want to see your face when you tell me that. I want to look into your eyes. The eyes don't lie!"

The preacher's demand infuriated Mollie, but she decided that the wisest course was to go along with him. She and Anson had done nothing wrong, and if Septin wanted to look at her face while she told him the truth, she would damn well let him. She slid over on the seat to Anson's side of the buggy and climbed down.

Septin approached her and stared directly into her eyes. He stood so close that Mollie could feel his warm breath on her face.

"Now tell me again, child, that the two of you wasn't doin' nothin' you shouldn't." Beneath the odd smell of spearmint on his breath, Mollie realized, was a faint scent of whiskey.

"I don't see that this is any of your business at all, sir," Mollie replied, standing her ground, "but we were just talking, and Anson was about to take me home when you came along."

"Then what about this?" the preacher demanded, pointing an accusing finger at the center of her chest. Mollie looked down and for the first time realized that she had never refastened the buttons that Anson had opened earlier. She glanced quickly toward Anson, realizing that he must have been aware of this.

"I was going to tell you before you went in the house," Anson explained, scarcely concealing his amusement. It was easy enough for him to laugh, Mollie thought angrily. He didn't have this preacher breathing accusations into his face, and it would not be him who paid the price for this night's business when word spread over the community.

Quickly, Mollie raised her hands to button her blouse, but Septin grabbed one of her wrists and pulled her hand away. "It's too late to cover your nakedness now, you shameless harlot!" he roared. "Your sin is alreay blazed in crimson acrost your breast!"

"What are you talking about?" Mollie cried. "Have you gone completely out of your mind?" She twisted her arm to the side, freeing it from Septin's grasp, and stepped back.

"The punishment you have to suffer is clear," Septin

proclaimed, advancing on her again. "You gotta be stripped naked and flogged for the abominable act you've committed with this man." They struggled briefly, and at one point the preacher grasped a handful of her blouse and ripped it off her shoulder.

"All right, preacher or no preacher, you've gone too far now, mister!" Anson exclaimed. He stepped forward and spun Septin around by one arm, then struck him in the stomach with a blow that made him stagger. For an instant the preacher stood still, his shoulders hunched forward, one hand clutching his abdomen. Then as he slowly began to straighten, Mollie saw that he had pulled a pistol from somewhere in his clothing.

The gun wavered unsteadily in Septin's hand, pointing first at Mollie, then at Anson.

"Look, this thing is getting out of hand, Reverend Septin," Mollie exclaimed. "I swear to you, I swear on my mother's grave, that I committed no sin with Anson! I don't think you're feeling too well tonight, sir. Why don't you just go your way, and we'll go ours, and nothing will ever be said about what happened."

Septin simply stood there with the gun in his hand, saying nothing.

"I don't think it's about that anymore," Anson told her guardedly, not taking his eyes off the preacher or the gun he held. Mollie knew that Anson's own gun belt was rolled up and tucked away under the seat of the buggy, too far away to do either of them any good now.

"Then what is it about?" Mollie asked. "Why is he doing this to us?"

The expression on Anson's face told her. The situation no longer had anything to do with punishment for an imagined sin, but had evolved into something more primal, something she was loath to consider longer than a passing instant.

"Sir, it's been a long night, and you're tired," Mollie

said, trying to placate Septin once again. "You're not feeling well, and —"

"Silence, harlot," Septin hissed. "For your sins the Lawd's turned his face from you. He's withdrawn his grace, and it don't matter now what happens to you. It don't matter to him what I do to you no more."

The words filled Mollie with terror. Septin had the look of a man who had gone utterly mad, and when he began to advance toward her slowly, she could do little more than cower against the buggy.

Suddenly the muzzle of the gun dipped toward the ground, and Anson chose that moment to make his move It went off just as Anson grabbed the hand that held it, but the bullet plowed harmlessly into the ground several inches from Mollie's foot.

The two men were immediately locked in combat. Anson was clearly stronger than the tall, spindly Septin, but the preacher fought frantically to raise the gun. Anson was too busy keeping that from happening to strike an effective blow, but he shouted to Mollie, "Get my gun! Get my pistol from under the seat!"

Mollie turned to the buggy and scambled to retrieve the weapon. She managed to get the cartridge belt unwrapped from around it and was just drawing the pistol from the holster when Septin's weapon discharged again behind her.

Anson's scream of pain pierced the night. Fear and desperation lanced through Mollie as she spun, gun in hand, to see what had happened.

Anson lay on his back, clutching his midsection and writhing in agony while Septin knelt above him, almost as if in prayer. His weapon lay on the ground at Anson's side, but he seemed to have no more use for it now that it had done its work.

A rush of mindless fury swept over Mollie, and during that first instant the only thought she had was of killing

Boone Septin. With both hands, she raised the pistol she held, pointed it toward the preacher's head, and pulled the trigger. The roar of a third shot split the night, and without a sound, the preacher slumped to the ground.

Mollie ran to Anson and dropped to her knees. He looked up at her, and though he did not cry out again, the expression on his face told everything about the excruciating pain he was in. Even in the moonlight, Mollie could see the stream of blood that flowed freely over the fingers that clutched his stomach.

Anson tried to speak but coughed instead, bringing up a bloody froth for his efforts. Then, before Mollie could speak or think about what to do for him, his chest heaved a final time and his last breath left his throat. She knew he was dead even before his left thumb stopped its feeble twitching and the muscles of his face began to relax into the mask of death.

Mollie felt as helpless and alone as she ever had in her life. Unable to tear her eyes away from Anson's face, she found it impossible to believe that he was actually dead. How could he be when he had been so strong and vital, so very alive, only moments before? In a minute he would look at her again with recognition in his eyes, he would move and talk, he would be alive again. Then she would take him to someone who would tend his wound, and then after he was healed . . .

"Oh, Anson!" Mollied wailed, collapsing across his body as the realization came crashing down on her. Her body was racked by sobs which stole the breath from her chest with their intensity and caused her to quiver and shudder uncontrollably. A limitless span of time passed before the overpowering rush of grief started to wane and she began to be aware of her surroundings once more. She struggled to her knees, then tried to muster the measure of strength required to stand up.

It was at that moment that the fingers closed around her wrist.

Boone Septin was alive!

She had not given him another thought since the instant that she saw him fall away from Anson's side, but now she realized in a flash of terror that the bullet she fired had not completed its mission. He was alive and clutching her wrist with a grip that seemed to crush the very bones of her arm.

Mollie struck out blindly with her free hand, but her frantic blows seemed to have no effect on the bloody head that rose from the ground only inches away.

A sudden flash of pain burst into her consciousness as Septin's fist crashed into the side of her head. A bolt of white light erased her vision, and Mollie could feel consciousness slip away. After that, the whole world consisted only of a few vague impressions, which somehow managed to penetrate the cottony fog in her mind.

The preacher struggled to his feet . . . he took something from the ground beside her . . . he moved away . . . in the distance a horse snorted as it responded to a command . . .

The neat mound of dirt in the small church cemetery was completely concealed beneath armloads of bright spring flowers.

Mollie had not been at the funeral service for Anson Younger which had been held only a few hours earlier. His family had sent word the day before that they did not want her to come. But later in the day, after she was sure that the churchyard would be empty, she had come here alone to say her own private goodbye.

The two days that had passed since Anson was killed had been terrible ones for her. There had been what seemed like hours and hours of questioning, first by various members of hers and Anson's family, then by the county sheriff when he arrived, and then again by Anson's cousins and uncles in preparation for the manhunt that they conducted throughout the area. No one had been particularly kind or understanding to her but Arethia, and, to some degree, Jason; beneath the surface of every question put to her, Mollie sensed scorn and disbelief.

But even worse than the extensive interrogations were the hours she spent alone, trapped in the solitary prison of her own grief and lingering terror. She had hardly slept at all since the night Anson died, so afraid was she of the recurring scenes of violence and death that immediately invaded her mind every time she lowered her guard even briefly.

Yet what could she have done to prevent what happened? She had asked herself that question a thousand times, but still no answers came. Boone Septin was responsible for this tragedy. He alone had killed Anson Younger, and Mollie doubted that there was anything she could have done to thwart the fate which awaited her young friend.

That was the truth of it, but bringing herself to fully believe it, and finding a way to make the members of Anson's family believe it, was quite a different matter. In fact, she had already resigned herself to the possibility that they might always blame her for his death.

Staring at the grave, Mollie found herself wondering what the future might have held for her and Anson. There had not been time for the two of them to become very close, but there was no denying they had begun to build something good and valuable.

Would they have married? Mollie wondered. Would Anson Younger have become the man who could have helped her purge her mind and soul of the lingering yearning for Kurt Rakestraw? It was possible, she decided. It was possible that soon she would have wanted that to happen, would have worked to make it happen.

But she would never know. Now, instead, her legacy was the memory of two men who had passed forever beyond her reach.

Sitting alone on the grass beside the grave, Mollie was suddenly aware of someone standing a few feet away. She looked up and saw, without pleasure, that it was Cole Younger, Anson's cousin.

His simple work clothes were dusty and sweatstained, and he wore a pistol in a holster strapped to his right side. He stopped at the edge of the grave but said nothing as he stared down at the mound of flowers.

Finally, Mollie stirred, disturbed by his silence, but when he glanced over at her, there seemed to be no anger or accusation in his expression.

"I missed the funeral," Cole explained at last, his voice calm and natural as if she were simply another mourner. "Late yesterday I picked up what I thought was a good lead on Septin south of Buckner, and I decided to run it down rather than coming back for the service." Then he added, "It turned out to be nothing. When I caught up to the fellow they told me about, it was just a drummer."

Mollie knew very little about the tall young man who stood beside her. He had several brothers, four or five, she thought, and he lived with his family on an average-sized farm farther north in the county. Seeing him this close, she realized he was not as old as she had thought, but if Anson's stories of their escapades were to be believed, he made up with daring for what he lacked in years.

When the silence began to weigh heavily again, Mollie said slowly, "I'm so sorry about Anson, Cole. I just wish there was some way I could make your family understand how terrible I feel."

"You couldn't. Not right now," Cole told her bluntly. But then he added, "Right now I guess they're just desperate to blame this on somebody, and you're an easy target because nobody's been able to lay their hands on that bastard Septin. At least not yet."

"But surely you'll be able to trace where he went," Mollie

cried. "I don't know how badly I wounded him in the head, but it was bad enough that he would have needed to get some help."

"Yeah, I've been thinking about that," Cole admitted, "and I've been considering what I would have done if I was in his boots. I spent the whole ride back from Buckner thinking of nothing else."

"And?"

"I figure I would have gone to Kansas," Cole announced.

"Why?"

"Several reasons," he told her excitedly. "First of all, he's spent so much time damning Kansas Territory and everybody in it that we wouldn't think right off that he'd head in that direction. Second, all he'd have to do to make himself welcome in a hundred places across the borderline is to tell folks he'd done away with any relative of Judge Thomas Younger. And finally it would be a lot harder for a bunch of Missourians to ride over there and bring him back than it would be if he was hiding out anywhere in this state."

Everything he said made good sense to Mollie, and she was impressed by his logic. But everything he said pointed toward another, thornier question.

"So if he did go to Kansas, what can anyone do about it?" Mollie asked.

"Find him and kill him," Cole said flatly. "After what he did to Anson, I wouldn't care if he found himself a warm place to curl up in the devil's hip pocket. Me or one of us would get to him even there. We Youngers are that way. Scratch one of us and we all bleed — attack one of us and we all fight back."

Cole's words reminded Mollie of those Anson had spoken a few days earlier, and looking up at the firm lines of determination etched on his youthful features, she felt no doubt that he would do what he said.

"I'm going to help you get him, Cole," Mollie announced with such intensity that he quickly glanced down at her. "I want to see him dead as bad as anyone in your family possibly could."

"I'm sure you do, but I don't see how you can do any helping," Cole replied. "And I'm not sure anybody would accept your help anyway."

"Would you accept it, Cole?" Mollie asked. "If I found a way to do something about this, would you let me?"

"Of course," he told her without hesitation.

"All right then, I'm going to Kansas and start looking. I'll leave as soon as possible, and I'll find some way to get word to you if I pick up any lead about Boone Septin's whereabouts."

Her statement caught him off guard, but surprisingly, he did not immediately begin to argue against her idea. Instead, he seemed to mull the matter over. Finally he said, "No, I don't think you should go right now, and not by yourself. If you did happen to turn him up, he might be to hell and gone before I could get over there and kill him. But we might go together. Having you along might be just what I need to let me travel anywhere I want without suspicion."

"But Anson told me you were already recognized once in Kansas," Mollie pointed out.

"Well, the truth is, it was Anson that was recognized by a man that had traded some mules with his daddy on his way through the county last fall, and there was just a handful of men that saw us in that place anyway. Besides, we wouldn't have to go to Lawrence right off. Kansas is a big territory, and there's plenty of other places to look."

"We could go as brother and sister," Mollie suggested. "I don't think anyone would believe we were married."

"That might work," Cole mused. "I can look and act a lot younger when I need to. And, of course, I'd put this thing somewhere out of sight," he added, patting the gun on his hip. "We'd just be a brother and sister looking for a place to settle."

After talking for a few minutes more, the two of them left the cemetery and went their separate ways. On her way home, Mollie felt better than she had since the night Anson was killed.

She and Cole had agreed on a number of things before they parted. They would leave for Kansas Territory within the next few days. Mollie knew that the decision she had made was bound to bring her trouble from her family, and if word got out about what she was doing, it would certainly earn her universal scorn from the community.

But all that mattered less to her than the fact that now, at last, she had found a course of action that would propel her out of the numbing depression and guilt that otherwise might overwhelm her. Of course, they might never find Boone Septin. Kansas Territory was, as Cole Younger had pointed out, awfully big, with a lot of obscure places for a man to hide. But at least they would be trying, and whatever the cost Mollie might have to pay at home, she felt that it would be no more than the debt she owed Anson Younger.

5

Rising from his chair, Jason went over and poured another measure of whiskey into the nearly empty glass that sat on the table beside his brother. It was good Kentucky bourbon, hoarded for guests and special occasions, and he usually didn't dispense it quite this freely, but tonight he hoped an extra draft might help to mellow William's foul mood.

The children had been in bed for nearly an hour, and in the adjoining kitchen Arethia was just putting away the last of the supper dishes. When William had arrived a few minutes earlier, she had understood by his curt greeting that this was something other than a social call and had quickly excused herself so the two men could be alone.

After a healthy sampling of the bourbon Jason provided him, William plunged right into the topic that was on his mind, which had to do with Mollie and the alarming rumors about her that had started to circulate throughout the community in the months since Anson Younger's death.

On three different occasions Mollie had disappeared for days at a time, with little explanation to her family about where she was going or what she planned to do. The first time Jason and Arethia had voiced few objections, believing that she simply needed some time away by herself to help recover from the shock of what had happened to her. The second time she left, it had been more difficult to remain sympathetic, but when she came back at last, they had tried to curb their curiosity.

Now she had disappeared yet again, and even Jason and his wife were beginning to feel the same concerns that William had come tonight to express.

Earlier in the day a neighbor, Silas Bledsoe, had seen Mollie riding south toward Independence and had stopped by William's farm on the way to tell him about it. Trying to hide his surprise, William had lied and said his sister was just going to visit friends in town. But he spent the rest of the day growing increasingly angry, and by the time he got to Jason's, he was seething over his sister's scandalous conduct.

"I don't know who she thinks she is, carrying on like this," William growled, picking up the glass for another impatient swallow of the liquor. "Doesn't she realize that she's becoming an embarrassment not only to herself but to her whole family?"

"She hasn't been the same since the shooting," Jason agreed. "But that was five months ago, and Arethia and I had hoped that she would have started to settle down by now."

"She could have lived all that down," William said harshly, "that business about the Younger boy and all that. It might have taken a long time, but if she'd behaved herself, eventually people would have started to forget. Now, though, I don't know if people's opinions of her will ever change. And I'm starting to wonder myself if maybe she isn't what they say she is — just a tramp with no sense of right and wrong. Can't you do anything with her, Jason? Can't you and Arethia find a way to drum some sense into that hard head of hers?"

"Well, I guess it's the same way for us that it was with Daddy back in Virginia," Jason admitted. "He'd lecture, and she would act like she was listening, and then she would just go ahead and do whatever she wanted without worrying about the consequences. Being headstrong and willful isn't just a trait that the men in our family possess. Mollie has a full share of it.

"But that certainly doesn't mean she's a tramp. I have no idea what she's up to when she goes off like this, but I'd be willing to stake everything I own that she isn't out whoring around like everybody seems so eager to believe. Mollie's not a whore."

"Well, whatever she's doing, it's got to stop!" William said, his voice hard. "If you and Arethia don't think you can find a way to pull the reins in on her, I might have to take the matter in hand myself."

"How, William? How would you do it?" Jason said, challenging him. "Mollie's twenty-one now, a full-grown woman, and I see no way, short of running her off, to make her act as proper as we think she should."

"If that's the case, it might come to the point of making her leave," William said stubbornly. "If we can't make her change, we might have to send her away so at least she wouldn't be such an embarrassment to the rest of us. We might have to ship her all the way back to Virginia."

Although Jason knew that his wife must be hearing their conversation, she had given no indication that she was listening. But now, looking past William, Jason saw Arethia step to the kitchen door and cast a worried glance in his direction. She and Jason had had a similar discussion that very morning after Mollie saddled up and rode away without a word of explanation, and they had already agreed that making her leave was not the solution to the problem.

"I'll have no part of sending her away," Jason told William flatly. "I promised our father that I would take care of her, and as long as I have a home, she does too, no matter what happens. And as far as sending her back to Virginia is concerned, I know for a fact that she simply wouldn't go. If we put her on a stage, I promise you she'd get off at the first stop, and then her situation *would* be desperate."

"Then what do you propose?" William asked angrily.

"I don't think we have any choice but to weather it out," Jason replied. "I don't like people talking about us either, but if our friends here are the kind to look down on our whole family because of what Mollie's doing, then it makes me begin to doubt that they were ever our true friends in the first place. And right now I'm more concerned with what is going on in our sister's life than what people say is going on."

By the sour look on his face as he drained his glass, it was obvious that William did not agree. They had reached yet another of those impasses that, Jason realized with regret, were becoming a common occurrence between the two brothers. William had yet to come out and say that he regretted his decision to encourage his family to move to Missouri, but Jason wondered sometimes if such thoughts were not in his brother's mind.

"So what are you going to do when she gets back this time?" William asked derisively. "Talk to her?"

"Yes, we're going to talk to her," Jason replied evenly. "We're going to try to make her understand that the way she is acting is bringing a lot of discomfort to a lot of people. She's not stupid, and she does care for her family. I think she'll listen this time."

"Well, I guarantee she'll listen to me when I get my

hands on her. Even if I have to tie her to a tree and make her listen."

With some effort, Jason let the remark pass. Surely William realized, he thought, how much trouble there would be between them if he ever actually laid a hand on their sister.

Nothing had been settled by the time William left. In fact, the visit had only served to widen the ever-expanding distance between the two brothers. Jason regretted the division as much as he had ever regretted anything in his life, but despite that, he could not bring himself to go against his own beliefs and best judgment to bend to his brother's will.

But even if the two of them seldom agreed on anything, he thought, at least they were still able to talk with one another and air their grievances, unlike the situation between William and Charles.

Over the past few months, Jason's thoughts had turned with growing frequency to their brother in Kansas, the brother who dwelled in his memories only as a vague figure in the faraway past. It bothered him to think that by now Charles was living no more than a two-day ride away, and yet they had not seen each other or communicated in any way for the past twenty years. The time would soon come, Jason realized, when he would have to do something about that.

There were deep, deep problems in the family, problems that could, if left alone, eventually turn them into embittered strangers who no longer felt any semblance of unity or love for one another. But he would not let that happen, Jason vowed.

After Arethia finished her work in the kitchen, she came into the parlor, where Jason sat. Stopping behind him, she silently began to knead the corded muscles of his neck and shoulders, relaxing him in a special way that only she had the ability to do.

"It's hard, honey," Jason muttered at last. "It's hard holding it all together when you don't understand why anything is happening the way it is."

"I'm here with you, though," Arethia assured him quietly.

"I know, and I don't think I could make it sometimes if you weren't. I'm not even sure I'd want to try." Jason settled back in the chair, submitting himself more fully to the skillful manipulations of her fingers. A quiet minute passed, then he said, "I think that feels about as good as anything I've ever felt in my life."

Arethia leaned forward to kiss his cheek, then she whispered playfully in his ear, "You might think that right now, but there's something waiting for you in the other room that feels much better." Then without another word she crossed the room and went into their small bedroom. A minute later Jason followed, smiling.

They camped on the open prairie, eating a supper of biscuits and beans heated over an open fire, followed by tinned peaches packed in thick, sweet syrup.

Mollie approved of the campsite Cole Younger had chosen. It was in a small depression deep enough to hide their horses, with escape routes on either side. A small creek nearby provided them with ample water, and there was plenty of thick grass for their mounts to graze on during the night.

Vick Miller and Matt Hardesty, two of Cole's friends from Clay County, had come along with them on this trip. Matt had been with them once before, but this was Vick's first trip into Kansas Territory, and he was obviously elated by the sense of danger and adventure such an excursion naturally aroused.

All of Mollie's companions were younger than she by three to four years. Before she met Cole Younger, she would not have considered undertaking a trip like this with such young companions, but now she felt no concern about the courage and abilities of the three young men. They raised their boys rough and rugged along the Missouri frontier, readying them at an early age to stand up to all sorts of trouble. Furthermore, their age stood them in good stead as she had seen on her two previous trips across the border; it made them less suspicious.

And besides, Mollie was not at all sure that any of the older men she knew would be willing to take off with her to search the Kansas haystack for a needle named Boone Septin.

At times even Mollie had her doubts. She realized full well that she was risking her own life and the lives of all who accompanied her when she crossed the border, and she knew that her mysterious disappearances were doing little to contribute to the peace and harmony of her brother's household.

Yet she was a driven woman. The months since Anson's death had only served to increase her desire to seek out and destroy the man who had killed him, and there had been enough scattered rumors of Boone Septin's whereabouts to cause her and Cole Younger to cling to their belief that he was still in the area.

In fact, such a rumor had prompted this trip. A week earlier a drummer had told Mollie about a flier he'd seen that told of a camp meeting to be held in the small community of Franklin, a few miles south of Lawrence. At first the man had not recalled the preacher's name on the flier, but when Mollie mentioned Boone Septin, he thought that it sounded familiar.

That was enough. It was as good as any of the other leads she and Cole had followed up. Within twenty-four hours she had contacted Cole, and they immediately laid their plans for the manhunt. Vick and Matt had been recruited with little difficulty to go along so they could cover more territory in less time. Both had been good friends of Anson Younger's and were eager to take part in any adventure that held the promise of avenging his death.

With the crops laid by for the summer, the boys did not have much trouble getting away for a few days, explaining that they were going hunting. As she'd done before, Mollie simply saddled Stony and rode away.

After their simple supper, Mollie and her three companions spent the next hour carefully going over their plans. They would split up the next morning, with Mollie and Cole riding toward Lawrence, and Matt and Vick heading toward Franklin. The two destinations were only a few miles apart and had a good connecting road, so they planned to meet again in two nights midway along that road. At that point they would decide whether to follow up on any information they might have discovered or to head home.

Cole, who knew the area best, detailed three different places along the road where messages could be left if either party had to change the plan.

"And just remember," he told his two friends, "we're over here in Kansas for only one reason, and that's to find Boone Septin. Don't try to be heroes if any of these damned abolitionists start asking a lot of questions about who you are and why you're here. If it looks like you're going to be stopped, try to hide your guns. Act as young and ignorant and scared as you can, and they'll probably let you go."

"But if we get close to Septin?" Matt asked tentatively.

"Kill him straight out if you think you can do it and not get caught," Cole said quietly. "Otherwise, one of you stick with him while the other comes as fast as he can for Mollie and me."

"And for heaven's sake both of you be careful," Mollie added. "I'd much rather we never find him than for either of you to be hurt or killed. One man is already dead, and I don't think I could live with the burden of knowing that I was responsible for another death."

"We'd probably be here even if you wasn't," Vick said matter-of-factly. "When I was eleven, I killed my first deer with Anson Younger's rifle and him standing to the side whispering to me just where to aim. Afterwards we both tasted the blood, and he smeared it all over my face. Then he cut my shirttail off, and he told me I'd become a man that day. He was just like an older brother 'cause he done things like that for me."

"It's pretty much the same with me," Matt added. "The Youngers have been good friends and neighbors to us all my life. Two years ago when my pa broke his leg at harvest time, I guess Anson and his daddy probably saved our farm by coming over and helping us get our crops in."

"It'll be all right, Mollie," Cole said gently. "These boys know how to take care of themselves, and they're not likely to do anything stupid that'll get anybody hurt. I wouldn't have them along if I thought otherwise."

Mollie smiled at her friend. It was amazing how much she had come to rely on Cole since that bleak day when they met at Anson's grave. He had become such a constant source of strength and reassurance that it was easy for her to forget how young he was. He had the confidence and abilities of a mature person, and she felt as safe here with him as she would have with men twice his age. It was good to have such a friend and ally.

When Cole rose and headed for a nearby stand of cottonwoods, explaining that he was going for more wood, Mollie quickly stood up and said she would go along.

Mollie had gathered most of an armload of the dead-fall when she stopped and looked over at her companion. "Cole?" she asked abruptly. "Are we doing the right thing?"

Cole turned and shot her a quizzical look. "What do you mean?" he countered.

"I mean us being here and bringing your friends all the way from Missouri to check out a vague rumor that's days, maybe weeks, old."

"If we didn't, who would?" Cole asked softly. "My cousins and uncles all tried to find Septin right after Anson was killed, but they gave up. They all have their own lives to lead, and none of them have the time to do what we're doing. It's up to us."

"It's just that I get so frustrated sometimes," Mollie sighed. "For all we know, Boone Septin could have left these parts long ago. He could be anywhere by now, anywhere on the continent, and we could all be risking our lives for nothing."

Cole said nothing for a moment, then spoke slowly. "I can't explain it, but I keep getting this feeling deep down in my gut that he's still close by. I never have been any big believer in fate or anything like that, but ever since you and I started this business, I've felt like I was supposed to be the one to hunt the bastard down and kill him. Sometimes I wake up at night seeing the look in his eyes when I pull the trigger on him."

"Have you ever killed anybody, Cole?"

Cole stared at her a long moment, his face pale in the moonlight that pierced the canopy of leaves. "There was a man once in Independence," he said quietly. "He was a teamster with one of those big outfits on their way to Santa Fe to trade. I've never told anybody about it, not even my brothers."

Mollie waited, though she was no longer sure she wanted to hear the rest.

"I'd gone to town with Mama to buy some supplies, and we were going to stay the night at my aunt Ellen's. This man stopped Mama outside a store and started insulting her, telling her how pretty she was and what he'd like to do to such a good-looking woman. I tried to stop him, but he cuffed me across the mouth, and I got the wind knocked out of me when my back hit a hitching post. And then he just strolled away, laughing like the devil.

"Later that night I was out and about when I saw him come out of a saloon and head around back to make water. I picked up a split wagon spoke, and I followed him. After he'd done what he came out to do, he started to turn around, and I hit him full in the face with that spoke. He went to his knees, and that might have been enough for me, but then I saw his hand go toward his gun, so I hit him again.

"They found him there the next morning, dead as a rock, and the sheriff figured it was a robbery. I didn't take anything off him, but somebody else must have come along later and cleaned him out, 'cause even his gun was gone."

"How old were you?" Mollie whispered.

"Just turned nine," he answered simply. "I've shot at raiders since them, but in the dark it's hard to tell whether or not you've hit anything. So I guess there was just that one time."

Mollie tried to imagine the courage that it must have taken for a nine-year-old boy, armed with nothing more than a piece of wood, to go up against a full-grown man, an armed frontiersman who had probably spent years fighting Indians along the trail to Santa Fe. It was almost beyond belief, and yet from the calm, detached tone in Cole's voice, Mollie knew it must be true.

"So now you know something about me that nobody else in this world knows," Cole said. Then before Mollie could reply, he turned and started back to the camp.

Vick and Matt were already spreading their blankets on the grass, and after dropping the wood she carried, Mollie did the same. After making her bed a short distance away from the others, she rolled her riding boots up in her coat for a pillow and lay down. The last thing she saw before dropping off to sleep was Cole sitting by the fire, staring at the dancing flames.

Although Mollie had been to Lawrence twice before, there was always something new to see when she returned. Founded only the year before, in 1854, the little town was growing fast as more and more Easterners made their way to this frontier settlement. Unlike many other parts of Kansas, Lawrence was an abolitionist stronghold, and few Southern sympathizers dared even visit the place for very long, let alone settle there.

Riding up the long main street, past the shops and houses, Mollie and Cole drew very little attention. Lawrence was used to strangers, and a woman and a youth traveling alone were hardly something to remark upon.

They stopped their horses in front of the Free State Hotel, dismounted, and tied the animals to a rail there. The three-story stone building was by far the most impressive structure in town, and Mollie knew that it was probably not by accident that it was constructed as much like a fortress as a refuge for weary travelers.

After taking two rooms at the hotel and depositing their scant luggage in them, Mollie and Cole headed in separate directions to do some sleuthing. Cole took the horses and went to the livery stable nearby, which he knew was tended by a garrulous old man.

Finally on her own, Mollie took a leisurely stroll around town, looking for fliers that might mention a camp meeting or revival in the area. When she found herself approaching the Free State Hotel however, she turned into a dry-goods store and pretended to examine the merchandise. Actually she was waiting for two other women to finish their business and leave so she would have a better opportunity to strike up a conversation with the owner. As the women closed the door behind them, she selected a packet of needles and a spool of thread and approached the counter.

"This all for you, miss?" the man asked. He was a pleasant-looking middle-aged fellow, a round-faced man with a white apron tied over his starched shirt and trousers.

"Yes, thank you," Mollie smiled as she produced a few pennies to pay for her purchases. "I tore a hole in my best frock during the trip down from Iowa, and this is the first chance I've had to get the right color of thread to repair it." She was careful to mention the route to Kansas that many abolitionists chose to take rather than risk the perils of crossing Missouri.

"Just in from the East, are you?" the man asked.

"Actually my brother and I have been here in the territory something over a month now. We came from Massachusetts with friends of our family, and now we're staying with them up north of Fort Leavenworth until our mother and father arrive. But we got bored just being at their farm for so long, so we decided to come into town for a few days."

"Well, there's not that much more to do here, I'm afraid," the storekeeper offered. "Except for the saloons, the whole place shuts down at dusk. People in these parts get pretty edgy after dark, what with all the trouble with Missouri lately."

"I had heard talk that there might be a camp meeting planned for Lawrence sometime soon," Mollie said. "A drummer who visited the farm a couple of weeks ago said something about a traveling preacher who was working his way through this area holding revival services."

"Well, we've got a couple of preachers in town, but I haven't heard anything about any camp meeting."

"The drummer said the preacher's name is Septin," Mollie persisted. "He doesn't have any regular church. Instead, he just travels around from place to place, holding services wherever he can."

"Now that you mention the name," the man said, looking thoughtful, "it seems to me there was a fellow through here by the name of Septin. I didn't pay much mind to him 'cause I don't go in for that sort of thing, but my wife went to see him. She said after he got himself wound up, the devil didn't stand a chance against him, and neither did the congregation when it came time to pass the collection plate."

"Hmm. How long ago was that?" Mollie casually asked, trying to suppress her excitement.

"Let's see. It's been at least a month, more like six weeks. Like I told you, I don't pay much mind to that sort of carrying on."

A minute later Mollie gathered up her purchases and left the store. Her excitement had been replaced by disappointment. Apparently the parson had made a single pass through the area, holding services in Lawrence, Franklin, and probably a number of other communities to the south as well, and the trail was now pretty cold.

But the conversation had been fruitful, too; now they had proof that Septin had not fled the area after killing Anson Younger, and it appeared he was still using his own name.

I guess he thinks he's safe just because he left Missouri, Mollie thought. I wonder how he would feel if he knew that we haven't given up and that we're here right now sorting out his trail.

She met Cole at the hotel at a prearranged time, and the two of them eagerly compared notes over supper in a small restaurant. Cole's inquiries had been even less productive than Mollie's, and they decided that there was no reason for them to remain in Lawrence. They would leave at first light for the meeting with Matt and Vick on the road to Franklin.

Against Mollie's wishes, Cole elected to stop in at a couple of saloons before going back to the hotel, so she returned alone. Despite her confidence in his ability to take care of himself, Mollie lay awake in bed for nearly an hour, remembering the trouble Anson and Cole had encountered in a saloon in this very town only a year before.

But at last she heard footsteps in the hall, then the door to the room next to hers opening and closing, and finally she relaxed and let sleep claim her.

They rode south out of Lawrence at a gallop. Mollie could not explain the feeling of happiness she felt this morning. Perhaps the guilt she felt over Anson's death was finally ebbing, she thought, or maybe it was because of the sense of adventure that automatically accompanied each new incursion into enemy territory. Whatever the cause, she was enjoying the morning immensely, and from the rare smile on Cole's face, she decided that her happiness must be contagious.

They covered the distance quickly, stopping briefly to check the places where their friends might have camped or left a message. Only when they had ridden to within a couple of miles of Franklin did either of them give voice to their growing concern.

"We should have met them by now," Cole said at last, a frown creasing his face. "It can only mean one of two things. Either they came across something, or they've run into trouble."

"Well, from what we learned in Lawrence, it seems likely that Septin was headed south," Mollie said. "Maybe they've found out where he is."

"But the plan was for them to leave a message," Cole reminded her. "Either that or one of them was supposed to bring us word."

"I guess we'll find out when we get to town," Mollie said and spurred her horse.

About a mile outside of Franklin, the road dropped

down a hillside and passed through a small grove of trees. As they entered the grove, a shrill whistle sounded a few yards ahead and to the left of them.

In an instant, Cole was off his horse, crouching on the ground, gun in hand. Mollie was almost as quick to dismount and take cover. When the whistle sounded again, Cole responded with one of his own. It seemed to be a signal that he understood, but he was taking no chances.

"Cole? Is that you?" a voice called out hoarsely from the bushes. It was Vick.

"Damn, Vick!" Cole exclaimed, standing up at last and holstering his gun. "What's going on?"

Vick waved to them from his hiding place in the trees a dozen yards away. "Come on over here!" he said urgently. "Get off the road first, and then I'll explain."

He led them to a spot where there was no chance that any passersby could see them. He had hobbled his own horse there, and from the clipped grass around the animal, it appeared that he had been waiting for several hours.

"Where's Matt?" Mollie asked immediately.

"He's OK," Vick assured her, grinning broadly. "He's waiting for us in a safe place a few miles east of here. We ran into a little trouble during the night, but I think when you hear about it, you'll agree that it couldn't have turned out better!"

"Did you find Septin?" Cole asked impatiently.

"No, but that's about the only thing that didn't happen to us since we saw you last," Vick said. "Come on. I'll tell you about it on the way." And with that, the three of them mounted up and started off across country, heading due east, toward Missouri.

Vick and Matt had finished their inquiries in Franklin earlier than expected the previous afternoon, and instead of paying for a place to sleep in town, they decided to ride a few miles north and find a place to camp. About dusk they came across a party of half a dozen men who had already made their camp along the roadside. The men had meat cooking and coffee already made, and when they invited the two youths to join them, neither Vick nor Matt saw any harm in it.

"They looked like they had done some traveling," Vick explained, "and we thought there was a chance they might have heard something of Septin along they way. They hadn't, but we judged them to be safe company anyway because they weren't from anywhere around here. It turns out they had formed a company in Indiana and were on their way to try their luck in the California gold fields."

In the middle of the night, however, Vick and Matt discovered that they had misjudged the strangers badly.

"I woke up with a knee in my chest and a big ugly fellow grinning down at me," Vick said. " 'Now you be a good lad,' he says, 'and maybe I won't have to send you back to your mama all busted in pieces.'

"Well, I looked around and Matt was in about the same shape with another fellow on top of him. And the rest of them was breaking camp and saddling horses, ours included. Then this ox on top of me says, 'Plowboys like you don't need to be riding such fine horseflesh, so we're just gonna take them two horses off your hands. We got a long trip ahead of us, and we're gonna need a few extra animals to get us through.' "

"So?" Cole asked.

"Hell, I shot him, Cole," Vick exclaimed. "My gun belt was rolled up with my jacket a few feet away, so I guess he thought I was unarmed, but I'd taken my pistol under the covers with me. I raised it up a little ways, and I meant to shoot him in the head, but I hit his knee instead.

"You never heard the like of hollering in your life as that fellow did, but in a second I had my gun barrel poked in his ear, and he started to calm down right away.

Between the two of us, we talked the rest of them into laying down their guns and backing off, and then me and Matt high-tailed it out of there. It was mighty convenient, 'cause they already had our horses saddled up for us."

"Didn't they come after you?" Mollie asked.

"They probably did," Vick said. "But it would be mighty slow going for them on foot, 'cause we took their horses. And they had a wounded man, too, don't forget."

By this time both Mollie and Cole could do little more than shake their heads in amazement.

"I know what you told us about staying out of trouble," Vick said, "but we just couldn't help this. We were right in the middle of this scrape before we knew what was happening, and by then there wasn't nothing to do but fight our way out."

"So what did you do with the horses?" Cole asked.

"Matt's got 'em," Vick said. "We left their gear where they could find it and didn't even keep the cash we found, but we figured fair was fair. If they could take our horses, we could take theirs. I know a horse trader over south of Westport who doesn't ask too many questions, and he pays cash money for anything with four legs."

They pushed their horses hard across the open countryside, and within an hour they had reached the woods where Matt Hardesty waited, rifle in hand. Another hundred feet into the woods they came to the place where Matt had the stolen horses, and his own, tied to a long rope strung between two trees.

"I'm sure glad to see the three of you," Matt admitted. "I don't believe I could handle horse thieving as a regular trade. It's just too blamed hard on a fellow's nerves."

"Have you seen any sign of the six men?" Cole asked.

"I've stayed on the move all around the edge of these woods ever since Vick left, but I haven't seen anyone."

"Well, let's don't push our luck." Cole paused. "The sooner we get back into Missouri, the better off we'll be. If we push it, we can be across the line before dark. Then we can unload the horses in Westport tomorrow morning and still be home by supper time."

It took the three only a moment to organize the horses for the trip back to Missouri. Five minutes later they were racing from the woods, venting the exhilaration they felt. The chorus of wild yells would have made any charging band of Indians proud.

6

Tyson Hartman skirted a meadow at the base of the forty-foot cliff, moving stealthily on moccasined feet, blending in so completely with his surroundings that a chance observer only a few yards away might very well have missed his passing.

The sun had been up less than half an hour, but everyone was already in place. Jason had taken a stand somewhere on the cliffs above, and his two oldest sons, John and Daniel, were in position about a quarter mile ahead and slightly off to the left. Unlike the others, Tyson knew this area thoroughly, having scouted and hunted it many times in the two years he had been in Missouri, so he had selected the best positions for everyone else.

This particular chunk of territory, which lay east of where the Missouri River made its wide curve and started north, was too rocky to farm and too broken by bluffs and rugged hills to cut roads through, so it had remained wild and inaccessible despite the encroachment of civilization all around. Tyson had found it to be a haven for a variety of game, especially deer and bears, and because of its comforting remoteness, he had found himself drawn to it again and again since coming west with his sister and Jason's family.

The four of them had traveled most of the previous day to reach this spot and had camped last night on the bluffs. This hunt was particularly important because it was the first for Jason's middle son, Daniel, who had turned eleven three months earlier. They needed meat for the table, and beyond that, it was the hope of both Jason and Tyson that the boy would get at least one opportunity to become the provider of that meat.

There were seven deer in the herd Tyson was tracking, six does and a buck. From the depth and spacing of their tracks, he could tell that they had not yet detected his presence and were leisurely working their way north along the base of the cliffs. If they kept on like this, they would pass right in front of the two boys, and directly below where Jason was positioned.

For the next half hour, Tyson trailed the herd, making no sound or movement that might send them into flight. Once when they stopped to graze, he actually came in sight of them for an instant and could have dropped the big eight-point buck with one quick shot. Instead, he vanished from sight and waited for them to move on. He wanted the boys to have at least one chance for a shot before he himself went for the kill.

When the ground began to rise to the north, Tyson knew they were approaching the spot where the trap was laid. The hill he was climbing rose steadily for about seventy-five yards, then dropped off steeply on the other side. Unless the boys had moved, they should be waiting at the base of the hill where two game trails converged at a convenient creek crossing.

When he reached the crest of the hill, he spotted the

deer about fifty yards ahead, descending the wooded hill-side and heading for the crossing. He stopped behind a thick oak and raised his rifle, poised for a shot in case the boys had moved from their stand.

While still about thirty yards from the crossing, the big buck seemed to realize instinctively that something was wrong. He stopped and tested the wind, then snorted and pawed the ground a couple of times to warn the others. The does stood patiently behind him, waiting for guidance.

At last the buck appeared to decide that the danger lay ahead, because he turned back on the trail. Tyson knew that if the herd backtracked, he could easily kill the buck, but that would mean that the boys would never even see the deer, let alone have a shot at them.

Tyson stepped out from behind the tree and stood in full view of the approaching herd.

The instant the buck spotted Tyson, he spun once more and bounded toward the creek crossing with the does close behind.

When the deer drew to within ten yards of the creek, Tyson saw two forms rise from the brush nearby, rifles already raised. Two shots sounded in close succession, and one of the forms, undoubtedly Daniel, pitched back out of sight as the recoil from his rifle knocked him off his feet.

One of the does dropped like a stone out of the herd, but the rest of the animals bounded forward and in another second were out of sight. There was seldom time for a second shot in situations like this.

Uncocking his rifle, Tyson moved quickly down the hillside to where the two boys were just wading out of the brush and starting toward their kill.

"I don't know which one of you got her," Tyson said, looking down at the dead doe, "but it was a good shot, especially on the run like that."

"It was John," the younger boy admitted. "It must have been him, 'cause I aimed at the buck." He leaned his heavy rifle against a nearby tree and then began to rub his sore shoulder. "I bet I didn't even come anywhere close," he added in a voice heavy with the burden of his failure.

"Well, it's like I said," Tyson told him, "a running shot is the hardest one there is to make. I've missed many of them myself, and I don't know of any other hunter that hasn't as well. The important thing is, we've got meat to carry home." Then turning to John and handing him a long hunting knife, he said, "Here, you need to slit the throat and then hang the carcass up to bleed awhile. You help him, Daniel."

With obvious distaste, the older boy knelt beside the dead doe and sliced through the thick hide and meat of her throat until it was laid open. Daniel took a length of rope that Tyson provided and tied it around the deer's back legs, then the two boys began to drag the carcass to a nearby tree. Tyson knew they would probably need some help getting it off the ground, but he wanted them to take care of as much of this business as they could manage. That was part of hunting too.

Suddenly a shot rang out in the direction the deer had fled.

"It looks like your father got a crack at them too," Tyson noted.

"Yeah, he probably got the buck," Daniel grumbled, pausing in his labors long enough to stare wistfully into the distance.

"Well, are you grown up enough to be glad for him if he did?" Tyson asked sharply. Both boys stopped working again and stared at him, surprised by the tone of his voice. "When men go hunting together, not all of them always make a kill," Tyson said. "I didn't get one either."

"Yes, sir, Uncle Ty," Daniel answered quickly. "I'll be

glad if Daddy got the buck. About as glad as if I did it."

For the next fifteen minutes the three of them were busy preparing the deer. Tyson showed them the proper way to slit the abdomen open and pull the innards out, then identified the heart and the liver in the warm pile of entrails and instructed them to wrap them in leaves and place them in a cloth bag that he had brought along for that purpose.

A short time later they heard Jason call out, and Tyson responded with a yell to indicate where they were. Soon Jason emerged from the north, a doe slung across his shoulders. His sons ran over to him to examine the kill.

After Jason had dropped his deer on the ground, the first words out of his mouth came as a surprise to the other three.

"You know, Ty, I've tried to raise all my children good and to teach them right from wrong," he said, "but I guess I've been a failure with these two."

The boys were stunned by the apparent rebuke, but Tyson simply asked, "How's that, Jason?"

"If you remember how it was back home," Jason replied, "we considered it a shame and a disgrace for a man to shoot game just for sport and then to leave it lying in the woods. But I guess that's what one of these two boys has done. Not fifty feet on the other side of that creek over there I came across a fine buck lying dead on the ground with nobody to claim him!"

With a whoop, Daniel shot past his father and bounded across the creek to find his prize.

The final rays of sunlight were sinking in the horizon when Jason stacked the wood for the evening fire and touched a match to it. Tyson was sitting on the ground across the small clearing, restoring the razor edge to his hunting knife with a small whetstone.

Overall it had been a good hunt, and when they headed

home in the morning, they would carry enough meat with them to last the family for several weeks. The four of them had spent most of the day in the woods, and in addition to the three deer carcasses that now hung from a tree limb in the camp, they also had a dozen rabbits and perhaps twice that many squirrels.

The boys were still in the woods, hunting squirrels in a deep hollow south of the camp, but with daylight quickly fading, Jason expected them to return soon.

"We're going to have our work cut out for us curing all this meat when we get home," Jason commented. "And if the ground is dry enough when we get back, I might have to turn the job over to you and the boys and start my spring plowing."

Tyson raked the stone across the blade a couple more times, then tested it on his arm by neatly shaving the hair off a small patch of skin. Satisfied at last, he replaced the knife in the sheath on his belt and stuck the whetstone in his pocket.

"I guess I haven't been much help to you around the farm, have I?" Tyson asked.

"Not much," Jason replied without malice, "but it's not exactly a secret that there's not an ounce of farming blood in you. And the meat you bring in does help a lot. What with you keeping us in game most of the time, I haven't had to slaughter near as many cows or hogs to keep the family fed."

"Well, there's more to it than just not wanting to be a farmer," Tyson said. "I've been studying on it for a spell now, most of the winter, and I think I've got it figured out."

"What have you got figured out, Ty?" Jason asked, taking a seat near the fire and giving Tyson his full attention.

"You know that fellow that Mollie used to be so crazy about? That Kurt Rakestraw? Well, when he used to come over to visit, sometimes we'd get to talking, about the places he'd been, the places over toward the Rockies and beyond, places where a man could live the way he liked and go for weeks or even months if he wanted and never lay eyes on another living soul. I got me a hankering to see some of those places, Jason."

Jason took his pipe from his pocket, filled it with tobacco, and lit it with a burning twig he'd pulled from the edge of the fire. "I can't say that surprises me very much, Ty," he sighed. "Ever since you were a kid, you spent more time in the hills by yourself or with your Cherokee friends than you ever did at home. Even Mama used to say that if she hadn't been there when you were made, she'd swear you were half-Indian yourself."

"I just feel more comfortable in places that are still the way God made them," Tyson tried to explain. "The thought of going away and not seeing any of you again for years, or maybe ever, puts a knot as big as a crab apple in my chest, but staying in these parts is like having a terrible itch that I just can't scratch."

"Have you given any thought to what you might do out west?" Jason asked.

"Well, I can ride and shoot, and I can hunt and trap and track. I guess I'll do whatever falls into my hands to do. I'll scratch the itch any way it feels right."

Jason couldn't find it in himself to argue with his brother. If Tyson went west, they might never see one another again, and that thought lay like a stone in the pit of his stomach. But he had always known that this day would come. For years now it had only been a matter of when Tyson would decide the time was right.

And now apparently it was.

"I met a man in town a couple of weeks ago who's putting together a wagon train bound for Oregon," Tyson said. "He's got thirty families waiting to leave now, and he said when he has fifty committed, he'll be on his way.

He needs a hunter to keep his people fed along the way, and I figure that'll be me."

"The way folks are pouring in from the East this spring," Jason mused, "it shouldn't take long for him to get the numbers he needs."

"About a week, he says. Two at the outside."

"And then you're gone."

"And then I'm gone."

The words had a ring of finality that Jason found hard to bear, but he turned his head away and busied himself with the fire so his brother would not see the moisture glistening in his eyes.

Jason and William rode into Independence with Tyson on the day he was scheduled to join the wagon train. They had held a big family dinner for their brother the night before in honor of his departure, but Jason wanted to ride along with him this morning as well, and at the last minute William decided to come too.

While most other people would have been bursting with excitement over the journey they were about to undertake, Tyson was quiet and calm, talking very little with his brothers even during these final hours.

He was traveling as light as possible, carrying everything he would need in a roll on the back of his saddle. His gear consisted of two wool blankets, an oilcloth slicker, extra powder and shot for his rifle and pistol, and a few miscellaneous personal items, such as a razor, soap, and a small New Testament. He wore his customary buckskins and moccasins, and in a pouch he carried a folding knife, a flint and steel for fires, a whetstone, a length of cord, and a small compass.

The three brothers rode straight south through the center of Independence to the broad meadow where wagon trains usually gathered. In addition to the group Tyson was joining, two other wagon trains were also being assembled in the area. One train, consisting of heavy, high-sided, canvas-covered wagons filled with trade goods, was on the verge of departing for Santa Fe, and the other, much smaller than the rest, had the ambitious destination of California.

Tyson introduced his brothers to the leader of his group, a weathered frontiersman by the name of Ezekiel Slade. Like others of his breed, Slade had spent most of his fifty years in the western wilderness, first as a trapper and then when the demand for furs began to dwindle as a trader, scout, and leader of bands such as this one. He was being sponsored by a group in the Willamette Valley, in Oregon, that hoped to attract new settlers to the area.

"I can't say I envy you the journey you have ahead of you, Slade," William said to the wagon master. "The talk is that the Oregon Trail is none too safe these days, what with all the Indian country it passes through. And this bunch you're leading looks to be about as green as you could find anywhere."

"It ain't no picnic out there," Slade admitted, aiming a stream of tabacco juice with great precision at a nearby rock. "Never has been, even back before the Sioux an' Cheyenne an' Crow commenced to gettin' their dander up 'bout all the palefaces crossin' their land. But give me a month on the trail with this bunch, an' you won't recognize most of 'em." Then turning to Tyson, he added, "We'll put some leather on 'em, won't we, boy?"

"I don't know all that much about what's ahead of us," Tyson grinned. "But I figure we'll do all right."

"Sure, we will. Sure!" Slade exclaimed with bravado. "Hell, we'll lose a few along the way. Always do. But out of the two hundred or so folks that start out with us in the morning, I don't s'pose we'll plant more'n a dozen or so beside the trail. Maybe twice that many if the Indian raids is rougher'n I expect."

The numbers seemed unacceptably high to Jason, and it occurred to him to wonder if Slade had informed the people he would be leading of these expected losses. But it probably wouldn't have stopped most of them from going. He understood how it could be for a man who had his heart set on reaching a region of abundant, fertile, and practically free land like the Oregon country.

The final parting between the brothers turned out to be brief because Slade already had a dozen things he wanted Tyson to take care of, and as he insisted, "Time was a'wastin'".

When the time came for Jason and William to leave, Tyson solemnly shook hands with them and promised to send word when the trip was finished. His brothers didn't linger; they felt that they'd already become a part of his past, and that he was impatient to get on with his future and the big adventure he'd been yearning for.

On their way back through Independence, Jason and William stopped for a meal. Over steaks and fried potatoes they discussed their brother's departure.

"I wrote Daddy and Sarah a couple of days ago about Tyson leaving," Jason said. "I guess they won't be any more surprised than we were that Ty had to see what was out there, but it feels odd having our family even more scattered than we already are."

"Yeah, what with Edward in the navy in New York," William said dryly, "when Ty reaches Oregon, the family will stretch from coast to coast."

"And Milton's down in Mississippi raising cotton —"

"Uh huh. And Charles is over in Kansas raising nigger lovers."

"I've been thinking a lot about Charles lately," Jason said, refusing to acknowledge his brother's remark. "I've been thinking I'd like to go to Kansas and see him. I'd like to get to know him."

"You'll be wasting your time," William told him flatly,

"because after you get to know him, you won't like him. Twenty years ago he was a sanctimonious bastard, and I don't know of any good reason to believe he's changed one whit since then."

"Well, he might be a lot of things, but he isn't a bastard, William," Jason said sharply. "He's our brother, born of your mother and of our father, and I feel bad about the fact that I've never even tried to contact him once in the two years we've been out here."

"You do what you want, Jason," William said stiffly. "I can see there's no use in me offering any more advice in the matter because your mind is made up. You go to Kansas and find out for yourself."

"I guess that's what I'll be doing before much longer."

They ate in silence, their conversation at an impasse, and would have gone on this way had not an acquaintance of William's come into the restaurant and made his way to their table. He was a man in his late forties with handsome features and the manner of one accustomed to taking charge. By the way William rose and shook the man's hand, Jason could tell that the event must be of some importance.

'Here's a gentleman I've been hoping you would have the chance to meet, Jason," William said expansively. "Senator, may I present my brother, Jason Hartman. Jason, shake the hand of Senator David Atchison!"

Jason stood up and took the senator's hand. As a stalwart supporter of the rights of slaveholders in Missouri, Atchison's name was practically a household word in this part of the state, but Jason was surprised to learn that the senator was familiar with him as well.

"My friend Judge Younger mentioned you to me a short time after your arrival," Atchison told Jason. "As a matter of fact, he said he nearly hung you."

His casual, almost jovial tone in mentioning the event irritated Jason, but he didn't let it show. "It couldn't have been much closer," he shrugged. "When I found out what was going on, I understood how they could make that kind of mistake. As worked up as everybody was that night, it's a wonder they didn't leave the countryside littered with corpses."

"So I hear." Then without changing his tone or expression, Atchison popped a question that took Jason completely by surprise. "Tell me, my friend, after living here for two years and seeing the kind of trials we've been going through, are you sound on the goose?"

Jason glanced quickly at his brother, but he could see that William was going to be no help. In fact, Jason thought, his brother was probably as interested in hearing his response as the senator was.

"Well, sir," he replied at last, "because I own no slaves, my interest in the matter is probably not as great as the interest of those who do. But I do soundly disapprove of those fanatics who keep riding over here to attack us and disrupt our lives, and I am concerned with the situation that is shaping up in Kansas."

"I see. I see," the senator said, but he didn't sound convinced. He was obviously aware that Jason hadn't really answered his question and seemed about to toss it out again when all of a sudden he equivocated. "Because you're William Hartman's brother, I had no real concerns about your loyalties, but in these troubled times it's always good to make sure."

"My brother can be trusted," William said, coming to Jason's relief at last.

"Then if that's the case, and if you gentlemen have a few minutes, I'd like to discuss something with you." Jason did not relish the idea of being a party to any sort of insider discussion, but decided that it would be easiest to just go ahead and listen to what the senator had to say.

Atchison wasted no time in getting right to the point.

"As you're probably aware, the territorial elections in Kansas are coming up within a few weeks, and their outcome will undoubtedly be crucial to our cause. A territorial legislature and a number of local officeholders are to be selected, and if the abolitionists carry the day, the problems that we've suffered up until now will be nothing compared with what we will face in the future." He paused for a moment to take out a long cigar and light it.

"Our efforts to relocate faithful, supportive Southerners in Kansas Territory have not been as successful as we had hoped," Atchison continued. "We hold a few enclaves here and there, but they don't begin to provide the numbers we will need to do well in these elections."

William nodded frequently, agreeing with every word. He seemed, in fact, to know where the conversation was going, but Jason still had no idea.

"I've made a special trip back from Washington just to travel around this part of the state and stress the importance of the Kansas elections," the senator said. "The territory is being taken over by outsiders from the East whose only true interest in this part of the country has to do with the particular misguided and radical point they are trying to make. I think that it is entirely possible that once they have voted in an abolitionist legislature and packed most of the county offices with their lickspittle lackeys, the majority of them will go back east, rejoicing in the fact that they have loosed a terrible monster at our very doorsteps."

Suddenly it hit Jason like a brickbat, and he blurted it out before he had a chance to catch himself. "So you think the people of Missouri should go over and vote in the Kansas elections?" he asked incredulously.

"Exactly!" Atchison replied, unfazed by the amazement in Jason's voice. "I know on the surface it sounds dishonorable and, in fact, downright illegal. But consider this. Most of us who have lived here for years have based our life styles and fortunes on certain institutions, and our concerns in preserving our way of life simply do not end at some arbitrary line drawn on a map. What happens in Kansas is of crucial interest to us, much more so than it is for any interlopers who have moved only recently into the territory.

"And when you consider the matter in that light, we here on the western edge of Missouri have far more right to express our opinions at the Kansas polls than do those outsiders. By the strictest interpretation of the law, we might be legally in the wrong by going over to vote in Kansas, but it is my firm belief that morally we will be doing the right thing."

"I see no other course for us," William agreed immediately. "Who has a greater right to cast a vote in Kansas than those who must live for the rest of their lives with the outcome?"

"Precisely!" Atchison exclaimed.

Jason knew that at this point his own sentiments would displease both of his companions, so he refrained from saying anything. Atchison did not seem to mind, and William was probably thankful for his brother's silence.

"We are very discreetly beginning to organize the resources that it will take to get enough men of legal age over into Kansas at the correct time," the senator said. "Transportation for hundreds will be needed, and once there, they will need places to sleep and food to eat. There's been some talk of providing some financial incentives to increase our numbers, but I'm opposed to that unless it becomes absolutely necessary. And of course," he added guardedly, "we must be prepared to defend ourselves in case our efforts are opposed."

William's eagerness to be a part of such a massive undertaking was readily apparent. "I promise you, Senator, that I could muster a hundred men for you overnight," he announced grandly. "And given the time we have to prepare, I believe I can come up with five times that number."

"We'll need that many a dozen times over to pull this off," the senator said, "but by God, we can do it! We can save ourselves from this terrible menace if we pull together!"

For the next quarter hour the two men were immersed in their discussion, each feeding his own enthusiasm on the excitement of the other. By the time Atchison left, William was so elated that he acted as if the battle were already won.

"There goes a very interesting man," Jason said as Atchison swept out the door, no doubt to sound the call to arms in other quarters.

"He's a great man," William beamed. "A hero!" Then, unexpectedly, he turned to his brother and let the warmth of his mood spill over Jason. "And I want to tell you right here and now how appreciative I am for the way you conducted yourself during our discussions."

"A couple of times there it was hard to keep quiet," Jason admitted. "But I kept thinking, 'What good will it do?'"

"What good indeed?" William said. "I know we are of different minds on this subject, but a least you are learning to keep our differences between ourselves, and I'm grateful for that. To speak out at the wrong time could only embarrass me and put you under a dark cloud of suspicion."

"Well, when you're passing out campaign posters," Jason told him, "just don't expect me to hang one on my front door. Until all this is over, don't ever make the mistake of thinking that my silence implies support."

7

The increasingly cold wind blowing down across the plains from the northwest plagued Jason for the last twenty miles of his journey to Lawrence. It emphasized what needed no emphasis — that winter was on the way.

Jason could ill spare the time he had taken off to ride across the border into Kansas in search of his brother Charles, but he tried to turn his mind away from all the work he had postponed to make this trip. There would never be a good time, yet this was better than most. Now, in late October, the crops were harvested, the stockpiles of winter feed for the stock were safely stored in the barn, and the small storeroom he had added to his house over the summer was filled to overflowing with the food they had preserved for winter. There were a multitude of lesser tasks still to be done around the farm, but at least the necessities had been taken care of.

During the summer he had sent two letters to Lawrence for his brother but hadn't received a reply to either of them. He had only the word of Sarah, faraway in Virginia, that Charles was still in Kansas, and the letter she based her information on was nearly a year old now.

There was no way to tell what he would run into once he reached Lawrence. Charles could be anywhere in the territory by now or could, conceivably, even have moved his family back to Pennsylvania by this time. And in addition to that uncertainty, there was also the inherent risk that was constantly present for any Missourian who dared penetrate this deep into abolitionist territory. The suspicions that had developed in these parts toward Missourians had reached almost fanatic proportions, and he knew that there were plenty of men in Lawrence who would shoot him on the spot, with no questions asked, if they happened to learn who he was and where he came from.

But still he had to try.

Jason crossed the Kansas River a few miles east of Lawrence and then headed southwest along a well-traveled wagon road. He had ridden no more than a mile from the river when he spotted a band of four men approaching from the direction of Lawrence. His first impulse was to turn his horse and try to outdistance them, remembering all too well the time only two years before when another chance encounter along an isolated road had nearly meant his death.

Instead, though, he simply stopped Ned in the middle of the road, cocked both hammers on the double-barreled shotgun he carried and opened the front of his coat so he could quickly reach his pistol if necessary. He had a right to be here, and the reason for his journey was too important to be abandoned simply because of a chance encounter with a band of strangers.

But if these men meant to do him harm, he resolved,

this time would not be a repeat of the last. He would not fall into their hands without a fight.

As they neared, Jason saw that each of the four men was as heavily armed as he was. One carried a shotgun, another a muzzle-loading rifle, and two were armed with Sharps rifles. There had been many rumors all summer that abolitionist groups in the East were sending cases of the new and deadly Sharps rifles to their brethren in Kansas, and here was formidable proof that there was at least some substance to the talk.

The men stopped a full thirty feet away, respecting the threat that his shotgun presented and seeming to sense his resolve.

"Good morning to you," one of the men said. He was an ordinary-looking man, Jason thought, dressed in simple work clothes similar to Jason's own, and by the tone of his voice he seemed no more eager to plunge headlong into a gunfight than Jason was. In fact, none of the four came across as the wild-eyed sort of fanatics that Jason realized he had been expecting.

"It's a fair morning, I suppose," Jason replied. "A little chilly for my tastes, maybe."

"Headed to Lawrence?" the man asked.

"That's right," Jason said.

"Might I ask on what business?"

Jason considered the question for a moment before answering. He disliked the idea of being interrogated like this by strangers, but he realized that their purpose in being here was probably to intercept border ruffians or troublemakers approaching Lawrence. He decided that the matter was not important enough to raise trouble over.

"I have a brother there," Jason answered finally. "His name is Charles Hartman, and mine is Jason Hartman. I'm going to visit him."

The men conferred among themselves for a moment,

and though they spoke quietly, Jason happened to over-hear the words *Missouri* and *one of them*. Apparently the people of Lawrence knew that Charles had family in Missouri.

Finally the leader turned back to Jason and asked, "And where do you hail from, Mr. Hartman?"

During the ride over, Jason had decided that if asked, it might be best to simply say he was from Virginia, but now it struck him that if he used that story with these men, he might be caught in his lie.

"Clay County, Missouri," he replied, "but I hope you men will not make the mistake of thinking that that auto-matically means I've come here looking for trouble. Like I told you, I've only come to see my brother."

"Your brother owns a store in Lawrence," the man said, "and you're welcome to pass through and visit him. But I would like to give you a word of advice before you move along. "After your visit is finished, you'd do well to get on back across the border as quickly as you can. There's those among us in Lawrence who believe everyone who crosses over that line comes with mischief on his mind, and if you had happened to meet up with some of those instead of us this morning, you'd probably be lying dead in the road already."

"I believe you," Jason replied, "and I appreciate the warning."

He was a quarter mile down the road to Lawrence before he uncocked the shotgun hammers and allowed himself to relax. Although the encounter with the four men had, on the surface, been almost amiable, he had not for an instant let himself forget how quickly the whole thing could have exploded into gunfire and death.

As he neared the outskirts of Lawrence, Jason expected to be challenged again, but he drew little attention as he rode into town and started down the long main street. The cold drizzle that had started a few minutes before had driven most people indoors, and those who were out seemed intent simply on getting where they were going as quickly as possible.

Jason stopped one of the first men he met to inquire about Charles and was directed to a one-story building about midway down the street. In the style of the day, Charles's store had a false front, across which were painted the words *Lawrence Hardware and General Mercantile.*

Jason stopped Ned out front, tied him to a rail, and then paused at the entrance to brace himself for what was to come. He cherished no illusions that he would receive a warm welcome. William's warnings had had some effect after all. But he did hope that Charles would realize the import of this visit — that his family still cared about him and wanted to reestablish some of the closeness that had once existed.

A small bell above the door announced Jason's entry, and a pleasant warmth enveloped him as he closed the door behind him and started across the room toward a long counter. A woman at work there arranging rows of canned goods into a neat pyramid looked up as he approached, taking his measure with an immediate glint of suspicion in her eye.

Her steel-gray hair was pulled into a tight bun, and her plain black dress bore no trace of lace or ribbon to temper its drab austerity. Her features were sharp, with high cheekbones and a long, straight nose. The directness of her gaze did little to reassure Jason that he was doing the right thing. This, he thought with a flash of disappointment, was probably his brother's wife, Gertrude.

"Yes?" she asked as Jason stopped directly in front of her.

"Good morning," Jason said pleasantly. "I'd like to see Charles Hartman if he's here."

It was obvious that the woman was curious about his business, and she seemed on the verge of asking him what it was, but instead she replied, "My husband is in the storeroom, in back. If you'll wait here, I'll see if he can come out."

"Thank you," Jason said. As she turned and started toward a doorway to her left, he thought how easy it would be to dislike this woman if he were to simply give in to his instincts. But he had vowed that at least during this first contact he would be completely accepting about anything that came his way and would try to avoid any hint of controversy or conflict. He realized full well that if he handled it badly, this visit could serve to drive the family further apart.

As he waited, Jason gazed at the household goods and farm implements displayed around the store. Back in Virginia he had heard that his brother's store in Pennsylvania had become a thriving enterprise, and it appeared obvious that Charles was doing equally well here. The shelves were well stocked with the types of goods people in a frontier region such as this one needed, and the tables in the center of the room were as full of useful items and necessities.

A minute later a man emerged from the doorway to the storeroom. He was tall, with the sturdy, well-proportioned frame of all the Hartman men, and his close resemblance to both William and their father, Will Hartman, left no doubt about who he was. Although he was about forty now by Jason's reckoning, he looked to be several years older.

"May I help you?" Charles said in a completely impersonal tone that echoed that of his wife. A moment later his wife came out and stood in the doorway to stare at Jason.

"There's no way you could be expected to recognize me, Charles," Jason grinned, excited by the meeting in spite of himself. "It's me, Jason, your brother!"

Charles's brows furrowed, and he scrutinized Jason's

features closely. "Jason?" he said incredulously. "You're right. I never would have known you. You were only a little boy when I left our father's farm. What are you doing here?"

The tone of his voice left something to be desired, but Jason wrote it off to the shock of the moment. "I came to see you. I live just across the border, in Clay County, Missouri, now. Didn't you get my letters?"

"Uh, yes," Charles said hesitantly. "They're here somewhere. Back in my office, I think."

Jason paused. If Charles had received his letters, then he should have known Jason planned to come to Lawrence to see him — unless he had never opened them!

"Well, it doesn't matter," Jason announced, sticking to his resolve not to let anything bother him. "The main thing is that I'm here now, brother, and it's very good to see you." He held out his hand across the counter, and Charles accepted it and shook it briefly.

"I don't believe you've ever met my wife, Gertrude," Charles said formally. Then turning to his wife, he said, "Gertrude, this is my brother Jason Hartman."

"How do you do?" Gertrude said, taking Jason's hand and shaking it as a man would. "Will you be in Lawrence long?"

"I hadn't really thought about it," Jason admitted. "I can't afford to be away from my farm and family for too long, but I guess they can do without me for another day or two."

"I wish we could invite you to stay with us," Gertrude said abruptly, "but as you may know, we have nine children, and our home is very crowded."

"I wouldn't want to impose," Jason said, a little surprised by her announcement. "I'm sure there's a hotel somewhere in town."

"The Free State Hotel is just down the street," she said. "The rooms are clean, and the food is good."

"Well, then, I'll stay there," Jason replied with a smile. A moment of awkward silence followed, and Jason wondered if they expected him to leave now that the issue of his housing was settled. But he would not be dismissed so easily.

"I've ridden for a day and a half to get here, Charles," Jason told his brother, "and now that I'm here, I'd like to spend some time with you. I'd like to find out how things are going for you, and to tell you about my family and my new home —"

"Most of our customers are provisioning their homes for the winter," Gertrude interrupted. "It's a very busy time of year for us."

Jason glanced around the empty store, then aimed a sharp glance in the woman's direction. "Yes, I can see that." It would be easy to dislike this woman, he thought, but that was not why he had come. Looking back at his brother, he said, "I understand that you have a business to run, Charles, but it's been twenty years since we've seen one another. When you left, I was only seven years old, for Christ's sake! Can't you find some time for me?"

"Yes, of course I can, Jason," Charles said quickly. With a glance at his wife that stopped her from objecting, he added, "It's nearly ten now. You get yourself settled in the hotel, and I'll meet you there at noon. We'll have lunch together and a good long talk."

Jason left feeling resentful and ill used not only by his brother's wife but by Charles as well. Would he have to go back and report to his brother William that he had been right all along? he wondered. Was Charles a lost cause, a prodigal who had no intention of ever returning to the fold? Certainly this first encounter had contained nothing to contradict William's predictions.

But perhaps, Jason hoped, Charles would begin to relax after he got used to the idea of Jason's being here and they had a chance to spend some time together away from the dour Gertrude.

Jason checked into the Free State Hotel, made provisions for Ned's care, and changed into the dry set of clothes he had brought along wrapped in an oilcloth. When Charles arrived, precisely at twelve o'clock, Jason was waiting in the hotel lobby.

Charles seemed to be in a better frame of mind and even mustered a trace of a smile as they went into the hotel dining room.

"I wanted to explain about the way my wife acted toward you this morning, Jason," Charles said after they were seated. He cleared his throat. "Gertrude comes from an old Pennsylvania Dutch family whose code has always been rather strict and straitlaced. They believe in tending to their work, their families, and their religion to the exclusion of all else, and I'm afraid my wife believes in devoting little time or attention to strangers."

"I may be a stranger," Jason chided, "but I'm also family."

"Well, I'm just explaining how she is," Charles said defensively. "But she is also a good wife and mother, a hard worker, and a dedicated helpmate in the difficult work we have undertaken here. I offer no apologies for the way my wife is."

"Nor should you," Jason said easily. "I'm here to get to know you, Charles, not to pass judgment on the woman you married."

After they had ordered their meal, Jason spent some time priming his brother with questions about his life in Kansas. Although Charles never directly discussed the abolitionist work he was involved in, the subject drifted into the conversation several times. Jason was careful, however, never to broach the subject himself, knowing that he might bring suspicion on himself if he showed too much interest in it.

"But enough about me," Charles announced midway through the meal. "Tell me about your family. Let's see, how many children did Sarah write that you have? Three or four?"

"Five," Jason grinned. "John, the oldest, is thirteen now,

and the youngest one, Cassie, is seven. They're all good children, and they've done well in our new home."

"And what about the others who came out here with you?" Charles asked. "Tyson was just a babe in arms when I left, and Mollie wasn't even born yet. It's odd sometimes to think I have a sister that I've never even met."

Jason spent a few minutes explaining about the journey that Tyson had begun in the spring and then told him of the lovely young woman Mollie had become. He avoided the topic of Mollie's recent disappearances, not wanting to influence Charles's opinion of her before they had even met. If there were other visits after this one, there would be time to fill in the details.

"And that leaves us with only one more member of the Missouri branch of the family," Charles said at last, his voice tinged with bitterness. "But I don't suppose I really need to ask about our dear brother William. Rumors of his activities and exploits reach us with some regularity here in Lawrence."

"William is doing well for himself," Jason replied. "He has a large, prosperous farm, and his holdings have been increasing steadily over the past few years."

"Such is usually the case for those conscienceless individuals who are willing to base their fortunes on the enslavement of other human beings," Charles pronounced. "From time to time, Sarah writes me that Milton is doing equally as well in Mississippi by the same foul means."

"I suppose," Jason said cautiously. He knew the subject was bound to come up sooner or later, but he was determined neither to defend nor to condemn William in front of Charles.

"You know, Jason," Charles continued, "it is a tribute to the goodness of our friends and neighbors here in Lawrence that they are able to accept me and my family in spite of the fact that I have a brother as notorious as

William nearby. I have never concealed the fact of my Missouri relatives from the people here, though I bear the shame of it."

"That sentiment really warms my heart," Jason answered, tempering the severity of his words with a quick smile.

"Of course, you know I am referring primarily to William," Charles said impatiently. "But I admit that I have been curious about you as well. Where do you stand, Jason? As a newly inducted Missourian, are you as dedicated to the abominable institution of slavery as those around you are?"

"So far I've had success at staying completely out of it," Jason answered. "I don't own any slaves, nor do I ever plan to, but I can't find it in my heart to condemn men like William because they do. As long as people will let me, I'll be content simply to live my life and raise my family the best way I know how, and let those around me do the same."

"That may seem the wisest course right now," Charles cautioned him, "but when you're sitting on a powder keg, it isn't wise to try and ignore the fact that someone has lit the fuse. Living where you do, amidst all the upheaval that is going on around you, some day you will be forced to take a stand."

It was ironic, Jason thought, that his brothers, whose beliefs were as different as day and night, would make the same prediction for him.

"Why?" Jason asked.

"Because this is a war, and you are in the middle of the battleground," Charles replied with conviction. "There is no safe middle ground, no neutral territory in which you can hide."

"I'm not hiding from anything, Charles," Jason insisted. "But why should I choose to fight for one side or the other when what I truly believe is that neither side should be bracing itself for a fight in the first place? We're a country of laws, and laws have been passed to take care of this situation."

"This is beyond the abilities of the law to deal with," Charles said sharply. "Believe me, if I thought otherwise, I would be very happy to simply sit back and let the law take its course. But we cannot. Men like Senator David Atchison and, sadly, men like my own brother William have forced us into the position of taking matters into our own hands, and we are determined to do so aggressively."

"Since I've been in Missouri, I've seen a few of your fellows who have taken matters into their own hands. A lot of them end up dancing on air with ropes around their necks."

"Those are the risks we take," Charles said carefully. "Any man who takes up our banner knows the road ahead will be a long and dangerous one. I didn't bring my family to Kansas thinking that we were moving to a land of milk and honey."

"It could be, though," Jason said.

"Yes, and perhaps some day it will be, when all men who live here are free to share in the bounty equally. But before that day arrives, there will most certainly be more sacrifice and bloodshed. There is no alternative."

"I hope you're wrong, Charles."

After spending more than an hour with Charles, Jason had come to the opinion that the reason William and Charles could not, and would never get along, was that they were so much alike. Each was mired in his own convictions, so blinded by the cause he served that he could see no value in any other point of view.

For his part, however, Charles seemed pleased to learn that Jason was not firmly entrenched in the proslavery camp. By the end of their lunch, the man Jason found himself with was far different than the one who had greeted him in the store that morning, and finally Jason began to believe that his long trip to Lawrence might not have been in vain after all.

As they rose to leave, Charles told his brother, "A few of us are getting together this evening to welcome a comrade who has recently arrived from the East. It would please me to show some of my local acquaintances that not all of my Missouri relatives are two-headed ogres, and you might be interested in meeting the man we are gathering to honor. His name is John Brown."

Jason was hesitant to accept the invitation, thinking of the awkwardness he usually felt when William involved him in such clandestine activities for the other side. But he understood that Charles's invitation was a sign of his growing trust, and he was unwilling to do anything that might damage that. He decided that the best decision was to go along as he sometimes had to with William and to keep his mouth shut as much as possible.

He would meet this man Brown and Charles's other abolitionist friends, and perhaps by his actions and demeanor he could show them that all Missourians were not inhuman, slave-thrashing brutes.

"Just tell me what time to be ready," he told Charles.

The gathering was held in the back room of Charles's store, which had been rearranged and filled with more than a dozen chairs for the occasion. Among those present were two of the four men who had challenged Jason on the road earlier in the day. Like most of the others, they treated him with an impersonal courtesy that reflected their inherent suspicions of him.

Wisely, Charles made no secret about where Jason was from, but he also let it be known that his brother was not a slaveholder and preferred to remain a neutral in the conflict that swirled around him.

Only one man among them seemed actually interested

in Jason and treated him with cordiality and respect. Charles had introduced him as Dr. Charles Robinson, and immediately upon hearing the name, Jason was startled to realize that this open, friendly man was, in fact, one of the most ardent abolitionist leaders in Kansas.

The guest of honor was late, and so for the first half hour the men simply sat around, sampling the cake and punch that Gertrude Hartman had provided as they talked about various local issues. Heading the list of topics were the recent elections, in which hordes of Missourians had packed the new territorial legislature with a majority of proslavery advocates, many of whom did not even make a pretense of actually living in Kansas Territory.

Robinson had buttonholed Jason and was earnestly explaining the outrage that the abolitionist residents of Kansas felt over the elections.

"There was a time not so long ago," Robinson revealed, "when all of us had high hopes that all of this could be settled by the process of law. I was here at the founding of this town, and the last thing I ever want is to see it turned into a battleground. Sadly, I have to admit that we haven't always been able to convince our brothers to turn away from violence, but until recently I have always been among those who tried.

"The situation now has reached such crisis proportions that even I am beginning to believe that we have little choice anymore. What can we do when your Missourians invade our homeland by the hundreds and thousands to fill our public offices with their own kind? I appeal to your sense of reason, Mr. Hartman," Robinson implored. "What choice do we have?"

"I was against that election business all along," Jason admitted. "I refused to come over here back then, and a number of my neighbors did the same. You must realize, Dr. Robinson, that you're not being forced to make a stand against all Missourians."

"It's not just all of Missouri that we feel we're up against sometimes," Robinson said, "but the entire South as well. We have proof that some of the trash who showed up at our polls last spring were from as far away as Tennessee, Virginia, and South Carolina. Knowing that, I ask you again, what choice do we have?"

"Feeling as you do," Jason conceded, "perhaps you have none." Robinson seemed startled to hear such an admission from a Missourian, and Jason was quick to amend his remark. "But to my thinking, taking a stand on your own home ground and riding across the border to murder and pillage indiscriminately are two different matters. I know of a number of innocent people who have died at the hands of nightriders from Kansas, and I see no way that murdering people can serve the abolitionist cause."

"I am opposed to such excesses as strongly as you," Robinson said, "but I can understand why they are taking place. There are many among us who believe that if the master must die to free the slave, so be it."

Jason was starting to realize that Robinson had drawn him much deeper into the discussion than he wanted to be and that a number of the other men present, including Charles, were beginning to listen in. He decided that the time had come to try, as gracefully as possible, to back away from the topic.

"This John Brown who's coming here tonight," he said to Robinson. "His name sounds familiar to me, but I can't recall why."

"John Brown devoted his life to our cause long before the freedom of Kansas became a national issue and the abolitionist movement became so popular," Robinson explained. "If you've heard of him, it is probably due to his service to the cause in Pennsylvania."

"A number of us knew Old Brown through our underground railroad contacts back east," Charles revealed.

"We've been trying for over a year to persuade him to come to Kansas, and finally last spring he sent some of his sons on ahead to get a farm started."

As if the mention of John Brown's name was meant to serve as his introduction, a firm knock sounded at the back door and one of the men nearby slid the bolt back and opened it. All eyes turned toward the entrance as three husky, bearded men, each carrying a rifle, entered the room.

Charles stepped forward and greeted one of them with a warm handshake. He was beaming. "Welcome to Kansas, John!" he exclaimed. "It's so good to have you here with us at last!"

The hearty greeting seemed to have little effect on Brown, who scanned the room as if looking for danger. Finally he let his gaze rest on the still-smiling face of his host.

"The road has been a long one, Charles," Brown replied in a deep voice that seemed to give every word he spoke import. "It's good to be here."

Brown, in his late fifties, was dressed in a drab, heavy coat and trousers that bore the signs of many years of use. As he removed his hat, his hair spilled out, a great, shaggy mane. The lower half of his face was concealed behind a thick, wiry mat of graying whiskers.

The two men with him, obviously his sons, were in dress and general appearance younger replicas. Their presence in the room was almost completely obscured by the commanding presence of their father, but both seemed accustomed to going through life in his shadow. Neither offered more than a mumbled reply when Charles reached out and shook the hands of each in turn.

Robinson was the next to greet Brown, and he assumed the responsibility of introducing the new arrival to everyone else in the room, including Jason.

Jason experienced a sensation quite unlike any he could

ever recall when he grasped Brown's callused hand and gazed into his dark, unfathomable eyes. The first thought that raced through his mind was that here was a truly dangerous man, a man so steeped in what he believed in that no other truth or morality existed to him except that of the cause he served.

It was with a palpable sense of relief that he watched John Brown move away and focus his penetrating, unyielding gaze on the next man he was introduced to.

For the first time the gathering took on the semblance of a meeting as Robinson, Charles, and their fellow abolitionists settled into chairs and prepared to listen to John Brown's comments on the work that faced them in Kansas.

"Two weeks before we left our home in Pennsylvania to begin the journey here," Brown began, "the Lord delivered into my hands a man named Marsh Titus, a farmer, the father of four, a resident of the northeastern portion of the State of Virginia. He had in his pocket a warrant for another man who was staying in my home at the time, named Toby Woodson, a Negro human being which Marsh Titus claimed he owned."

Brown paused to turn his massive head left toward his sons, who had taken seats off to the side and slightly behind him. One was munching on a slab of cake, and the other had just filled his jaw with a large wad of chewing tobacco. "Owen," he said, "where is Marsh Titus today?"

"He's dead, Papa," the son with the cake answered. "You killed him." There was no noticeable change in his expression when he answered, no indication that the event was any more momentous than slapping at a fly.

"I killed Marsh Titus because the Lord delivered him into my hands, and it had to be done," Brown said in a voice as sharp and deadly as the blade of a straight razor. His eyes roamed over the faces around him, as if recording the reaction of every man there. "It's not the sort of thing a man should be proud of, and the only reason I'm telling you about it now is that I want you to understand very clearly why I've come to Kansas."

Jason tore his eyes away from John Brown's hard countenance long enough to glance over at Charles. He was curious to see what his brother's reaction to this brutal announcement might be, but he could read very little from Charles's rapt expression.

Robinson, on the other hand, was noticeably disturbed by Brown's remark. More from habit than need, he took a handkerchief from his pocket and mopped his face, then glanced around, as Jason was doing, to observe the reactions of the others.

"We have a bloody job before us here in Kansas," Brown continued, "and I want you good men gathered here to understand that I've come here itching for a fight. If ever there was a cause in this world that was plain and just, it is ours. The road we must travel is laid out clearly before us, and before we reach the other end, the way will be littered with the bodies of those who tried to stand against us."

The abolitionist's remarks were surprisingly brief, and his closing words were chilling. "That's all I've got to say," Brown told them gruffly. "You know where I stand, and you know what I plan to do, so any of you who don't have what it takes to side with me, all I ask is that you stay out of my way."

Over the past two years, Jason had grown accustomed to the potential for violence. It was hard to imagine any man living in this part of the country not owning at least one firearm, and few if any would hesitate a second to use their guns in defense of themselves, their families, their homes, or their beliefs.

But in this man Brown, Jason sensed a difference that stood out as starkly as a full moon against a sky without stars. He wasn't simply willing to fight; he was *eager* to do so. His mind was so set on the infallibility of his own beliefs that he probably found it easy to justify any act he committed, no matter how brutal, with the same logic that he used to explain the death of Marsh Titus. *It was necessary!*

John Brown was more than just dangerous, Jason decided. He was insane.

Jason packed his bag and left Lawrence that night. During his brief farewell to Charles he tried to explain the feelings that Brown's harangue had stirred in him, but he had yet to fully understand them himself. All he knew was that some power within was driving him to get out of this town and away from these people as quickly as possible.

By midnight he was riding across country, pushing Ned due east, toward home, toward the place that suddenly seemed the only safe haven in the world. He kept off the roads for the first few miles, not wanting to be responsible for controlling his temper in case he was again challenged by one of the bands of men who seemed constantly on patrol in the countryside around Lawrence.

After more than an hour of steady hard riding, Jason realized that he was probably nearing the Kansas River, and he cut back to the road so he wouldn't miss the ford. In places the river's currents were deep and treacherous, and a nighttime crossing under such conditions could be extremely dangerous.

Almost as soon as he started Ned down the moonlit, relatively level road, he spotted a band of five horsemen about fifty yards behind, riding in the same direction as he. They had been riding along at a leisurely pace, but as soon as they spotted him, the men pushed their mounts into a gallop. Then in the distance, Jason heard one of them call out to him, "Wait up, mister! We want to have a word with you!"

"Not tonight, fellows," Jason mumbled to himself. "No, thank you!"

He put the spurs to Ned and the horse bolted forward.

At every bend in the road his pursuers dropped out of sight momentarily, only to reappear again on the straightaways. After the first few minutes their horsemanship and the quality of their mounts seemed to dictate the order in which they rode. Soon a couple had dropped so far behind that they no longer posed any immediate threat, and another was beginning to lose ground.

The other two, however, continued in hot pursuit. Glancing back, Jason decided that they were gaining little, if any, ground on him, but they certainly weren't losing any either.

Then a rifle shot cracked out behind him, and an instant later he heard the unmistakable sound of a bullet singing past. At this point he wasn't too worried about being shot because he knew how difficult it was to achieve any accuracy from the back of a running horse, but the mere fact that they had chosen to shoot at him at all was like an announcement of his fate in case he was caught.

Being unfamiliar with the countryside, he was caught off guard by the sudden appearance of the Kansas River ford. He had known it was somewhere up ahead, but he thought he had at least another mile or two to go and planned to get off the road before he reached it. But when he rounded a slight bend and saw the broad channel before him, there seemed no alternative but to plunge straight into the chilling currents and try to make it to the other side.

As Ned splashed across the shallows and bounded gamely into the main channel, Jason slid off to the side and began to swim by the horse's side, gripping only the saddle horn for buoyancy and support.

He recalled hearing William tell about the time they had caught up with a band of raiders just as the men were attempting to escape across the Missouri River into Kansas. It had been a moonlit night much like this one, and his brother had enthusiastically described the event as a "turkey shoot." At this moment, Jason realized the panic those men must have felt at being caught floundering in such a helpless, frustrating situation. Not only was he completely exposed, an easy target even for a pistol, but there was not any way he could return the fire of his pursuers once they opened up on him.

Ned and Jason had reached midstream before the first two men rode into sight, and then they wasted the first few seconds of their golden opportunity by excitedly blasting away at Jason from the backs of their prancing horses. The current was carrying Jason and his horse downstream as they struggled to reach the opposite bank, but they weren't passing out of rifle range nearly fast enough.

When the bullets began to strike within feet and inches of him, Jason realized that his pursuers must have dismounted to go about this business properly. The first bullet that found him merely plucked the hat from his head, but it was quickly followed by another that slammed solidly into the back of his left shoulder.

His head slipped under the water briefly, and he nearly lost his grip on the saddle horn, but he managed to regain control an instant later.

Then as if from a dream a man's voice called out ahead of him, "Hang on, Jason! You've just got a few yards to go! We'll keep them off your back till then."

His head was beginning to swirl, but Jason was still aware of the salvo of four or five shots that was fired in quick succession from the bank in front of him. Behind him a shriek of pain sliced through the night, and for a moment the shooting on that side stopped.

"Come on, Jason. Come on!" the voice urged.

Jason recognized the voice now. He knew who it was, but he couldn't put a name to it.

His grip on the saddle horn began to slip, but he couldn't seem to do anything about it. There was more gunfire from somewhere . . . ahead, he thought, but maybe from behind as well. Water rushed into his mouth and nose as he gasped for breath, and his head went under again.

Then someone was in the water beside him, drawing him back to the surface, and his feet sank into the soft mush of the river bottom.

"It's Cole, Jason, Coleman Younger."

Yes, that was who the voice belonged to, Jason thought, and the face that hovered above him also belonged to that name. He didn't quite remember how he had got up out of the water, but he was lying flat on his back in a small stand of cottonwoods.

"I don't know what you're doing here, Cole," Jason mumbled, "but thanks anyway. In another few seconds they would have nailed me."

"Perhaps," Cole said dryly. "But they didn't, and it sounds like we bloodied one or two of them for their efforts."

A moment later a form emerged from the brush and then another. One of the new arrivals knelt on the ground beside Jason, and he felt a shock nearly as powerful as the bite of the bullet that hit him. It was Mollie.

"Mollie! What in the hell —" Jason exclaimed.

"There's no time for explanations, Jason," Mollie said hurriedly. Then turning to Cole, she asked, "How bad is it?"

"Straight through the meat," Cole said, "in the back and out the front."

"Well, those men that were after him have dropped out of sight," Mollie told him. "Matt said they might have decided to cross somewhere else and then come after us, so we'd better get away from here fast."

"Just give me a minute to cover up these holes so he doesn't bleed to death," Cole said, "and then we'll go. You and Matt get the horses ready, and find a piece of rope so we can tie him in the saddle."

Mollie started to rise, then paused to look down at her brother. The pain of his wound was beginning to gnaw into his consciousness, and his features were drawn and stark in his attempt to resist it. "Don't worry, Jason. We'll take care of you," she said, touching his cheek with her fingertips. "And I'll tell you everything when we get home, I promise."

"From the looks of things, there'll be a lot to tell," Jason rasped.

"I guess there is," Mollie said. "And I guess it's time."

As she moved away, Jason closed his eyes and gritted his teeth, bracing himself against the pain as Cole rolled him onto his right side and began to cut away his shirt.

8

May 1856

Homer, Jason's plow mule, stopped in his tracks when he reached the end of the row, waiting as Jason paused to brush the sweat off his face with a dirty handkerchief. He was a good mule, dumb as a turnip but a steady worker and seldom inclined to balk, kick, or bite. In the fields he responded with almost mechanical precision to spoken commands and to the light tugs on the reins Jason sometimes used to turn him left and right.

A dull pain throbbed in Jason's left shoulder as he reached around to return the handkerchief to his hip pocket, reminding him of his close pass with death the previous fall. It had been a rough winter for him, and the ragged hole in his shoulder had given him plenty of trouble before finally healing properly. But he still counted himself lucky that the rifle slug hadn't taken a heavier toll. Back in November, when the pain had been at its worst, waking him night after night with its burning and throbbing, he would think that no matter how bad the wound felt, he was fortunate to be here to feel it.

He and Homer were nearly finished turning the middles of the field, and Jason decided to call it a day after this one was done. Though nearly seven months had passed since the shooting, he still had not regained his full strength, and he had promised Arethia that he would continue to take it easy until he'd achieved full recovery.

Glancing across the broad field where he stood, Jason could not help but smile with satisfaction. The corn was knee-high already, and thus far this spring the rains could not have been more perfectly spaced if Jason himself had been granted the power to control them.

Jason had used the excuse of his wound and the urgency of planting season to draw even more deeply into the protective cocoon of his farm and family. He took little part in community activities except to attend church on Sunday, and he adamantly refused to be drawn into any of the plots of men like his brother William, David Atchison, and Judge Younger.

He seemed not to be missed. During the fall and winter the problems and conflicts had intensified to the point that in December it appeared that open warfare between the Kansas abolitionists and the Missouri slaveholders was inevitable.

Leading a well-armed "army" of hundreds of men, Atchison had crossed the border into Kansas and besieged the city of Lawrence for several days. Only the intervention of the U.S. Army had ended that crisis, but not a single point of contention had really been settled.

Nevertheless, the ensuing winter months had been relatively quiet, but with the arrival of spring the trouble had started anew.

At this very moment, in fact, William was somewhere

in Kansas with a band of locals and newly arrived Southern ruffians he had assembled. William had armed and
provisioned his little company with his own funds and
led it with an almost military deportment. It was rumored
that he had even got hold of a small cannon.

William's group was only a small component of an
army of several thousand men that David Atchison had
again led into Kansas. The excuse for this particular invasion had to do with the killing of a Missouri man and
the fact that the Kansas abolitionist who had done the
deed remained at large. A posse of several thousand men
was hardly needed to bring one miscreant to justice, but
the real truth was that if Atchison had not come across
this excuse to invade Kansas, he would have invented
one.

The invasion had begun several days before, but Jason
had not yet received any word about how things were
going. William had left his farm in the hands of a man
named Milt Bailey, and Jason rode over there daily to
make sure things ran smoothly.

The sun had dropped nearly to the treeline by the time
Jason finished his plowing. He directed Homer to the
gap in the fence that opened onto the road to the house,
and there he unhitched the plow. Then he hopped up
on the animal and rode off toward the barn.

As he dismounted to open the gate to the feed lot,
he looked toward the house and saw a rider approaching.
When the rider saw Jason at the barn, he passed the
house and rode up to him. It was Cole Younger.

Cole had been a frequent visitor at Jason's farm since
that night when he, Mollie, and Matt Hardesty had saved
Jason's life. He usually came to see Mollie, but Jason
also welcomed visits, and the two of them had spent a
number of spring evenings on the front porch talking.
Despite the difference in their ages, Jason enjoyed the
young man's company, and he particularly appreciated

the fact that Cole never presumed to stand in judgment of Jason because of nis decision to remain neutral over the question of slavery.

"Evening, Cole," he said. "I'm surprised to see you here. I figured you'd be over in Kansas where all the excitement is."

"Matter of fact, I just came from there," Cole grinned. "But I heard some news that made me think that maybe I should make a quick trip back here."

"I hope it isn't another rumor about that damned Boone Septin," Jason said. "Mollie's got no business riding over there and getting mixed up in all that trouble."

Since the night when they fished Jason out of the Kansas River, Cole and Mollie had made one more trip into Kansas to investigate yet another rumor about Septin's whereabouts. Jason had not tried to talk her out of going, knowing that it would do no good, but he and Arethia had spent three long, sleepless nights before she finally returned.

"No, it's not about Septin this time," Cole said. "This news is for you. It's about your brother."

"Has something happened to William? Has he been wounded . . . or worse?"

"No, it's the other brother — Charles. The one that has that store in Lawrence. He was one of the first ones arrested when they took the town, and now they've got him locked up."

"They took Lawrence?" Jason exclaimed. "I didn't really think things would go that far. I figured it would probably just turn into a standoff like the last time."

"Well, Atchison's men took over the place without hardly firing a shot," Cole informed him, "and after they had things under control, they started rounding up all the abolitionists, like Charles Robinson and your brother. They've got a passel of them locked up right now, supposedly awaiting trial on trumped-up charges like resisting arrest and obstruction of justice. But I spent the night before last in the camp of one of the Missouri outfits, and the talk there was that none of the men that was arrested would ever live long enough to face a real judge. A lot of the fellows I heard talking said they figured this was as good a time as any to clean out that nest of troublemaking abolitionists once and for all."

Jason's face was grave.

"It's getting worse all over," Cole went on. "The word is that when John Brown heard about Atchison taking Lawrence, he and some of his kin rode into a little pro-slavery settlement down near Pottawatomie River and murdered five or six people. And they say that Jim Lane is marching south from Nebraska right now with an army of several thousand abolitionists, all armed with new Sharps rifles and out for blood."

"Damn it, what's the use in all this, Cole?" Jason cried. "Has every single man in the state of Missouri and the territory of Kansas gone mad at the same time?"

"Beats the hell out of me, Jason," Cole replied calmly. "But I did think you might want to know about your brother."

"I'm grateful to you for telling me. But surely you didn't ride all the way over here just for that reason."

"That and a decent meal, I guess," Cole grinned. "Six days of my uncle Paul's cooking is about all any normal gut can stand, so I figured I'd slip away while nothing much was going on and get some of Mama's good vittles in me before I started back."

After Cole had left, Jason started toward the house. Arethia, who had been working in the kitchen and had seen Cole ride past, was waiting for Jason when he walked in the kitchen door.

"Is it bad news?" she asked anxiously as she handed him a cup of coffee.

"Not so bad as it might be, but bad enough," Jason

told her. "William's all right, I guess, but they've got Charles locked up in Lawrence along with a bunch of his friends. Cole said it doesn't look good for them."

Arethia said nothing until he was finished speaking, but by the look on her face, Jason could tell that her mind was racing. Probably, he thought, they were both thinking the same thing.

Finally, Jason reached out and took his wife's hand in his, as if to soften the impact of what had to be said next. "I've got to go, you know."

Arethia just stared at him, her eyes wide.

"I don't think I could live with myself if one of my brothers was killed and I hadn't made any attempt to stop it," Jason reasoned. "I don't know if I'll be able to do anything or if Charles will still be alive by the time I reach Lawrence, but I have to try. You understand that, don't you, Arethia?"

"Would he do the same for you?" his wife asked pointedly, her eyes locked on his.

"Probably not," Jason admitted. "I couldn't swear to you that he'd walk across the street to save my life, let alone ride a hundred miles into the middle of a war to do it. But that's the way he is, and this is the way I am."

"I know, Jason," Arethia said sadly. "But don't expect me to tell you that it's all right with me and give this thing my full blessing. Not after what happend last time. But I won't try to stop you. Do what you think you have to do, but no matter where you go, don't ever let yourself forget that you have a wife and five children here on this farm who love you and depend on you." She put her arms around his neck and hugged him, then added quietly, "You know, sometimes it can be quite a burden being married to an honorable man."

The second week after the capture of Lawrence, the road west into Kansas from Westport, Missouri, was still alive with travelers. A few were trickling eastward, toward their homes in Missouri, but most were new arrivals on their way into the territory, lured by the exciting happenings there and by the prospect of having a part in something so important to the cause of slavery.

Instead of taking the northern route, which crossed the Missouri River above Independence and then turned southwest and crossed the Kansas River before reaching Lawrence, Jason had chosen, for safety's sake, an alternate, southern route this time. At this time of year both the Missouri and the Kansas rivers were swollen with spring runoff; there was no use risking his life in two difficult crossings when he could cross the Missouri by ferry at Independence and complete the rest of the journey on land.

Soon after crossing the border, he fell in with a band of eight men who had recently arrived from Tennessee. They had been traveling for several days, and all were eager to reach Lawrence, but after talking with them for a short time, Jason quickly got the impression that their motives in coming had more to do with adventure than with any belief in slavery.

And judging by the dress and manner of his new companions, Jason guessed that none of them had ever come close to owning a slave or anything else in life more valuable than the ragged horses and mules they rode and the assorted weapons they carried.

The leader of the group, however, was an exception. His name was Simon Crump, and he stood out from the others like a peacock in a chicken yard.

Crump was a young man, no more than twenty or twenty-one, Jason guessed. He wore a frock coat, tailored wool trousers, and kidskin boots, all of which he had somehow managed to keep brushed and clean during the long journey, and he carried a matched pair of shiny, nickel-plated pistols in tooled-leather holsters. His horse was a magnificent blooded roan that would probably sell for more than the collective value of all the mounts his companions rode, and he spoke in a deep, melodic Southern drawl that contrasted markedly with the dialects of his men.

The men called him Mr. Crump or Young Mr. Simon, and it was obvious that none of them questioned his social superiority and leadership. During his first hour with the group, Jason learned that all of them were residents of Fayette County, Tennessee, which lay about forty miles due east of Memphis. Simon's father, Colonel Marlin Crump, owned a good part of the county; the other men either worked for the colonel or were sharecroppers on his land.

During the first day's ride, Jason provided the newcomers with what details he could about the situation in Kansas but said nothing of his own mission. He liked the idea of traveling with a band this size because of the security that their many weapons provided, but he realized that he would not be at all welcome if they learned he was actually on his way to free an abolitionist leader.

When they stopped for the night, they were less than twenty miles from Lawrence, but Jason had advised against riding after dark because of the numerous patrols that were bound to be all over the countryside.

Within thirty minutes of stopping to make camp, they were well into a meal of fried pork, tinned beans, and hardtack. When supper was over, pipes came out, and cups of coffee were spiked with splashes of homemade whiskey.

"We heard tell back home," one of the younger men told Jason, "that these here Yankee ab'lisionists don't just steal niggers when they go raiding into Missouri. They also steal white babies so they can take them back over into Kansas and teach 'em to be nigger lovers. And sometimes they'll make the niggers they take kill their masters a'fore they'll ship 'em on north to Canada."

"As far away as Tennessee," Jason replied evenly, "I guess you're bound to hear a lot of different stories, some true and some not. But I've lived here three years now, and I've never heard of a white child being kidnapped. And as far as the killing is concerned, the abolitionists seem to be able to handle that without any help. Whatever else they might be, they certainly aren't cowards."

"Well, for brave men, they shore gave Lawrence up easy," another pointed out.

"That was mostly a matter of numbers and firepower, though," Jason said. "Atchison's got several times more men behind him than the people of Lawrence could ever hope to muster, and he has artillery. And don't forget that the men in Lawrence also had their families to think about. It's a hell of a lot easier for a man to risk just his own life than it is to risk the lives of his wife and children."

"It sounds almost as if you feel some sympathy for the white abolitionist trash who have infected Kansas Territory, Mr. Hartman," Simon Crump said. The subtle disdain in his voice was not lost on Jason.

"Not for the raiders who think they have the right to cross over onto the Missouri side of the border and do as they please," Jason replied. "But I have to feel a certain respect for any man brave enough to make a stand on his own home soil against the invasion of outsiders."

Crump bristled. A couple of the others read the full meaning in Jason's words, and made as if to reach for their weapons, but their young leader discouraged them with a single sharp shake of his head.

"I would like for you to understand, Mr. Hartman," Crump said stiffly, "that were we in Tennessee, this conversation might well lead to a duel. However, since we are not in that great state and I am, indeed, a stranger here, I am inclined to let the matter pass — this one time."

Jason's first impulse was to reply as sharply as he had been addressed, but even as the harsh words were gathering in his mind, he remembered Arethia's final remonstrance. He was not here to trade insults with a blue-blooded dandy from Tennessee, and he had an obligation to Arethia and the children not to encourage a fight that he was so certain to lose.

"I feel the same way, Mr. Crump," Jason replied as he stood up. "It would probably be better all around if we just let it go. If things don't get better soon, there'll be plenty of fighting to go around without those who are basically on the same side mixing it up amongst themselves."

With that, he turned and walked to the place several feet away where he had spread his blanket. He pulled off his boots and shirt, but lay down with his trousers on and placed his gun belt within easy reach beside his head.

The others remained by the fire awhile longer, bolstering themselves with whiskey and talk of what they would gladly do to any and all abolitionists who crossed their path. But as the fire was reduced to a bed of glowing coals, they moved off one by one to their blankets.

Jason lay awake for a while longer, despairing of what the future would hold if men such as this were permitted to take part in deciding it. Even when he finally did drift off, he slept fitfully, jolting awake at the slightest sound. He was up and on his way at dawn just as the others were beginning to stir from their bedrolls.

Most of Atchison's forces were bivouacked on the east side of Lawrence in a sprawling, filthy tent city that made the town look small by comparison. Now, with the opposition firmly under their control, most of the invaders had little to do but sit outside their tents, smoking and grumbling, growing more restless and hungry for action as each new day arrived. As Jason rode through the camp, searching for familiar faces, the stench of dirty bodies, poorly placed latrines, and animal dung assailed him from all sides. He passed through the area without pausing and entered the outskirts of the town.

Lawrence was barely recognizable as the thriving frontier town he had visited only seven months before. Scattered around the perimeter were the remnants of the barricades that had evidently been thrown up in anticipation of Atchison's attack. A number of homes and shops had been reduced to heaps of ashes, with only an occasional iron bedstead, potbellied stove, or stone chimney still standing amid the wreckage.

As he advanced into the center of town, Jason saw that even Lawrence's most noteworthy landmark, the Free State Hotel, had been devastated by the invaders. The hotel, built mostly of native field stone, with walls that were more than a foot thick in places, would have been immune to the flames that had claimed so much of Lawrence. But the formidable structure had been no match for Atchison's cannons, and now the two-story building lay in ruins.

Spotting Charles's store, Jason saw, with great relief, that the building was still standing. The front door was wide open, indicating that Gertrude Hartman might be carrying on as usual despite her husband's imprisonment, so Jason dismounted and went inside. He was hardly prepared for the scene of chaos that awaited him.

The small number of goods that had not already been carried off by looters lay scattered about on the floor. Most of the fixtures, including the shelves, counters, and tables, had been destroyed with axes and sledgehammers, and the round black stove that had greeted Jason with such welcome warmth last fall now lay on its side in the middle of the room, battered and split by whoever had ravaged the place.

A rustling behind the counter where Jason had first met Gertrude last fall caught his attention, and he reached for his pistol instinctively. "Who is it?" he asked loudly. "Who's over there?"

A man raised his head from behind the counter and, seeing Jason, said, "Take it easy. I'm just picking myself up a few cartridges from the mess back here. Seems like a man can't buy a blessed thing he needs in this town 'cause so much has been stole already."

Jason was about to say something when he stopped and smiled. He was looking at Abe Drury, one of the men who had come to Kansas with William.

"My stars an' garters, Jason! What in the hell are you doing over here in Lawrence? I thought you figured on staying out of this business."

"I did," Jason said. "And I still want to stay out of it as much as I can. But I have urgent business with my brother William."

"I bet it's about that other brother of yours," Drury said. "The one named Charles."

"That's who it's about," Jason replied. "Did you know this is his store?"

"Yup. It's a mess, ain't it?" Drury grinned, obviously pleased by the devastation. "Some of the boys done it the first night after we took the town. The only reason it ain't burnt up is that it shares a wall with the best restaurant in town, and Dave Atchison said he wanted to leave at least one decent eating place standing."

"Where is my brother now, Abe?"

"If you mean Charles, why he's still locked up tight," Drury chuckled. "And the other, he's down the street at the headquarters the senator set up."

Jason got directions to this headquarters and left his neighbor from Missouri to sort through the wreckage of Charles's store.

Senator David Atchison had set up his base of operations, and his temporary residence, in a white frame house near the western edge of town. Jason led his horse the hundred yards to the house, then tied him to the neat picket fence that surrounded the front yard. He recognized one of the two men who stood guard out front and so had no trouble being admitted.

Jason found William seated behind a long table in the dining room with a large map spread out before him. Three men Jason didn't know were with him, and they were engaged in a discussion of the terrain to the north and east of Lawrence. Jason wondered if they were still bracing for the expected attack from Jim Lane, who was rumored to be on his way with his "army of freedom."

William seemed not the least surprised when he looked up from the map and saw his younger brother standing in the doorway. "Jason!" he exclaimed, getting up and coming around the table to greet him. Jason decided the warm handshake and hearty clap on the shoulder were for the benefit of the other men, who were probably fellow "officers" with William under Atchison's command. Certainly, William's attitude toward him had been markedly different during their last meeting.

As if to verify Jason's suspicions, William introduced him around the room and was quick to let the other men know that his younger brother had "caught a Free-Soiler bullet in the back" the previous fall. The other men appeared suitably impressed, and Jason didn't bother to explain his reason for being in Kansas at the time.

"So what brings you to Kansas, little brother?" William asked. "I thought you had decided to sit this one out."

Jason was sure William knew why he was here, but he played along for the sake of appearances. "I came because I needed to see you," Jason answered quickly. "An important matter has come up that we need to discuss, and I didn't think it would wait until you got home."

William nodded and excused himself from the others, and the two of them went outside.

Once they reached the street and were out of earshot,

Jason got right to the point. "I came because of Charles," he announced. "I want you to know that I won't stand by and let these people kill our brother."

"I figured that the minute I laid eyes on you," William snorted. "But I might as well tell you right now that you're wasting your time."

"You could get him out, William," Jason insisted. "You're one of the leaders of this affair, and you know David Atchison well enough to talk him into releasing Charles. Even if you really don't give a damn whether Charles gets hauled out of his cell and murdered by some of these border ruffians you've led over here, think of the rest of us, and think of Charles's family."

William gave Jason a sharp look and said angrily, "It will probably surprise you to hear that I have already thought of all those things, little brother. And I have considered what our father would think of me for the rest of his life if Charles was killed and I didn't do a thing to try and prevent it."

He paused long enough to take a long, slender cigar from his pocket and light it. "Four days ago I went to the senator, and he agreed to release Charles under the condition that Charles leave Lawrence. I figured Charles would agree to that quickly enough, since his store is wrecked and his family has already left town."

He exhaled. "But when I went to tell him the news, he refused to even speak to me. Then when one of the other men explained the bargain to him, he turned it down."

"He turned it down?" Jason asked incredulously.

"He said that he wouldn't leave unless all his companions were freed as well, and that if he was forcibly removed from jail, his first act would be to find a gun and kill David Atchison."

"I can't believe he would be so stupid!" Jason exclaimed. "He's not doing anybody any good sitting there in jail.

If he was out, at least he could be taking care of his family."

"I guess they're safe for now. Apparently, Charles loaded them in a wagon before we got here and sent them away. The word is they're staying at John Brown's settlement south of here at Osawatomie. But," he added, "if the senator decides to head down that way and clean out that hornet's nest after he's finished here, they could be right back in the middle of things again."

"I'd like to speak with Charles," Jason said quietly. "Maybe I can reason with him and convince him to get out of here while he has the chance."

"When will you learn the truth about this man, Jason?" William asked irritably. "Believe me, I admire your loyalty to the family and all those other noble sentiments that you're always spouting about. But when are you going to realize that we're dealing with a complete stranger here, a true zealot who is ready, and maybe even anxious, to throw his life away for the sake of this abolitionist nonsense? When are you going to understand that this man is our brother only through a quirk of birth? Beyond that, any other bonds which might once have existed have long since been broken!"

"I guess it hasn't soaked in yet," Jason answered stubbornly. "I'd still like to see him."

"All right, I'll arrange it," William said with a sigh. "It will probably take a day or two. While you're here, you can bunk in with me, but for God's sake keep your mouth shut about this and try to refrain from telling every Missourian in this town how stupid you think he is for being here."

"I'll try to keep my spouting off to a minimum, William," Jason promised.

William came to his brother late the next afternoon with word that Atchison had signed the pass that would admit Jason to the jail. They went together to the two-room brick office of the city marshal, which was now being used as a prison for over a dozen abolitionist leaders.

After inspecting the pass, one of the guards led Jason into the rear cell area. William remained in the front office, well aware that his presence in a meeting with Charles would only serve to make matters worse.

All the prisoners were crammed into two small cells that were meant to hold two or three men each. In one of the cells, Charles Robinson was reading aloud to his companions from a Bible, but he stopped when Jason and the guard came in. Glancing at the faces of the prisoners in the two adjoining cells, Jason recognized a number of the men who had attended the meeting in the back of Charles's store last fall.

Charles was sitting on the stone floor at the back of the cell but rose and came to the cell door when he saw Jason. They shook hands through the bars, and Jason thought Charles seemed sincerely glad to see him. Then Jason greeted Robinson and the other men he had met before.

The mood of the imprisoned men was surprisingly relaxed, which made Jason wonder if they had any idea of the great danger they were in. For the time being, Atchison and his lieutenants had things under control, but there was no telling when the bored and restless throngs in the camp outside town might grow impatient and decide to take matters into their own hands.

"It's good to see you again, Jason," Charles announced, "though these circumstances leave much to be desired."

"I came over as soon as I heard they had you locked up," Jason told him. "I was hoping there might be something I could do to get you out of this place — and out of this mess."

"I appreciate that," Charles said quietly, "but at present our best hope seems to be Jim Lane. We're expecting him and his army to arrive any day now and drive these rascals out of the territory. We've also sent word of our predicament to Colonel Chapman at Fort Leavenworth, but he seems hesitant about bringing troops into town under these conditions."

"Things really are a mess all over," Jason observed. "I don't know if you've heard, but down south of here Old Brown has gone on a killing spree, and that has served to make Atchison and his men even more determined than they were before."

"At least some of our number are still free to fight back."

Jason knew the time was not right to debate the morality of the murders John Brown was committing, so he turned instead to the reason for his visit. "William tells me that he got permission to let you out of here, but you turned him down."

"I did."

"We tried to talk him into leaving, Jason," Robinson explained, "but he wouldn't go." He was sitting on a cot a few feet away and made no attempt to hide the fact that he was listening to the conversation, as were the others.

"Would you expect me to accept such a favor from a man like William?" Charles asked.

"Well, if I obtained the permission, would you accept it from me?" Jason asked.

"No, I would not," Charles said firmly. "Who the offer came from was only part of the problem. The rest of it has to do with deserting my comrades at such a crucial time. What kind of man would I be if I did that?"

"Perhaps the kind of man who has a wife and children to look after," Jason suggested.

"But practically every man here has a family out there somewhere, Jason."

"Then I would say to any man here that if he has

a chance to get out, even alone, he should take advantage of it."

"I told him the same thing," Robinson said.

"Yes, my friend," Charles said, turning to Robinson. "But what was your answer when I asked what you would do in my position?"

Robinson smiled slyly and replied, "If I recall correctly, I believe you did win that argument."

"I believe I did," Charles agreed.

For a moment, Jason considered telling his brother what an ugly mood the men in Atchison's army were in and trying to convince him that remaining in this cell could be tantamount to dying. But what was the use? It would probably only harden Charles's resolve to remain with his friends, and it would certainly inject needless worry and fear in the hearts of every man there.

"This whole thing is very frustrating," Jason said at last. "I feel like I have to do something, but I don't know what to do anymore. I don't know how I can help you if you refuse to be helped."

"Well, as you told me when you were here before," Charles reminded him solemnly, "you have chosen not to make this your fight. But even if you had, only one of two things would have happened by now, depending on the side you chose. Either you would be in here with us, or you would be outside helping to make sure we remained imprisoned."

Jason chose not to reply.

"There is one thing you could do for me, though," Charles said finally. "The last time I saw Gertrude and the children, they were on their way to Osawatomie, but I never received word that they arrived safely. Is there any way that you could find them and get a message back to me?"

"Yes, of course I will, Charles."

"We could give you a letter to John Brown so you wouldn't have any trouble with him," Robinson suggested.

"I would prefer not to have anything like that in my possession in case I'm stopped and searched along the way. I met Old Brown in your company last fall, so he should remember me. And as soon as I find your family, I will either come back or find some reliable way to get a message to you, Charles. I promise."

As the two brothers shook hands, Jason could not help but wonder if by the time any message arrived about the safety of Charles's family, Charles would be alive to receive it.

The countryside was in chaos. Every man on the road bore a gun, and few dared travel in groups of less than four or five. Conversations among strangers whose paths happened to cross were conducted with rifles and pistols leveled at one another. Two times on the way to Osawatomie, Jason passed bodies of men lying in ditches, but he didn't know either of them, so he paused only long enough to gaze with morbid curiosity at the agonized expressions on their lifeless faces.

He was challenged twice by patrols, but both times he was fortunate enough to be interrogated by men who knew and respected William. The leaders of both groups cautioned him that he could not ride much farther south without entering territory controlled by "the other side," but he was allowed to move on after hinting that he was on a vital mission for the forces that now occupied Lawrence.

After the meeting with Charles, Jason had spoken briefly with William before leaving Lawrence. Something was going on, something important, which William was apparently involved in planning, but he hadn't chosen to let Jason know what it was, and Jason hadn't asked. William had, however, hinted darkly that Jason's intention of riding south in search of Charles's family was "a very bad idea right now."

Most of the farms and homesteads Jason passed seemed deserted, but he never stopped at any of them to find out.

He had left Lawrence in midafternoon, which meant he couldn't reach Osawatomie before dark. He still did not wish to be caught on the open road at night, so when the sky began to darken and every shadow become a threat, Jason left the road and found a secure little clearing by a stream where he made his cold camp. The next morning he was up and riding again before the sun made its full appearance in the eastern sky.

It was surprisingly easy to locate John Brown's stronghold at Osawatomie, but entering the place would be far more difficult, Jason realized as he gazed down at it from a hilltop about a quarter mile to the north.

Brown and his sons had arranged their assorted cabins and outbuildings with security in mind. The several log buildings were laid out in a square, each facing an inner yard about fifty feet across. The gaps between the buildings were sealed with five-foot stone walls, and the windows on the backs of the buildings were much smaller than normal, scarcely big enough for a grown man to crawl through.

A second line of defense had been created by the strategic placement of the family barn and various other sheds and storage buildings. These had been lined up in an L shape on the north and east sides of the main compound, the most likely points of attack. To the south and west, a number of low stone walls, overturned wagons, and earthen berms provided excellent shooting positions from which to fight off an assault.

It was precisely the sort of fortress he would have expected Brown to establish, but seeing it now, its belligerent message unmistakable, he could only wonder again at the blind, savage devotion of its inhabitants. From the first moment that he entered the territory, John Brown must have realized that he would soon be committing the sort of atrocities that could only inspire fierce counterattacks.

The first warning Jason had that he had been spotted was when a rifle shot roared out from somewhere to his left and a slug furrowed the sod a few feet in front of Ned's hooves. The shot had come not from within the stronghold but from some concealed position a couple of hundred feed outside its perimeter.

Jason didn't try to draw his rifle from its scabbard and return the fire, knowing that if the person who fired the shot had wanted him dead, he would be dead already. Instead, he held both hands up and called out loudly, "Don't shoot me. I'm Charles Hartman's brother, and I've come here looking for his family."

"Step down and walk away from your horse," a voice commanded. The speaker was not the same man who had fired the shot. The instructions came from off to the right and slightly behind Jason. As he complied, Jason looked in that direction and saw a man step out from behind the trunk of a cottonwood tree two dozen yards away and start in his direction. His rifle was casually leveled at Jason's middle, and Jason was careful to give him no reason to pull the trigger.

"Do you have a handgun on you?" the man asked.

"Under my jacket," Jason replied.

"Get it out, slow and careful, and put it on the ground."

Again Jason complied.

As his captor neared him, Jason recognized beneath his flop hat and full beard the dark, stolid features of Owen Brown, one of the two sons who had accompanied John Brown to the meeting in Lawrence months ago.

"You're Owen, aren't you?" Jason asked. "I'm Jason

Hartman. We met in my brother's store in Lawrence last fall."

"I 'member," Owen Brown answered impassively. "And I also 'member finding out later that Charles ain't the only brother you got in this part of the country. You jus' play it slow and easy if you want to live through the day."

"Look, I'm disarmed and I've already told you that my reason for being here is a peaceful one," Jason replied impatiently. "What else do you want? An oath signed in blood?"

"Don't get smart, mister."

"Just tell me if my brother's family is here," Jason said. "If they are, I want to see them for a few minutes, and then I'll be on my way. You can even leave my guns out here if you're worried that I might try to pull a trick on you."

"No need. You try anything and you're a dead man."

By this time the second man, the one who had fired the warning shot, had reached Jason. He was considerably younger than Owen, but the similarity of their features made Jason believe that he was another brother. Brown was said to have fathered more than a dozen children, most of whom had come here to Kansas with him.

Owen instructed the new arrival to take charge of Jason's horse and guns, then used his rifle barrel to push Jason down the hillside.

As they approached the compound, Jason spotted men watching them from behind walls and partially opened wooden shutters. The place seemed to be well defended, and Jason guessed that Brown must have gathered other supporters in addition to his own family in preparation for the expected attack.

After entering the center yard through a narrow gate, Jason was directed to the front door of one of the log buildings, a two-story affair with heavy-shuttered windows and shooting slots. John Brown was waiting inside.

The room where Jason was received was as austere as the man it belonged to. All of the furniture was homemade, including a long pine table, a matching sideboard, and an assortment of high-backed, uncomfortable-looking pine chairs. A drab young woman of about sixteen was clearing a stack of dishes from the table when Jason and Owen entered, but a quick gesture from Brown sent her scurrying through a doorway at the back of the room.

Brown was seated at the head of the table, a dirty plate and a half-empty cup of coffee in front of him. On one side of the plate lay a folded newspaper, on the other a cocked pistol. He looked up at the new arrival and took Jason's measure with cold, expressionless eyes.

"You're not welcome here," Brown abruptly informed Jason. "Why have you come?"

"I'm here to see my brother's family," Jason replied. "I've just come from Lawrence, where Charles is locked up, and I promised him I would find out if his wife and children are all right. I asked your son here, but he never gave me an answer, so now I'm asking you. Are they here?"

Jason knew he was taking a chance by not acting more submissive and conciliatory, but some instinct told him that Brown would better understand directness and persistence than he would meekness.

"We know all about the abomination that is taking place in Lawrence," Brown announced. "I warned Dr. Robinson and the others, your brother included, that it would come to this if they didn't make better preparations for their defense, but they kept clinging to the foolish hope that they could deal with an irrational opponent in a rational matter. Didn't I warn them, Owen?"

"Yes, sir, Papa," Owen replied mechanically. "I heard you warn them."

"But what about Gertrude and the children?" Jason insisted. "Are they here? Are they safe?"

"Your brother's family is under my protection," Brown

announced magnanimously. "In fact, three of his sons are now members of the civil guard I have formed to deal with this crisis. If that is truly your reason for being here, then you can leave right away. In fact," he added, "I insist that you leave."

"I want to see her," Jason said.

"No."

"I have a right to see her," Jason replied doggedly. "She's a member of my family, my brother's wife, and I have a right."

"You got a right to die if you don't do what Papa says," Owen said, goading him from behind. Jason ignored the remark, knowing the son would make no move without instructions from his father.

"Don't you think she would like to hear it directly from me that Charles is all right, that he and the others haven't been mistreated by their captors?" Jason asked. "What harm can it do?"

Brown considered for a moment, then shifted his gaze to his son and commanded, "Get the woman, Owen. Bring her here."

After Owen was gone, Brown tried to interrogate Jason on the situation in Lawrence, but Jason had little to offer. He was glad that William had told him nothing of Atchison's plans so that now he could be honest about his ignorance. For the last few minutes that they were alone, a stony silence filled the room.

When Gertrude Hartman arrived at last, she seemed, if anything, slightly irritated by Jason's presence here. Her greeting was terse, and it was obvious that she was no more inclined to waste time on him now than she had been last fall, when they first met.

Jason quickly relayed the message Charles had sent to his family and tried to explain, as near as he understood them, what his brother's prospects might be.

"Things were pretty quiet when I left," he said. "Atchison had the men well in hand. But a lot of them were getting restless for some kind of action, so I can't predict what the situation might be like in another few days."

"What about the store?" Gertrude asked.

"The building is still standing," Jason told her, "but that's about all. I was told that the store was looted the first night, but Atchison ordered that it not be burned because he wanted to save the restaurant next door."

"I see. Now what else do you have to tell me?"

"I don't have anything else to say to you," Jason said. "But I thought you might like to send some message back to him in case I can make it back to Lawrence."

"All right, tell him this," Gertrude replied. "Tell him I'll try as best I can to work up an inventory of everything we've lost. I don't suppose we'll ever be able to get restitution from anybody, but at least it will serve as a good working list when we begin to restock."

"I'm sure that news will warm his heart in that cold jail cell," Jason said wryly.

"This is not a time for weakness and sentimentality," Gertrude shot back. "To survive this crisis, we must deal with realities, and at the moment the loss of our means of support is one of the most important realities."

"I suppose it is," Jason said coldly. "To you, at least."

Within thirty minutes, Jason was on his way back to Lawrence, his arms and horse reluctantly restored to him by Brown's sons.

He had one obligation left to fulfill, that of carrying the news to Charles that his family was safe. But after that duty was discharged, he vowed, it would take something akin to an act of Congress to get him involved with this ridiculous affair and its lunatic combatants again. He was powerless to help, powerless to affect in any way the destructive whirlwind of events, so why shoud he try? Why should he waste his time and risk his life trying to reason with men who stubbornly refused to listen to reason?

Of all that he had seen and heard over the past few days, one image began to emerge more powerfully than any other. It was something he had seen during those final few frustrating moments at Osawatomie as Owen Brown was leading him out of the compound.

Jason had caught sight of a youth of about sixteen lurking behind a stone barricade. The boy held a rifle in his hand that was nearly as long as he was tall, and the expression on his face matched in every detail the look of cold, stubborn determination that Jason had grown accustomed to seeing on the features of men such a John Brown and his own brother Charles.

The youth was one of Charles's sons. He was sure of it.

Jason's own son John was thirteen now, and Daniel was eleven. How long would it be, he wondered, until he saw that look in their eyes?

9

Mollie sat on the creek bank popping pebbles into the water, thinking about all that had gone on since Anson Younger was killed. It seemed as if the whole world had gone insane, and even she had not been immune to the madness. More than a year had passed now, and she could not begin to count the number of trips she and Cole had made to various parts of Kansas and Missouri in their compulsive, fruitless search for Anson's killer. Boone Septin had become a specter, a wicked spirit that haunted her every waking hour, and seeking him had become an addiction from which there seemed no escape.

But she was tired now, tired of sneaking and lying and hiding, tired of pumping herself full of hope and determination every time they rode out, and tired of dealing with the disappointment each trip produced.

She was waiting for Cole now. He had sent word to her that one of his neighbors, who had just returned from Kansas, had heard a rumor about Septin's possible whereabouts, and he wanted to ride over and investigate it. Mollie and Cole had suspended their trips into Kansas for more than two months while Atchison's forces occupied Lawrence and the surrounding countryside, but now that federal troops had intervened and Lawrence was back under the control of its founders, the crisis seemed to be past. It was safe for Mollie to go back into Kansas, or at least as safe as it had ever been, and Cole was eager for them to continue the search for his cousin's killer.

Things had changed for Mollie, though. The two-month interlude had given her time to think about their mutual obsession, and she was no longer sure she wanted to renew the crusade.

She heard Cole's horse as he approached the small clearing that had become their customary meeting place, and she rose to meet him. He seemed surprised to see her there.

"I didn't think you were here yet," Cole said as he tied the reins to a sapling. "I didn't see Stony anywhere around when I rode in."

"I walked over from the house," Mollie explained. "It's not so far, less than a half mile."

"Yes, but now you'll have to go back for your horse," Cole said impatiently, "and that will give your brother another chance to lecture you about what we're doing. I want to leave right away."

"Cole," Mollie said hesitantly. Now that he was here, it was difficult to say what she had to say. "About the trip . . ."

Her expression and tone of voice told him that something was different this time, that she had something on her mind. "What is it, Mollie?" he asked quickly. "Is something wrong at home?"

"No, it's nothing about home." She looked away. "It's about me. I don't want to go with you this time."

His eyebrows shot up, but he didn't hesitate. "All right," he answered coldly.

"Come on, Cole," she urged him. "Let's sit down over here. I want to talk to you. I want to explain why I'm not going to go."

Wordlessly, Cole followed her to the bank and sat down on the soft grass next to her. She could sense that he was already beginning to withdraw from her, mentally preparing himself to go on alone with his quest, but that was not at all what she wanted.

"How long have we been going off like this?" Mollie asked him. "Do you know how many of these trips we've made?"

"No, I don't know how many," he answered. "Anson died in April of last year, and we've been going ever since."

"That's right. It's been over a year. And what good has it done? Are we any closer to catching up to Boone Septin than we were that first time we went over into Kansas?"

"That's a damn fool question," Cole muttered. "Of course we aren't. He's still out there."

"The only thing we know anymore," Mollie reasoned, "is that we haven't killed him, Cole. Half the rumors we've tried to run down have disappeared like smoke, and it's been months since we've come across any real evidence that he's in this part of the country or even that he's still alive. Knowing the kind of man he is, it's possible that some husband or father or jealous boyfriend has already done away with him."

"Anything's possible, Mollie, but I can't rest until I'm sure. If a year has passed, or two, or five, that doesn't make any difference to me. I won't give up until I know he's dead."

"I felt that way too, and part of me still does sometimes," Mollie admitted. "But I also feel like this thing is eating a hole in me. It's like he took Anson's life away from him first, and now he's taking mine away from me a chunk at a time."

Mollie reached out and placed a hand on her friend's arm, staring intently at his determined face. His eyes were fixed on a jagged stone in the middle of the creek.

"While we've been about this business," Mollie continued, "I've shut myself off from the rest of the world. During these past two months, while you've been away most of the time and there weren't any trips to take, I started to realize how lonely I've become. I couldn't let any new lover enter my life because I wouldn't let my past one rest peacefully in his grave. You're my only friend, Cole, but even you and I seem to be friends for only one purpose."

Cole turned his head and looked at her at last. For a long moment his eyes stared deeply into hers, as if searching for all the unspoken meanings in her words.

"I'm probably the best friend you'll ever have, Mollie," he told her softly. "There isn't much on God's green earth that you could ask of me that I wouldn't try to deliver."

"I know, Cole," she smiled. "That's been the best part of all this. But can you understand that that's not enough, that having a friend like you is not enough?"

"Sure, I can, sure," Cole answered, glancing away abruptly. He began to close the door again, shutting her out. Mollie gave his arm a slight squeeze with her fingers, but he made no move to acknowledge her touch.

"Twice in my life there have been men that I cared very deeply about," Mollie said, trying to explain. "One was a man back in Virginia, and the other was Anson. When I was with them, they made me feel like the world was a wonderful place to be. I want that feeling again, Cole. I want to feel happy without having to worry about what I'm supposed to do to make myself happy. But I don't think that's going to happen as long as the only driving ambition in my life is to kill a man."

A minute of heavy silence passed. When Cole looked back at her at last, all the coldness had left his face. He seemed hesitant now, unsure of himself for the first time since Mollie met him.

"I know what you are, Mollie," he said slowly. "That's the part that's worried me most since we started this business. Don't you think that sometimes at night, when we were sleeping side by side . . . You know more about these things than I do, Mollie. Surely you knew what I was thinking about sometimes . . . that all I would have to do was . . . "

"Yes, I knew." Mollie flashed him a shy smile. "And you know what's funny? There probably were times when both of us were thinking the same thing at the same time. So there we were, a foot apart, both wide awake, and both acting like we were sound asleep so the other one wouldn't discover our secret."

Her admission caught him by surprise, and his mouth opened, but he couldn't speak.

"It's natural to think those things, Cole," Mollie said reassuringly. "For you, and even for me. You're younger than me, but you're a grown man still, strong and brave and not hard to look at even after three days on the trail." When she raised her hand and touched his cheek, he smiled at last, obviously enjoying the caress.

He leaned forward clumsily to kiss her, his lips pursed and his body tense. It surprised Mollie to realize that, despite the bold confidence with which Cole plunged into most other situations, he was a rank amateur at romance. After a second he withdrew his lips from hers and turned his head away.

"I guess you can tell I'm not much good at that," Cole mumbled.

"Maybe you just need more practice," Mollie teased. With a light touch of her fingers, she turned his face back to hers and kissed him again. He gasped when her breast brushed his chest, but a moment later he put an arm around her and pulled her to him. Despite Cole's awkwardness, having a man hold her like this again after such a long time filled Mollie with a long-forgotten feeling of contentment.

When they pulled apart, Cole was grinning broadly. With a pleased sigh, Mollie lay back on the grass, and Cole stretched out next to her, his head propped up on one hand.

"I always figured if I ever tried anything like that, you'd probably beat me till I couldn't stand up straight," Cole said playfully.

"I probably would have at one time," Mollie laughed, "but not now. I never had any idea that something like this would happen today, but I'm glad it did."

"So am I," he said.

She watched his eyes glide down across the curve of her neck to her breasts, and her breath quickened. His free hand started involuntarily toward her body but stopped a few inches short of its objective, as if restrained by some invisible bond.

"Go ahead," Mollie said. "We've come this far, so we might as well go a little farther."

"I just wondered what they feel like," Cole said huskily. His hand closed over one breast and held it firmly.

"Gently . . . gently," she whispered, her eyes closing. His touch lightened in response, sampling the shape and texture of her flesh as his breathing grew louder and faster. A familiar feeling, like an old friend long absent, began to course through Mollie, quickening her pulse and sending pleasure to all parts of her body.

Cole unbuttoned her blouse down to where it was tucked into her cotton skirt, then gently loosened the satin bows that held the front of her undergarment closed. His fingertips felt warm and delightful when they came in contact with the bare skin of her chest, but she reached up and stopped him before his hand slid completely inside her clothing. When she opened her eyes and looked up at him, he was gazing back at her, his eyes filled with uncertainty.

"If we let this go any further, things will never be the same again," she warned him quietly.

"They'll never be the same anyway," Cole answered. "It's been too late since that first kiss."

She smiled and nodded. He was right, of course. In fact, it had all started months ago in some forgotten camp while the two of them lay side by side, each yearning to hold the other.

"Get the blanket from your bedroll and find some smooth place to spread it out," Mollie suggested. "As long as we're going to change our lives, we might as well be comfortable."

Cole sprang to his feet and went to his horse. She almost laughed as she watched him fumbling with the straps that held his bedroll in place, but Mollie was careful not to let her amusement show, knowing her young, soon-to-be lover would almost certainly misunderstand it.

Mollie had her blouse off by the time Cole turned back to her. For a moment he stared at her, but then he ducked his head like a boy caught peeking in a window and busied himself spreading the blanket on a level, grassy spot under the trees. By the time he looked at her again, she had slipped her skirt and petticoats off and laid them aside.

From that point on, as she finished the job of undressing, there was no question of whether he would, or could, tear his eyes away from her again.

It occurred to Mollie that never before in her life had she so calmly, almost brazenly, revealed herself to a man. Even with Kurt Rakestraw, she had acted more restrained, always letting him take the lead in their lovemaking. But today it seemed perfectly natural, and quite thrilling as well, to be offering herself to Cole in such a free and open manner, and the look of hunger and delight on his face was all the reassurance she needed that she was going about this matter in exactly the right way.

"Mollie, you're so beautiful," Cole whispered. "Even after all the time I've known you, I could never have imagined you like . . . like this."

Smiling, her senses alive with anticipation, she went to Cole and drew his lips down to hers. Her flesh tingled as it brushed against his rough, masculine garments, and the feel of his fingers on the bare skin of her back sent an unexpected quiver through her.

After that first exciting kiss, she drew away from him and reached for the buckle of his gun belt. "Take this thing off, Cole," she told him huskily. "Take everything off . . . and hurry!"

Cole began to peel away his clothing as Mollie lay back on the blanket. His trembling hands, rendered clumsy and nearly useless with the urgency of their mission, fumbled with every button and buckle they encountered. But then at last, with his garments, gun and boots cast away in all directions, he stood naked above her. Mollie drew a deep breath, then held up her hand, inviting him to join her.

The first time didn't take so very long. Overwhelmed, Cole finally surrendered himself to sheer animal urgency. Mollie was surprised, but hardly displeased, by the force and abandon with which he used her body, and after it was over, she lay by his side, stroking his face and chest gently.

When they made love again. Mollie showed Cole with quiet words and soft responses how the most pleasure could be gained from their union. This time there was a quality of sharing, and when at last they lay back again, sated and momentarily exhausted, Mollie knew without even having to consciously consider the matter, that a new chapter in her life had begun.

"It's funny," Cole said at last, his body still and relaxed beside hers. "I feel like I'm supposed to say, I love you, or something now. But what's going on inside me isn't anything like what I ever thought love was supposed to feel like. It's better, if that makes any sense."

"I think I feel the same way, Cole," Mollie answered, "although I'm not sure I could put any words to it either. But maybe we're not supposed to. Maybe it's like our friendship. It's just there, and we know it's good and right. And that's enough, I think. More than enough."

When Cole finished checking the cinch on his sáddle, he looked toward the west, where the sun had dipped nearly to the horizon. "I guess I'll only try to get as far as Independence before I stop for the night," he said.

"It was terrible of me to delay you so long," Mollie grinned.

Cole looked over at her and nodded. "Terrible," he agreed with a smile. He tugged at the straps that held his bedroll in place, then turned toward Mollie and said, "Well, I guess I'm ready. You haven't changed your mind about going?"

"The idea does have a new appeal to it," Mollie admitted, "but I guess not." She put her arms around him for a final hug, then raised her face so he could kiss her.

"What happens now, Mollie?" he asked. "What happens when I get back, and next week, and the next time I hear talk about Septin and decide to go after him?"

"I don't know, Cole. I guess things will sort themselves out. From here on, I guess both of us will just do what we feel like doing."

"I know what I feel like doing," Cole chuckled. "But I guess you need to get back to the house before dark, and I've got miles to ride."

He turned and stepped up into the saddle, but Mollie

delayed him a moment longer with a light touch on his leg. "Now you listen to me, Cole Younger," she said sternly, sounding suddenly more like a schoolmarm than a lover. "If I ever find out that you've bragged to Vick or Matt or any of your other friends about what we did here today, I'll skin you out like a buck and hang your hide on a barn door somewhere."

"Yes, ma'am, I'll take those words to heart," Cole promised with a broad grin. He dug his heels into his horse's side and the animal bounded forward. Then Cole cut loose with a yell of sheer exuberance, which echoed through the trees like a panther's cry.

"Mollie Marie Hartman, you've really done it now!" she muttered to herself as she turned and headed toward home.

10

March 1857

Arethia was just finishing the last of the supper dishes
when she heard Jason ride by the house on the way to
the barn to stable his horse. Their evening meal was long
since over, and Mollie and the children were already in
bed, but Arethia had kept a plate of fried pork, potatoes,
stewed apples, and vegetables warm in the oven for her
husband.

Because Tyson was gone, there had been many times
during the past winter when there had not been any fresh
meat, but Jason and William had combined their efforts
to slaughter four hogs the previous week, so now they
were eating fresh pork or ham with almost every meal.

Several hours before, Jason had responded to a mysterious summons from William, delivered by his brother's
slave Hannibal. The mere fact that William had sent him

on horseback stressed the urgency of the request, and Jason had saddled his horse and left immediately.

Arethia had tried not to worry about him, but there was no denying the sense of relief she felt when she heard his horse and knew that he was home safely. A few minutes later, when she heard his footsteps on the back porch, she could tell by their heaviness how tired he was. His plate of food and a tall glass of buttermilk were waiting for him on the table when he entered.

Jason gave his wife a kiss and a tired smile on his way to the table, where he sat down and began eating immediately.

"I thought they were going to talk all night," Jason grumbled as he sliced off a chunk of pork and stuck it in his mouth.

Arethia poured herself a glass of tea and sat down across from him. "Was it a meeting?" she asked.

"Yeah," Jason answered noncommittally. "William and all his sound-on-the-goosers."

"Well, judging from the call he sent out to you, it must have been pretty important."

For a moment, Jason studied his plate as he chewed a mouthful of food, then finally he raised his head and looked directly at his wife. "Are the children all asleep?" he asked cautiously. "I don't see any need for them to know about this."

"Yes, they're all in bed," Arethia replied, concern spreading over her face. "What is it?"

"One of Atchison's spies over in Kansas has sent word that there's going to be a big raid across the border sometime during the next few days, and they want to be ready for it. They don't know exactly when or where, so the warning has gone out all over this part of the state."

Arethia was noticeably alarmed. "After such a quiet winter, I had hoped the trouble wouldn't start up again this spring and summer," she said. "When the troops came in last fall and took Lawrence away from Atchison, I thought maybe that meant they planned to put a stop to all this killing."

"One little garrison in Leavenworth isn't enough to keep a lid on all this hate," Jason told her. "Statehood for Kansas is the only answer, but the Congress is so split on the slavery question that they can't seem to get anything done about that."

"But it seems like after the scare Charles and his friends in Lawrence had last fall, they wouldn't dare antagonize Atchison's people again. From what you told me, they were lucky to get out of those jail cells alive, and a lot of them, including your brother, lost almost everything they had."

"A thing like that is only going to make them that much more determined," Jason said. "I guess if they were cautious men who always avoided trouble when they could, they wouldn't even be in Kansas in the first place." He took another bite, then added, "And besides, the word William received is that this raid isn't coming out of Lawrence. The men that are behind it live farther to the south."

"John Brown?" Arethia asked. By this time, Brown's ruthless reputation had grown to the point that the mention of his name seemed to fill her with dread.

"I guess so," Jason answered quietly.

After supper, Jason spent a few minutes closing and barring the shutters over the windows of their home, then he got out all the firearms in the house — two shotguns, two rifles and a pistol — and made sure they were all loaded and close at hand. He had tried to reassure his wife that there was no need to worry because there were no slaves on their farm, but his preparations made it plain how deep his own concerns were.

When everything was ready, Jason had his wife make a fresh pot of coffee, and he began gulping down cup after cup.

"If you stay awake all night," Arethia commented at one point, "you won't be worth shooting tomorrow."

"There's not much to do around here until the fields get dry anyway," Jason said. "I can sleep in the daytime."

"But if there's nothing to worry about —" Arethia said.

"Honey, we both know there's no guarantees when we're dealing with people like this," Jason explained. "I can't imagine any possible reason why they would want to come here and bother us, but I'll feel better being up and ready, just in case."

"And so will I," Arethia announced as she took a cup from the cabinet and filled it with coffee.

Jason roused himself enough to look at the clock on the mantle, and saw that it was almost four in the morning. He wasn't sure how long he had been asleep, but he thought it had probably been more than an hour. After the long day he had put in yesterday, even the coffee had not been enough to keep him awake and alert all night.

A few feet away, Arethia was slumped in a chair, wrapped in a blanket against the chill, and sound asleep. Jason set aside the rifle that was lying across his knees and got up to put more wood on the fire. Despite the impending arrival of spring, the nights were still cold, and the recent rains had filled the air with a discomforting dampness.

He had just laid a few sticks of kindling across the dying coals and was preparing to add an oak log when he heard Matthew's low growl out on the front porch. Normally he would not have paid much attention to the animal's warning. There were enough nocturnal creatures roaming the area to keep the small dog growling throughout an average night, and Jason seldom went outside to see what was disturbing him.

But tonight the dog's growl made him uneasy. He laid the log across the coals, then went to one of the windows and peered out through a four-inch notch cut in the shutter. The front yard, bathed in moonlight, was empty and still. He considered slipping outside for a better look, then decided there was no use getting so alarmed simply because Matthew was doing what he did practically every night.

He was on his way back to the chair when the small terrier erupted into a full-scale fit of barking. He returned to the window in time to see the dog racing across the yard to the road.

And then Jason saw them coming.

In the dim moonlight, it was impossible to tell how many riders were in the group. There were over a dozen of them, probably more like twenty, Jason thought, and they didn't try to conceal their presence as they entered the yard and stopped a few yards away from the door. Matthew, deciding that his task was finished, retired to a safe spot under the front porch to cower and growl.

By then, Arethia was at his side, clutching his arm. She didn't even bother to ask who it was outside. They both knew.

"Come out of the house!" one of the mounted figures outside commanded loudly.

"You'd better go see about the children," Jason told his wife hurriedly. "Send Mollie in here, and get the kids together in one room. Keep them flat on the floor in case there's gunfire." Without a word, Arethia hurried off toward the bedrooms.

"Come out!" the stern voice demanded again.

"You have no business with us," Jason called out at last. "We have no slaves here. Search the outbuildings if you don't believe me. But I'm not coming out."

Just then Mollie entered the room, alert despite the

abrupt awakening. The first thing she did was grab one of the loaded rifles and stand at Jason's side. "Who are they?" she asked.

"Jayhawkers," Jason told her. "They must have taken a wrong turn in the dark and ended up here by mistake, but they'll go away when they find out we don't have any slaves on the place."

The men outside conferred with one another for a moment, but instead of spreading out to search the farm, one man struck a match and lit a pitch-soaked rag wrapped around the end of a stick.

"This is going on the roof if you aren't out here in ten seconds," the man announced.

"Damn it, I guess I'll have to go out there after all," Jason muttered. "You bar the door after me, Mollie, but don't start shooting for any reason unless it's to protect yourself or Arethia and the children."

Jason opened the door and stepped out on the porch, then pulled it closed behind him. He heard Mollie drop the heavy bar in place as he had instructed.

The Jayhawkers had spread out in a broad line across the yard, and as Jason had estimated, there were twenty or more of them. He scanned the figures one at a time until his eyes stopped on the one he was looking for. John Brown was in the center of the line, next to the man who held the torch.

"I'm Jason Hartman, Mr. Brown. Charles Hartman's brother. You know me, and you know that I don't have any slaves on my place, so why are you here?"

"Get everyone out of the house, Jason Hartman," Brown commanded, his face expressionless.

"There's just women and children inside, and they're afraid," Jason answered. "There's no need to expose them to this."

Handing the reins of his horse to the man beside him, John Brown dismounted and came over to stand directly in front of Jason. Jason had squared off against men bigger and huskier than Brown, but he could never recall facing up to any man who was quite so intimidating.

"I won't argue with you," Brown told Jason in a quiet yet ominous voice. "Get everyone out here in the yard."

"But why?" Jason asked.

Instead of answering the question, Brown turned to the man behind him with the torch and said, "Burn the house."

"No, wait!" Jason shouted. "I'll get them out here, but damn it, don't burn our home down!"

Jason went back inside, and with Mollie and Arethia's help, they herded the sleepy, frightened children outside.

Brown inspected them briefly, then turned back to his men and ordered, "Some of you men search the house, and some others spread out and look the rest of the place over." A number of men immediately dismounted and scattered to do their leader's bidding.

While this was going on, Jason stood with his family huddled behind him, watching Brown with a growing anger and disdain. There was no sense in this, he thought. What cause was served by frightening children and harassing families who had nothing to do with slavery? But despite the fury that raged inside him over this sort of treatment, he realized the folly of letting such an emotion take control of him. If he and his family were to live through this thing, they must be completely submissive to Brown's irrational demands.

When the search was finished, the men began assembling in the yard once again. Finally, John Brown turned his attention to Jason again.

"You mentioned your brother Charles a few minutes ago," he said to Jason, "but I happen to know that you have two brothers. Where does the other one live? Where is William Hartman?"

"He lives miles from here," Jason lied. In fact, William's

farm was little more than two miles away, but he wasn't about to tell Brown that.

"You're a liar!' Brown rasped. "I know his farm is near here, but the map that was given to us is wrong. Where is his house?"

"Someone has given you some bad information," Jason said evenly. "My brother lives on the other side of the county, a good two-hour ride from here. You'd never make it there before daylight."

Brown brought his right fist up and landed a crashing blow on Jason's cheek. Jason staggered backward but recovered his footing quickly. He immediately leaped forward to attack the abolitionist, but before he reached Brown he was struck from the side by a short oak club. The first blow jarred his senses, and the second sent him to his knees. He remained there, dazed and unable to stand, until a kick in the stomach from John Brown's heavy boot toppled him over backward. Both Mollie and Arethia tried to reach him, but some of the men held them back.

Brown stood, panting and furious, over his victim. "Where is William Hartman?" he yelled. He accompanied the question with a second kick, which doubled Jason up.

"Long ways," Jason managed to gasp. Miles . . . from here . . . "

John Brown turned toward one of his men for an instant, and when he turned back, Jason saw through his blurry eyes that he held a long saber. This was it, Jason decided. It was said that the saber was Brown's weapon of choice for executions.

But instead the abolitionist leader turned toward where Jason's family was huddled. He reached out and grabbed Jason's middle son, Daniel, by the hair and hauled him clear of the others.

Arethia was frantic. It took three grown men to hold

her back, and nearly as much effort was needed to restrain Mollie. With a surge of agonizing effort, Jason started to rise, but someone forced him back to the ground with a shotgun barrel thrust against his chest.

"I'm going to kill this boy," Brown announced. He raised the saber up with his right hand while at the same time holding Daniel, limp with terror, in his left.

"Jason!" Arethia wailed.

"All right! I'll tell you!" Jason shouted. "Just leave my son alone!"

Brown immediately let go of Daniel's hair, and the boy crumpled to the ground at his feet. "If you lie to me, I'll kill them all," he vowed. "And you'll die last so you can witness the results of your treachery."

Jason was permitted to sit up and then to rise weakly to his feet. He staggered over and helped his son stand up, then handed him over to Arethia. Then he turned back and met John Brown's stern gaze with one equally cold and steady.

"This is a terrible thing you're doing, to make a man betray his brother," Jason said.

"Tell that to your brother Charles, who was imprisoned by this same vermin you are now so eager to protect," Brown snarled. "Now, where is he?"

Resigned, Jason provided the directions to William's farm.

"And how many men are there?"

"Just my brother and his overseer."

For a long, tense moment, Brown continued to study Jason's face, trying, no doubt, to determine whether or not he had been telling the truth. Finally he turned away and called back to the man with the torch, "Burn the barn. That should be punishment enough for the trouble they've caused us here."

The man turned and galloped away, and a moment later Mollie broke free from her captors and raced around the side of the house. Normally her horse, Stony, was allowed to run free in the pasture, but she had put him in a stall in the barn that evening because of a bruised hoof.

One of the men made as if to start for her, but Brown ordered him to let her go. "There's no need to put any of God's creatures to death because of this man's folly," he announced. "You, boy," he added, pointing to Jason's oldest son, John, "go and help her." He was feeling magnanimous now that he had gained such a total victory.

A minute later flames began to appear through the broken window of the barn where the torch was thrown, but soon after, the livestock that had been confined inside charged out through the doors Mollie had thrown open.

When the rider returned from the barn, Brown and the others mounted their horses. No other words were exchanged as the band turned and thundered out of the yard. Jason and his family watched until the last of them had disappeared down the road and the sound of their hoofbeats faded in the distance. Soon Mollie appeared again around the corner of the house, her face and cotton nightgown blackened with smoke and soot. John was right behind her, equally as filthy.

"Did you get all the animals out?" Jason asked.

"Yes, and we were able to save the saddles and some of the rest of the tack too," Mollie told him. "But there's no use trying to save the barn. That torch landed in a haystack and the fire has too good a start now."

"It doesn't matter," Jason replied wearily. "I can build another barn, but I could never replace any of you."

"But what about William?" Arethia asked.

"He'll be all right. He's not at home."

"But if they don't find him, then they might come back here!" Arethia persisted.

"Not tonight," Jason said. "They won't be back tonight."

"But . . . "

"No more talk, Arethia," Jason said with surprising abruptness. "You and Mollie get the children inside and back in bed. Then get out the bandages and ointment. I think this cut on my head is going to need some treatment before I leave. John, you go see if you can catch Ned and throw a saddle on his back. I want him ready to go in five minutes."

"Jason!" Arethia exclaimed. "You can't just —"

"We'll talk later," Jason snapped. "But for now, just do what I told you!" Before she could respond, he turned and started toward the house.

Pain rattled through Jason's skull each time one of Ned's hoofs struck the dirt road, but he scarcely noticed the discomfort. Behind him he had left a burning barn, a brood of terrified children, and a wife who was furious with him for deserting them at such a time, but at the moment even that seemed less important that the single, overpowering impulse that now dominated his thoughts.

Never before in his life had he felt such an overwhelming desire to kill a man.

Again and again in his mind he lived through that instant when John Brown had raised his saber up and Daniel's life had hung by a thread. Jason had no doubt that the fanatic would have killed the child if he had felt it was necessary. Youth was no barrier to Brown's savagery, and obviously the men who rode with him felt as he did; no act was too brutal if it served their exalted purposes.

Although he had yet to fully realize it, that single moment had changed Jason's life completely and irrevocably. Despite the bludgeoning and the intrusion into his home, until that second he was what he had always been, a man who placed his family foremost and a man who felt that the way to deal with conflict and strife was to avoid it whenever possible.

But the only emotion he felt now was hate. It seared his veins like liquid fire, blotting out everything else, driving him forward with such fury that at that moment he would have gladly taken on Brown's whole band in his urgent need to reach and destroy their ruthless leader.

The first cracklings of gunfire ahead reminded Jason that he would not have to fight alone, however.

William and his supporters had spent much of the evening planning an ambush at a strategic crossroads nearby. They had no way of knowing whether Brown's raid would be focused on this area, but they knew what route he would most likely take if he did come this way, and they were determined to be ready.

Jason had known about the ambush, and in fact, he had angered his brother and many of his neighbors by refusing to take part in it. But even after Brown had beaten him, and up until that final moment, when Daniel was about to die, Jason had hoped to remain uninvolved. To warn the Jayhawkers of the trap would have brought about the death of a number of his neighbors, and to steer Brown's band into it, he thought, would almost certainly bring about fierce retribution when the raiders realized what he had done.

The new Jason Hartman looked at things differently though. The best course would be to kill as many of the Jayhawkers as possible, to deal them such a devastating blow that abolitionists all over Kansas would live in fear of attempting to carry the war into the heartland of their enemy. Now, suddenly, the truth loomed, as stark and clear as the full moon hanging in the sky.

Killing was the only way. Nobody was going to change the way they thought or abandon the things they believed in. No one on either side was suddenly going to come around to the realization that logic and laws and a spirit of compromise should replace force and violence as a means to end the chaos.

Survival was the issue, and the key to survival was, simply, to kill.

By the time Jason advanced to within a quarter of a mile of the ambush, the gunfire reached a crescendo, then began to fall off. When the trap was sprung, most of those who were going to die were dead within a few seconds, downed by the first volley. After that it was just a matter of survivors scattering and running for their lives, which Jason guessed, the remaining men in Brown's party were probably doing at this very moment.

Knowing that it would be foolhardy to keep on when he was in their midst, Jason stopped Ned, dismounted, and sent the horse off into the woods at the side of the road with a slap on his rump. Then he crouched behind a bush at the edge of the road and waited.

In his haste to leave the house, Jason had strapped on his gun belt, then grabbed up a rifle and a handful of cartridges from the table in the living room. But now he was wishing he had brought along a shotgun instead. When they did come, if they came, the retreating Jayhawkers would be riding hellbent for Kansas, and there would be little time to aim a rifle properly. A shotgun was much better suited for such close-up, inaccurate shooting, but he would have to make do with what he had.

The sound of thundering hoofs announced the approach of some remnant of Brown's raiding party, and Jason braced himself. When they appeared a moment later around a bend in the road, Jason saw that there were four of them, riding close together and leaning forward in their saddles for speed. Each held a gun of some sort.

Their fatal error was that they looked behind them as they rode. For a critical two or three seconds none of them spotted the dark figure rise at the roadside and take aim.

Jason swung his sights to the center of the first rider's chest and squeezed the trigger. The bullet plowed into the raider's body from no more than ten feet away. At the same instant that he toppled sideways out of the saddle, his horse panicked at the gun's roar and tried to spin away.

The four men were riding so close together that when the lead horse stumbled and started to fall, the other horses had no chance to turn away before plowing into him. In an instant the middle of the road was filled with a tangled mass of terrified horses and men.

Casting the rifle aside and drawing his pistol, Jason sprang forward. He shot one man in the temple as he was struggling to rise, then spun and snapped off another round at a form writhing around on his left. The hastily fired round struck an injured horse in the throat, causing it to fall into a fit of helpless thrashing. From beneath the animal a crushed man screamed.

A shot exploded behind Jason, and a bullet ripped away a hunk of flesh from his side. He recalled seeing one man thrown clear of the tangle, but hadn't remembered seeing the man move after his body hit the ground. A second shot sounded even as Jason began to spin, and a burst of white light exploded inside his skull. But the necessary commands had already been dispatched to his hand. His finger jerked the trigger of his revolver, and the gun went off even as he tumbled, unconscious, to the ground.

"Good God, Will! Can you believe this mess? I wonder what happened here?"

"It looks like some of our boys ran into a bunch of them as they were running away."

"But I thought all our men were accounted for. We didn't put anybody this far away from the crossroads."

Jason heard the voices, but there was not enough life in him yet to speak or move. His left side felt as if it had been violated by a red-hot branding iron, and a thick, warm ooze was flowing from his forehead and down the left side of his face.

"Well, somebody had to have done this, unless these bastards got so scared that they just started shooting themselves —"

"And their horses. That dead black over there looks like a good animal too. It's a shame."

"Let's check them and make sure they're all done for, and then we'll send the wagon here to pick up their bodies."

Jason recognized his brother's voice and felt better knowing Will was here, and alive, but he didn't feel like talking yet. He was so tired . . .

"This one's still alive, I guess. He's got one eye open a little, and I thought I saw him blink."

Through the mist that clouded his vision, Jason saw a form loom over him.

"Underneath all this blood, he looks like —"

A rough hand brushed the left side of Jason's face.

"Christ, Will! It's your brother! It's Jason!"

A hand reached out, and a finger probed clumsily at the wound on the top of Jason's skull, sending pain slicing across the top of his head. "Yeow! Stop that!" Jason winced, reaching up to grab the offending hand.

In an instant, William was kneeling above Jason, staring down at him. With his help, Jason struggled up to a sitting position, with his back against the carcass of a dead horse.

"What the hell happened here, Jason?" William asked, his voice heavy. He had produced a roll of bandages from somewhere and was already covering the wound on Jason's head.

"They were going to kill my boy, Will," Jason told him weakly. "You were right about them all along. That devil was going to kill Daniel with a sword if I didn't, tell them where you were! Damn him . . . damn all of them!"

"Did you do all this, Jason?" William asked incredulously. "Did you kill all these men by yourself?"

"I wanted Brown," Jason replied resolutely. "It was him that I came after . . . but all these others, they would have let him do it. They were guilty too."

After wandering around the area briefly, William's companion returned to where William was just finishing bandaging Jason's head. Jason hadn't recognized him earlier, but saw now that it was Milt Bailey.

"There's four of them here, Will," Bailey reported. "Three shot dead, and one mashed flat under a dead horse. I guess that makes nine dead and one taken alive. Not a bad night's work, I'd say."

"Did you get him, William?" Jason asked urgently. "Did you kill John Brown?"

William shook his head. "We wounded three or four others, and there's men out looking for them now, so we still might get him. But he wasn't with those killed at the crossroads."

"We've got to get him," Jason said. "Even if we have to follow him all the way back to that snake pit in Osawatomie and shoot him like a dog. We've got to make sure he dies before he has a chance to come back over here and get his revenge for this. If you'll just round up my horse, I'll find my guns and we can —"

"Hold on, little brother," William said, holding Jason in place with surprisingly little effort. "From the looks of you, I doubt that you have the stuff left to even ride home alone, let alone cross over to Kansas and beard the lion in his den. I'm not sure why you've turned into such a firebrand since I saw you a few hours ago, but you took out four of them already tonight. That should be enough for anybody."

"All right, not tonight," Jason conceded tiredly. "But I've got to get him, Will," he said hoarsely. "As far as I'm concerned, after what he did to my family tonight, he's a dead man."

11

Jason considered it a poorly chosen campsite. The thick woods around them made it easy for anyone to slip up on them, and there was a small abolitionist settlement no more than two miles away, which greatly increased their chances of being discovered. The men he was with were not being careful either. The fires they built were entirely too large, and the wood they were burning was damp and green; it sent up clouds of thick, telltale smoke.

But Jason was not in charge, as Winston Singleton, the leader of the six-man party, had repeatedly reminded him when he tried to offer advice.

Jason didn't know much about Singleton or the men who accompanied him. They were members of a new breed who had begun to appear in western Missouri during the last year — hard-fighting, heavily armed ruffians who seldom if ever engaged in any honest toil but who always seemed to have coins enough in their pockets to indulge their vices and meet their simple needs.

Like most of his neighbors and friends, Jason felt little but contempt for men like Singleton and his followers, yet he had agreed to come along on this raid into Kansas Territory for one simple reason: Singleton's intention was to strike the heart of the abolitionist menace, and his objective was John Brown's stronghold at Osawatomie River.

William had sternly advised Jason not to make the trip with these men, and Arethia had tearfully pleaded with him not to go. Brown's abortive raid had taken place only two weeks before, and Jason had barely recovered from the wounds and abuse he had suffered. The bullet wound in his side was still a tender, livid welt, and the hair on the top of his head was only now beginning to grow back where the abolitionist bullet had scored his scalp.

But Jason could not be swayed. Night after night the vision of John Brown's saber sweeping down to slash Daniel's flesh invaded Jason's dreams, and the desire to have revenge against the man who had brutalized him and his family obsessed his every waking hour.

Singleton and his followers had ridden all night to reach this spot, where they intended to remain until darkness fell. Most of them had slept throughout the morning, and after their noon meal was finished, flasks had appeared and an afternoon of drinking started. A couple of them were close to being drunk already, and of all the men there, Jason was the only one who was cold sober and deadly serious about their mission.

When, about four o'clock, one of the men clumsily drew his pistol and took a potshot at a squirrel in a nearby tree, Jason decided he had had enough. He stood up and marched over to Singleton to protest.

"Wouldn't it be easier if we just passed out fliers with maps to this camp on them?" Jason complained.

"Take it easy, Hartman." Singleton shrugged. "Hell,

the boys are just blowing off a little steam before we get down to business tonight."

"At the rate they're going, there won't be a man among them who's even able to sit a horse by tonight, let alone take part in a raid against Brown's stronghold. You can bet that right now his men aren't getting liquored up and wasting their ammunition shooting at the treetops."

"So what? If we aren't in shape to take him on, we'll just hit someplace else," Singleton announced without concern. "The last time we were over here, we scouted a couple of cabins about ten miles south of here. There's a few head of livestock and two or three women on the place, and only a man and a half-growed boy to protect them —"

"Now wait just a damn minute, Singleton!" Jason said angrily. "I won't take part in anything like that. The deal was that we were going after Brown, and that's the only reason I came along in the first place. Do you think I'm just going to sit back and watch you attack families that might or might not even have a part in this trouble?"

"You can watch or not. I don't give a shit!" the leader snarled. "You and me don't have any goddamned deal. When I planned this thing, I figured I'd have more men along than I do now. From the way you described Brown's place at Osawatomie, we can't take it with six men anyway."

"Of course not, but we can hit him where he lives, just like he did to me and my family. We can let him know his home is not immune to attack, and that's what he'll remember the next time he considers taking his forces on a raid into Missouri."

"But if we just ride in, shoot the place up, and ride out again, what do we get out of it?" Singleton asked. "Just a long, hard run all the way back to the Missouri line, that's what! At least if we hit those cabins down south, we can have a little fun with the womenfolk and then ride away with a few head of cattle and maybe a couple of horses to show for our efforts."

"Damn you, Singleton! You're nothing but a belly-crawling snake. I'm sorry I ever got mixed up with you!"

Singleton's face went red, and he reached for the rifle that was lying on the ground beside him.

But Jason's hand was already resting on the butt of his revolver. "Do it, you bastard," Jason said, goading him.

Singleton was trying to remain calm, but fear crept into his expression as he realized how close he was to dying. "There's five of us," he announced with bravado. He laughed nervously. "You don't stand a chance, Hartman."

Jason's glance took in the other men, all of whom were watching the confrontation intently. "If you reach for that rifle, you'll never know whether any of them were willing to back you or not because you'll be dead," Jason said levelly. "But my guess is they'll let you go out alone."

Singleton was still trying to maintain his composure, but his face had gone sheet white, and he couldn't keep a slight quaver out of his voice when he spoke. "Get out of here, Hartman," he said. "I don't know whatever got into me to let you come along in the first place, but we don't want you with us."

Jason drew his gun and pointed it at his opponent's head. Singleton stared dumbly at it, mesmerized by its nearness.

"I'll be glad to go," Jason said, "but first I'll have your guns if you don't mind. Hand me the pistol in your waist-band and then the rifle." He accepted the weapons with his free hand and carried them across the camp to where Ned, still saddled, was tied to a long tether rope. There he laid Singleton's weapons on the ground, loosened the reins of his mount, and climbed into the saddle.

The eyes of every man were on him, but no one made

any attempt to stop him. He had proved how dangerous and unpredictable he could be, and all of them seemed content to see the last of him.

"It might not be too healthy for any of you back in Clay County when I spread the word that you're just a bunch of thieves and outlaws," Jason warned. "My advice is to haul your worthless hides off to some other part of the country where nobody knows what sorry curs you are."

With that, he pulled on Ned's reins sharply and touched his heels to the horse's flanks, causing the animal to spin around and leap forward. He half expected the men behind him to squeeze off a few parting shots in his direction, but no shots sounded as he disappeared into the thick woods.

Within a few seconds he was out of danger and riding down a game trail toward the road that skirted the patch of woods on its southern edge. His first impulse was to head straight for home now that the possibility of striking a blow against Brown was gone, but he couldn't rid his mind of the settlement to the south that Singleton had talked about raiding.

The chances were that if they lived in this part of the territory, the inhabitants of the cabins were hardened abolitionists. John Brown would probably not tolerate any other sort of people so close to his compound. But what if they were neutrals, as Jason had been not so long ago? He wasn't sure he wanted to live with the guilt he would feel if he learned later that Singleton's band had struck out against innocent families, raping their women and robbing them of their livelihood.

It would be risky, but Jason had no choice but to try to find the cabins and spread the alarm.

The man loomed up in the trail ahead of him so quickly that he hardly had time to turn Ned to avoid running over him. The man held a rifle, which discharged almost immediately, and Jason drew and fired an instant later, but neither hasty shot found its target. Before the stranger could fire again, Jason leaned forward and shouted a command to Ned that sent him bounding forward with a fresh burst of speed.

Another minute passed before the staccato of gunfire began to rattle through the woods behind Jason. The shooting lasted only a short time; the sound of the last shot echoed through the woods, and everything was silent again.

There was no doubt in Jason's mind what had happened. Singleton and his men had paid the price for their stupidity and lack of proper caution. Obviously some local had spotted the smoke billowing from their fires and had gathered up his neighbors for an assault on the camp.

It suddenly occurred to Jason that except for the merest coincidence, he would still be back in there in the camp, probably dead by now — or at least soon to be if he had happened to be taken alive. Few people on either side of the border bothered to turn prisoners over to local authorities. Usually they were either put to death on the spot or left to die slowly from their wounds.

But fate had intervened for him this time, and as he burst from the woods onto the open road, he realized that the killing of Singleton and his men would have one added advantage. Those people in the cabins south of here, whoever they were, could sleep peacefully in their beds tonight, free of the threat of harm from at least one band of marauding Missourians.

But so could John Brown, Jason thought grimly as he turned Ned east and started toward home. At least for now.

They met in the large tobacco barn that William Hartman had erected on some back acreage of his farm that spring. Entirely too many men had assembled tonight to meet in William's house, and the barn had the advantage of being way off the road and hidden from the view of any passersby.

Senator Atchison, back from Washington for a short visit, had asked William Hartman and Thomas Younger to call the meeting of local proslavers so they could plan their strategy for the summer months.

Waiting for the meeting to begin, Jason heard repeated rumblings about his recent trip into Kansas Territory. Word of the aborted raid had spread fairly quickly after his return, and opinions seemed to be mixed about its outcome. Some felt as Jason did, that the world was better off without Singleton and his men, no matter which side they claimed to support. There were others, however, who clearly had their doubts about the account Jason brought back. They recalled to one another how recently it was that Jason would have no part of the proslavery cause and wondered how it was that five men had died on the trip while the sixth suffered not even a scratch.

Although William was taken aback by the sudden change in his brother, he supported him completely. He was quick to point out to all listeners that if his brother was to be accused of cowardice or disloyalty, no such traits had been evident the night Jason single-handedly killed the four abolitionists after the ambush at the crossroads.

Jason didn't spend much time worrying about what anyone else thought. His mind was occupied with matters of more immediate concern.

Since his return from Kansas, it seemed that an emotional barrier had sprung up between him and his family. Arethia was aloof and distant, going about her household duties as usual but treating him almost as a stranger when they were alone. The children regarded him with a mix of awe and fear, unable to understand these sudden, unsettling changes in their warm and loving father.

Jason resented the isolation, especially because he felt that he was doing what he had to do for their sake. But he didn't try to explain anything. How could he make them realize that because of what had taken place, none of them would ever be safe again until John Brown was dead? Surely the burden of that knowledge would be worse than any temporary pain he caused them by simply doing what must be done.

He hadn't told Arethia that he would soon be going to Kansas again, but she seemed to know it anyway. The spring rains had stopped a few days before, and the ground was nearly dry, which meant that he would have to spend some time on the farm if he hoped to bring in a crop that year, but as soon as he had the opportunity and could tear himself away from the farm, he would be gone across the border again, to find and kill John Brown.

Over a hundred men had assembled before David Atchison finally mounted the back of a wagon bed and called for everyone's attention. Men had come from as far away as Cass County to the south, and Buchanan County to the north, but everyone there had one thing in common — an unshakable faith in the man who was now preparing to address them.

"It's good to see so many of you here tonight," Atchison told them. "There's hardly a face here that I don't recognize, nor a man present that I wouldn't trust to guard my backside till the devil took him. Welcome, my friends."

He was rewarded with a chorus of cheers and ear-splitting yells.

"I hear you gave Old Brown and his bunch a pretty hot reception a couple of weeks ago," Atchison continued. "I wish I'd been here to lend a hand, but I was up in Washington locking horns with the knotheads who are still letting him get away with all this foolishness."

"Bring 'em home with you next time, Dave," one of the men called. "We'll give them a taste of hot lead too."

"Sometimes I wish I could," Atchison laughed. "But you know how it is with politicians. They're happy enough to start the wars, but they stay snug in their beds while somebody else goes out and fights them."

The roar of laughter and cheers sounded again, but in a moment Atchison held up his hands for quiet.

"I didn't come here tonight to gripe about the riffraff I have to work with up there in the Capitol," he said. "I came instead to discuss with you men what we're going to do about our problems while the politicians are up there doing nothing. The way things are starting out, it's going to be a hell of a summer, gentlemen, and I hate to guess what the consequences might be if we aren't prepared."

He paused and turned to where William and Judge Younger were standing. "Can you help me with the map, Thomas?" he asked.

William and the judge stepped up on the wagon bed and unrolled a large map that depicted the western half of Missouri and the eastern third of Kansas. As the two men held the map, Atchison began to point out significant locations as he talked.

"We can expect the majority of our problems to take place in these four central border counties," he said, pointing to Platte, Clay, Jackson, and Cass counties. "Not only are they the most populous counties in the area, they also have the highest concentration of slaves, which makes them prime targets for Jayhawker raiding parties.

"In the past, you men have organized to defend your homes and communities on specific occasions, and I have nothing but praise for the courage and dedication you have shown. But from this day on, we are going to have to organize ourselves more efficiently than ever before, and to be ever alert to the threat of attack. Throughout the coming summer and fall, we are going to need twenty-four-hour patrols for all major roads, and roadblocks at all points where abolitionist raiding parties are likely to cross the border. It's going to call for plenty of sacrifice, and a lot of you will be spending a regrettable amount of time away from your homes and families, but I must impress on you that this is the only way we can remain safe from the maniacs and murderers who seem to have taken up residence in Kansas Territory."

"What about taking the fight to them like we did before?" someone called out. "We whipped them easy enough last year, and we can do it again if things get too rough."

"Yes, but what did we really accomplish when we took Lawrence last summer?" Atchison responded. "The army ended up making us give it back after all, and the whole episode stirred up a lot of adverse publicity for our side all over the country." He paused to let a ripple of protests pass through the crowd, then went on. "But that is not to say that we shouldn't, as you say, 'take the fight to them.' We not only should, we must." That comment seemed to appease the men.

"But that too must be an organized effort. Incidents such as the one which occurred a few days ago in Kansas not only waste lives, they also make us look like a pack of clumsy incompetents." Jason felt the eyes of a number of men boring into him when the recent raid was mentioned, but he ignored them.

"Our raids into Kansas must be thoroughly planned, excellently equipped, and intelligently led," Atchison insisted. "Each must be made against a strategic objective of some importance to our cause, and every man who participates must be sworn to secrecy. If we handle these raids correctly, if we hit hard and fast against the men who pose the most immediate threat to us, we can make these people afraid to even step out of doors after dark, and only the most foolhardy among them will ever consider crossing the line into Missouri."

That, Jason thought with a grin of satisfaction, was what he wanted to hear. The main reason that John Brown had gained such a deadly reputation and was able to operate so effectively was that he struck hard and fast with relatively small groups of supporters against specific opponents. Jason was convinced that the only way to operate against such a man was to use the same tactics that worked so well for him.

"You men for the most part will be the ones who have to go out there and risk your necks for our cause," Atchison continued. "So I don't want to go a step further with this until I know I have your full support for the plan of action I'm about to suggest. What I propose is that these two men here, William Hartman and Thomas Younger, each take charge of one part of our efforts. Judge Younger will organize and lead the home-defense effort, and William will coordinate the work to be done in Kansas Territory. Both will select their own lieutenants to assist them, and all efforts by any member of our organization will be approved by them before being carried out.

"If there is any man here who objects to this proposal, now is the time to speak up. We must be together on this. The success of our cause, and our lives, depend on it."

In the moment of silence that followed, no objection was raised. Then someone in the middle of the crowd shouted, "We're with you, Senator! Just tell us what to do!" An instant later a hundred voices roared their agreement.

Jason was as loud as the rest in his ready endorsement of Atchison's suggestion. Surely with the support of this many men, as well as that of others these men could enlist, they could strike an effective blow against the rabid abolitionists. If all went well, John Brown would very likely be dead by the end of the summer campaign, and when that blessed day came, Jason could at last begin to put his life in order again.

After the meeting, Jason sought out his brother to offer his support. William drew him aside where they could speak in private.

"I have some news from one of our operatives who just returned from Lawrence," William said. "I thought it might interest you because it's about our dear brother Charles."

"Well, what is it?" Jason asked anxiously. It had been months since he had received any concrete word about Charles and his family, and all the letters he had mailed to his brother in Lawrence had been returned unopened.

"Our man says that after Charles was released, he never reopened his store in Lawrence. In fact, he's moved away."

"I hope you're going to tell me he took his family back to Pennsylvania. I've thought for some time now that the only good which might come out of that business last summer would be for Charles to get discouraged and move back home."

"No such luck," William announced. "He's still in Kansas and still very much involved. The news is that he's moved to Osawatomie and is homesteading a quarter section which joins John Brown's land on the western side."

"Damn!" Jason exclaimed. "Damn him for his stupidity! What could he be thinking to move his family into a snake pit like that?"

William stared intently at his brother for a moment, then went on. "I agree that's bad enough, but I'm afraid it gets worse. Our informant says that Charles has apparently taken to riding with Old Brown on some of his raids. There's even a possibility that he was there that night at your house."

A cold, nasty sensation invaded the pit of his stomach as William's words sank in. "I can't believe that," he said dully. "It's impossible."

"I'm not saying it's certain," William said. "But I'm afraid the time has come for you to admit the fact that it certainly is possible."

"I can't believe it," Jason mumbled. "I refuse to believe that Charles would be a part of such a crime against his own brother. Who is this informant who has been supplying you with such nonsense."

"His name is Bill Quantrill," William said. "You've probably never heard of him because we've been keeping his identity a closely guarded secret, but all the information he's supplied us up until now has been reliable. He's the one who told us about Brown's raid three weeks ago, and that proved to be true enough."

"It just keeps getting worse and worse, doesn't it, Will?" Jason said, shaking his head. "I remember when I first came here, you told me this trouble would probably be settled in three or four months. That was three years ago, and now things are ten times worse than they were then. So what will happen next? Will it get so bad that you and I will have to gun down our own brother so that we can stay alive?"

"It seems to me it's already reached that point," William said quietly. "I don't like it any better than you do, but if they've already set their sights on us and have their fingers on the trigger, what choice do we have?"

"What choice?" Jason echoed sadly.

"Jason, I want you as the leader of one of the raiding parties I'm going to organize," William announced abruptly. "You know the country over there better than most of the other men I could choose, and you have the good judgment it will take to bring your men home alive after each mission. When I brought your name up in a meeting this afternoon, both David Atchison and Thomas Younger were opposed to the idea of making you a leader, but I assured them you had finally committed yourself to our cause. I didn't lie to them, did I, little brother?"

"I'm in," Jason said. "I didn't want to be, but those bastards didn't give me any choice. I'll take the job, but I have to tell you up front that I won't lead any raids against Charles or any member of his family. If you ever reach the point that you truly want them dead, you'll have to send somebody else."

"I don't want him dead, Jason. I never have," William told his younger brother earnestly. "But that doesn't mean that we won't reach a point some day soon when he has to die."

12

Jason slept so lightly that even the quiet footsteps of the sentry awakened him before the man had a chance to stoop beside him and call him for his turn on guard duty.

"Any problems?" Jason whispered as he sat up on his bedroll and began to pull his boots on.

"It's been quiet as a graveyard out there," the man replied. "You picked a good campsite. Ain't nobody likely to stumble across us out here, in the middle of this thicket."

"Probably not, but we can't risk our lives on it," Jason replied. He rose to his feet, strapped on his gun belt, and picked up his rifle to check the load. As he turned and started off into the darkness, the man he was replacing was already starting to unroll his blankets in preparation for a couple of hours of badly needed sleep.

The men in the raiding party were scattered across a twenty-yard radius of the pine thicket. Jason had instructed them not to make their beds close together, so that if they were surprised in the night, they would not be caught in a cluster, where they could be easily picked off.

It wasn't likely that they would be caught off guard, however. Two men had been on guard duty at all times during the night, circling the fringes of the area, and a third was stationed near the road to the south, which was the most likely direction from which to expect an attack.

There were twelve men in the group Jason led. Ten were in or around the camp, and two more had been out most of the night scouting possible targets for the raid. Jason had decided to take the second guard shift, from midnight to three in the morning, because that was when the scouts were most likely to return, and he wanted to be awake to receive their reports.

He tried to contain his excitement over what might yet take place before morning. They were camped a mere three miles from John Brown's stronghold, and one of the two scouts he had sent out just after dark had gone in that direction to try and determine the strength of Brown's forces.

Despite the counterattacks from Missouri, the abolitionist raids across the border had continued unabated throughout the spring, and it was believed that a number of those raids had originated in this very area, either led or inspired by the man who had come to be considered the most ruthless, uncompromising abolitionist in the territory. The logic that inspired the raid Jason was leading was that if Brown's prairie fortress could be attacked while at least some of his forces were away on a mission of mischief in Missouri, the chances were very good that it could be captured.

Two lesser, secondary targets had been designated as well, but Jason spent little time considering them. Whatever else they might accomplish, to his thinking the mission would be a failure unless they struck a decisive blow against Old Brown himself.

When he reached the fringes of the thicket, Jason paused and gazed out into the open area beyond. With only a quarter moon hanging in the sky, the darkness would have seemed impenetrable to the unconditioned eye, but Jason had begun to develop extraordinary night vision as well as a surprisingly accurate sixth sense.

But the night was quiet. All he could detect were ordinary nocturnal creatures, the chirrup of crickets, the whoosh of an occasional owl sweeping through the treetops, and the rustle of a raccoon or opossum.

He remained in one spot for several minutes, then began working his way slowly to the right, easing forward silently and staying far enough back in the trees to remain cloaked in darkness. He paused occasionally to probe the stillness, but he could detect no hint of danger. He had chosen this campsite well, and he felt confident that tonight there would be no senseless massacre like the one he had barely escaped a few months before.

Well into his first hour on guard, Jason was passing by the southern fringe of the pine thicket when a faint sound drifted toward him on the gentle nighttime breeze. In a moment he determined that it was caused by horses approaching through a band of trees south of the thicket. He cocked the hammer of his rifle and waited. He was fairly sure he knew who the new arrivals would prove to be, but he didn't want to take any chances.

Soon two mounted figures came into view, riding slowly toward the spot where Jason stood. One of them was talking in a low voice to the other, and after listening a minute, Jason stepped out into the open so they could see where he was. There was no mistaking the sound of Cole Younger's easy drawl, and Jason knew that the main reason Cole had been talking was so he and his companion would be identified by any hidden sentries in the vicinity.

The two scouts rode up to Jason and slid out of their saddles. Jason was barely acquainted with the young man who had accompanied his friend on the scouting expedition. Until recently, Bill Quantrill had been living in Lawrence, and it was said that he had supplied the leaders in Missouri with valuable intelligence about abolitionist plans on a number of occasions. He had been allowed to come along on this raid primarily because of his familiarity with the Kansas countryside, but as far as Jason was concerned, he was still an unfamiliar commodity and therefore subject to constant scrutiny.

Jason welcomed the two scouts back. "Well, what's it like out there? Did you get a look at Old Brown's place?"

"I did," Cole said. "Bill took a swing down south and checked out those other two homesteads we were thinking about visiting."

"So what did you see, Cole?" Jason asked eagerly. "Did you get the idea that some of them might be off somewhere?"

"I know you're not going to like this, Jason," Cole told him, "but it looked to me like the whole pack was home tonight. They had at least four sentries spotted on the hillsides, and there were about two dozen horses in that big corral west of the barn."

It was not the news Jason wanted to hear, for he was not willing to abandon the idea that they could mount an attack on the place.

"The sentries could be taken care of easy enough," he reasoned. "If we couldn't slip up on them, there's enough of us to just ride over the top of them. And as for the horses, two dozen horses doesn't necessarily mean two dozen men. Some of them could belong to the women and children, and some could be spares."

"That's true enough," Cole said, but Jason could sense he was far from convinced.

"Come on, Cole, out with it," Jason said sternly. "You know how bad I want Brown, but I hope you also know that I want to look the whole thing over top to bottom before I make any decision. What's on your mind?"

"OK," Cole answered, "what I'm thinking is that we could get into plenty of hot water if we go through with this. Sure, there's enough of us to take the sentries out, but I'd bet at least one of us would go down for each one of them we get. That would leave only eight men for the real attack, and by the time we got around to charging down that hill, whoever is inside would have plenty of warning that we were on our way. Even if it is mostly women and children in there, they can still draw a bead and pull a trigger."

Jason listened closely, trying hard to put his personal feelings aside and consider the arguments objectively. When Cole was finished, he turned to the second scout and said, "All right, Quantrill. Cole has put in his two cents' worth. What do you have to say?"

"Well, since you asked," Quantrill told him, "my guess is it probably wouldn't be as bad as Cole thinks, nor as good as we want it to be. Dark as it is, and with surprise on our side, I doubt if we'd lose as many men as he thinks, but not a one of us would probably see inside those walls either. Seems like the most we could hope for would be to ruin the old man's sleep for the night and maybe throw a good scare into them that's with him."

"Damn it, I still think we could do it," Jason said. "Every man in the group knew when he started over here that Old Brown's place would be guarded and that the folks inside would be shooting back when we started down that hill. I'm not trying to convince anybody that there wouldn't be some risks, but if we got the right breaks, I still believe we could do it!"

"Do you believe it, or do you wish it?" Cole Younger asked dryly. "You're my friend, Jason, and you know that for the right reason I'd ride beside you against a hundred like Old Brown. But right now I'm wondering if you're the right man to make this decision."

"Damn you, Cole!" Instinctively his hand tightened into a fist, but he checked himself before a blow could be delivered.

Cole seemed unaffected by the threat. "My question still stands," he said calmly. "Hellfire, we all want to get that murderous bastard. Maybe not as much as you, but enough to be here trying anyway. But that doesn't mean you have the right to throw even a single life away if there isn't a reasonable chance to do what we set out to do."

"I reckon I'll have to agree with Cole," Quantrill said. "And besides, the two places I checked out tonight look like prime pickings to me, so we wouldn't have to ride all the way back home without counting any coups at all."

Ever since they had crossed the state line from Missouri, Jason had been filled with confidence and with a determination to strike a decisive blow against his foe, but now he was forced to wonder if he might not be letting his own feelings overshadow his best judgment. With this many lives at stake, he couldn't afford to make a mistake.

"All right," he announced at last. "We'll let the group decide. Time's a-wasting, and if we're going to get anywhere and do what we came over here for, we're going to have to start within the hour. Quantrill, you build a fire and put a pot of coffee on while Cole and I round everybody up."

Within ten minutes all the men in Jason's raiding party were gathered around the small fire Quantrill had built, their eyes on the bubbling coffee pot. Knowing that some of them had slept less than an hour and would need some time to wake up, Jason waited until each of them had received a steaming cup of the dark brew before he opened the discussion.

"As all of you can see," Jason said at last, "Cole and Bill are back now, and they've just made their report to me. We came hoping that some of John Brown's men would be away so we could shoot our way in and capture his place, but Cole tells me there's no guarantee of that. We don't know for sure how many men he's got with him, but there's enough to make a fight of it. If we do what we came to do, I don't think all of us will be riding home again, and that's the reason I don't want to make this decision by myself. Each of you will have his life on the line, and you've got a right to have your say, so let's hear it."

One of the men, a burly farmer named Pittman from the northern part of Clay County, was the first to speak up. "What kind of numbers do you think we're looking at?" he asked.

"All I know for sure is that there's four on guard outside," Cole replied, "but I'd guess there's several more behind the walls. There could even be more of them than there are of us."

"So there's a good chance that Old Brown is there, then?" asked Colin Mathis, one of Jason's neighbors.

"I'd say he's there, Colin," Jason said.

"That would be good if we took the place," Mathis pointed out, "but it would be pretty damn bad if we messed it up. If we left Brown and some of his men alive, they'd be on our tails like a pack of wild dogs all the way back to the state line."

"What about the other men Will Hartman told us to

try for?" Pittman asked. "Do we know anything about them?"

"Their names are Stuart Bowles and Harv Coleman," Bill Quantrill said. "I went by both places tonight, and as near as I can tell, both of them are at home with only their wives and families with them. Bowles has a younger brother living with him, but he's only fourteen and not hardly worth worrying about."

"I say we go for Brown," a voice called out from the rear of the group. Several faces turned toward Bill Anderson who, at sixteen, was by far the youngest member of the raiding party. When he first asked Jason to take him along, Jason had flatly refused, but after Cole vouched for him, Jason had decided at the last minute to let the young man come along. "It's what we came for, and I say let's give it a shot," Anderson announced with bravado. "Hell, I been sharpening my sheath knife for a week just in case I'm the one that gets to cut Old Brown's balls off."

"Well, maybe some of us don't want to be quite as reckless with our lives as you do, son," said Colin Mathis. "Most every man here except you and Cole has a wife and children back home to think of, and I'm here to tell you that cuts back considerable on the amount of risks a man's willing to take."

"Then what are you doing here?" the young man said exasperatedly. "I knew this wasn't going to be no Sunday afternoon surrey ride, and I thought everybody else did too!"

"Look here, you little wise-ass bastard —" Mathis growled.

"All right, all right!" Jason interrupted. "Before we start fighting it out amongst ourselves, I think the best thing to do is take a vote. But before we do it, is there anybody who doesn't think he can go along with what the majority decides, no matter what it is?"

For a moment, Jason thought that Bill Anderson was going to speak up again, but he seemed to think better of it and refrained.

"OK. Who votes to go after John Brown as we planned to do in the first place?" To Jason's disappointment, only three hands went up, including Bill Anderson's and his own.

"Then I guess it's settled," Jason said. "We'll split up into two groups and head for the Bowles and the Coleman homesteads. Colin Mathis will lead one group, and I will lead the other. We'll do what we have to do, and when it's over, we'll head straight for the Missouri line." With the decision made, the men began to gather up their bedding and prepare to leave, but Jason was not quite finished.

"Before we go, I want to remind all of you of the rules we laid down at the start," he said. "There'll be no thievery — not a gun, not a knife, not anything. Nobody lays a hand on a woman or a child unless it's to defend himself. We're not here to show the world that we're the same kind of monsters that John Brown and his pack of hyenas are. Any killing that must be done will be done quick and clean, and there will be no mutilation of the dead." He looked hard at Bill Anderson. "Have you got that, Bill? Is that last part clear?"

"I heard you plain enough," Anderson answered sullenly.

Without even taking the time to eat, the men hurriedly broke camp and started on their way.

Stuart Bowles and his family lived in a crude hut built of thick slabs of sod cut from the flat prairie around them. The place was roofed with long pine poles that were covered with a layer of sod, which had sprouted a waist-high patch of weeds and grass. The barn was constructed of similar materials, and the small corral beyond contained only two weary saddle horses and a single milk cow. Beyond the house and barn were the family's meager crops of corn and barley.

The homestead was dark and silent as Jason and his men approached. They rode to within about a hundred feet of the place, then dismounted and led their horses forward. Near the house they tied their mounts to a low rail fence, then spread out in an arc around the front door, their guns ready. When everyone was in position, Jason and Cole went up to the door.

"Look," Cole whispered, pointing to a crude symbol that had been scrawled in charcoal on the doorsill. It was a cross enclosed in a small circle about three inches in diameter.

"Yep, he's one of them all right," Jason replied quietly. The symbol, which signified that the residents of the house were sympathetic to the abolitionist cause, was used throughout the territory.

Jason raised his fist and pounded loudly on the door, then called out, "Stuart Bowles, wake up. I need to speak with you."

There was a minute of silence, then Jason heard the sound of low voices inside. Soon a dim glow shone through the waxed-paper windows, and a moment later a man's voice just inside the door asked, "Who is it?"

"We represent the Territorial Vigilance Committee," Jason replied, using the name William and Atchison had concocted to lend an air of legitimacy to their activities. "I'm ordering you to open this door and come out."

There was more quiet discussion inside and then the sound of a wooden bar being slid from across the door. Finally the door eased open a few inches, and Jason got his first look at the man they had come to find. He looked to be about forty years old, with a dark, heavy beard and an unruly mat of graying hair. He was dressed in a ragged red union suit and held an ancient muzzle-loading rifle in his hands. In the dim lamplight, Jason caught a glimpse of a woman and several children huddled together in the middle of the single-room hut.

"I never heard of no Vigilance Committee," Bowles said gruffly.

"Well, you have now," Jason told him sharply. "Now come out of the house."

"Not till I know which side you're for," the man said. He started to raise the muzzle of his rifle, but Cole drew his pistol and stuck it in the man's face before he could threaten them.

"This man's in charge here, and you'll do what he says, Bowles," Cole warned. When he reached for the rifle, Bowles surrendered it without protest. Then Jason pushed the door open, and Bowles followed them out into the yard.

"You're from Missouri, ain't you?" Bowles said, gazing at the half circle of men surrounding him. "You're here to kill me!"

"We're here to persuade you to stay out of Missouri and to stay out of politics until Kansas is voted into the Union as a slave state," Jason told him. "And we'll do whatever it takes to bring you around to our way of thinking."

"I ain't no ab'litionist! I swear I ain't!" Bowles protested.

Jason's angry blow caused the man to stagger backward. "You're lying, Bowles," he hissed. "If you're not an abolitionist, then what's that sign doing on your door?" He hit the man again, knocking him to the ground.

Stuart Bowles remained where he fell. His lip and nose were bleeding now, and his eyes were wide with fear. "You gotta have one of them signs if you live around here," he claimed. " 'Cause of Old Brown. He kills anybody that he thinks ain't on his side. And he makes a man do things, things that maybe ain't right, things that maybe that man don't want to do, but he does them anyway because Old Brown will kill him if he don't."

"You're lying, Bowles. I think you're a stinking abolitionist who just came out here to meddle in our affairs. And I think the only way to keep you out of our hair is to blow your damn head off!" Jason drew his pistol, pointed it at the terrified man's head, and cocked the hammer. He had no intention of killing the prisoner unless it was absolutely necessary, but he did want to throw a mortal fear into Bowles by making him believe that he was about to die.

Suddenly, a boy shouted from the doorway, "Stop it! Leave my brother alone!"

Jason glanced up to see a half-grown boy burst from the house with a rifle in his hands. He started to raise his pistol to defend himself, but Cole got his gun up first and fired two quick shots at him. The youth tumbled face first into the dirt, where he lay writhing and screaming in pain.

"Barney!" Bowles cried. He tried to rise, but Jason kicked him in the head and knocked him back, then lowered the muzzle of his pistol until it was again aimed at him. Meanwhile, Cole had gone forward to see what damage his shots had done.

"How bad's he hit?" Jason asked.

"Looks like I got him in the knee and the wrist," Cole reported. "He'll live, but I expect he'll be a mite gimped up."

"All right. A couple of you get him in the house and let the woman take care of him," Jason instructed. "And while you're in there, look around and see if there's any more guns. We don't need any more surprises."

Jason turned his attention back to Bowles. "Now if you don't quit your lying, you're next," he warned.

"Please, mister," Bowles blubbered. His face was a bloody mess now, and he seemed only half aware of what was going on around him. "Please don't hurt us no more."

"I still might have to if you don't start talking straight to me," Jason warned.

"Please. I'll tell you anything . . . I'll do anything. I ain't no ab'litionist."

Jason knelt beside Bowles and held the muzzle of his pistol close to the man's face. "I don't believe you about that, Bowles," he said. "I guess the only way you could prove to me and my friends here that you aren't one of John Brown's bootlicks would be to just pack up and move clear out of the territory. And from the looks of this place, it seems to me that giving it up would be a small enough price to pay for saving your life."

Jason was beginning to feel some pity for the terrified man who lay on the ground before him, though he knew better than to let any such emotion show. Having been on the receiving end of such a raid himself, he could clearly recall the helpless frustration and stark fear of not knowing whether he, or his whole family, might die within the next few minutes. It was horrible and degrading, but it was also necessary.

"Please! Please . . . We'll go. I swear it!"

"All right then," Jason said. "It looks like we're going to reach an understanding after all." He started to rise, but Bowles continued his babbling.

"Just don't hurt anybody else," he pleaded. "We didn't hurt you —"

"Wait a minute!" Jason frowned. "What are you talking about?"

"Nothin', mister. I didn't mean it. I didn't mean nothin'!"

"What did you mean when you said, 'We didn't hurt you'?" Jason demanded. He jammed the muzzle of his pistol against the man's cheek for emphasis.

"It's Old Brown, like I said," Bowles stammered. "He makes a man do things . . . makes a man help him out even if he don't want to. But we're leaving. I swear to you —"

"Were you there?" Jason stormed. "Damn you! Were you there at my house that night?" He could feel the fury rising in him, raging and uncontrollable, as the memory of all the pain, fear, and humiliation of that terrible night came crashing back.

"I didn't do nothin'. He just made me ride along. I never fired a shot, not even during the ambush. But he made me go along . . . Old Brown . . ."

Jason slowly rose to his feet. His whole body was shaking now, and the men around him were beginning to stare at him in confusion and concern. At his feet, Bowles continued to babble his denials and apologies, but his words no longer registered in Jason's mind. Slowly, Jason's arm began to rise, and his finger tightened on the trigger.

A moment of complete silence followed the deafening roar of the pistol. The world seemed frozen for an instant, as if the sound of the shot had turned everyone within hearing to stone.

Then finally one of the men in the group muttered, "Goddamn, Jason! You killed the son of a bitch!"

An instant later an ear-splitting shriek sounded from the doorway, and Stuart Bowles's wife came stumbling forward to throw herself across her husband's dead form. She wailed like a wounded animal, soaking her nightgown in his blood, pleading with him not to be dead.

Still holding the smoking gun, poised at the same angle as when he had fired the shot, Jason was mesmerized by the scene. He had scarcely realized that he was going to shoot Bowles until the deed was already done, and now it almost seemed as if some other being had taken control of him for a minute and pulled the trigger.

Then he felt a hand on his arm, and a voice said, "Let's go, Jason. It's finished here. Let's go home."

Jason resisted at first as he watched the woman raise her head and stare blankly into his eyes. Her clothes, her hands, and her arms were bloody, and her features were as dull and lifeless as those of the dead man in front of her. "Jason," she mumbled, as if trying to memorize the name. "Jason."

The tug on Jason's arm became more insistent, and finally he allowed himself to be turned away and led toward the horses. The pistol nearly fell from his hand before someone took it and put it in his holster.

As he stepped into the saddle, he heard Cole's voice, as if from a long way off, speaking to the woman. "You tell them. You tell John Brown and all the rest that they're the cause of this. They're why he's dead. And you tell them that the killing won't stop here. It won't ever stop until they stay the hell out of Missouri!"

Jason woke in the middle of the night, drenched in sweat and filled with terror. The sound that had awakened him, the sound of his own scream, seemed to echo through the room. Beside him, Arethia was stroking his forehead, mumbling soft reassurances as she held him close.

It was the same dream, the one that had plagued him for days now, ever since his return from the raid into Kansas. He held a gun in his hand, one that he did not wish either to hold or to fire. But his finger was tightening on the trigger. Some power had claimed control of his hand, forcing him to squeeze the trigger, to squeeze and squeeze and squeeze . . . And the face below him, the face filled with fear and desperation, was his own.

"I'm sorry," Jason mumbled, still fighting his way back to reality. "The children . . ."

"It's all right," Arethia whispered to him. "I told them that something bad happened and that Daddy is just having some bad dreams. I told them not to get up anymore if they hear something."

"I'm sorry, honey."

"It will pass, Jason. It will go away like everything does. But you can't go back over there again. I don't think you can stand it, and I don't think we can stand it either."

"I'll have to go again," Jason said. "And again after that, and then again. Until this business is settled. I just wish there was some way I could make you understand that I don't have any choice anymore. I'm committed now. I don't have any choice but to see this thing through to the end."

"You're right, I don't understand," Arethia told him. "But I do understand what you're doing to me and the children. We can't endure much more." He could feel her body stiffen as she spoke, and her voice was cold and distant. The chasm between them was widening. He was doing what he did for her and his children, fighting for their very survival, but he saw that he was also turning them into strangers.

That realization filled him with a sadness as deep and profound as anything he had ever felt in his life. But he was committed. He was doing what he had to do, and some day they would understand.

"We'll talk about it in the morning," Jason told his wife at last. "I need to sleep now. It seems like I never get enough sleep anymore."

"The way things are, I never even know if there's going to be a tomorrow, Jason," Arethia said. Then she fell silent, and eventually he drifted back to sleep.

13

A cool nighttime wind from the northwest tempered the mid-August heat, making the buggy ride back from Cynthia Williston's party a pleasant one for Mollie and Cole. Jason had warned them before they left that the wind was sure to bring rain, but thus far the bad weather had held off and now, only a mile or so away from home, Mollie thought they would probably be lucky enough to make it back before the storm hit.

The evening had been an enjoyable one for Mollie. For the first time in years she had been able to relax among a group of young people her own age and simply have a good time without worrying about what everyone around was thinking about her or saying behind her back. Going with Cole had helped, of course, because he was admired and quite popular among the people his age, but Mollie also thought that the pleasure she felt had as much to do with the changes that were taking place inside her. She was happier now than she had been for a long, long time, more at peace with herself and the life she led than she had been since before Anson Younger's death.

Cole was in a gay mood as well. They had danced together until their legs were rubbery with fatigue, and the frequent nips of corn whiskey that he had sneaked outside to sample with his friends had only served to enhance his high spirits.

It was a funny thing about Cole, Mollie thought, as she listened to him rambling for most of the ride back about the things he would like to do and the places he would some day like to see. She loved him, but it was a different sort of love than she had ever experienced before. There was none of the desperation she had felt before when she realized she was in love with a man, no aching loneliness when they were apart, no surges of giddy euphoria when they were together.

Perhaps, Mollie thought, this is what came of falling in love with a friend. If that was the case, then she vowed never to let herself plunge mindlessly into another romantic involvement until she had taken the time to discover what sort of man she was getting involved with.

They were less than a quarter mile from Jason's house when Cole turned the buggy into a small grove of cedars and pulled on the reins. The wind rustled through the treetops like whispered promises, and the air was laced with the pleasant odor of the cedars. Cole turned to Mollie and smiled, still shy after all this time.

"I'd like to know what you think you're up to, Mr. Coleman Younger?" Mollie said in mock indignation. "You've certainly turned into a bold fellow these last few months."

"I guess I have," Cole grinned.

"You know, some day," she teased, "my brothers are going to get their shotguns and come looking for you when they find out what you've been doing to their frail flower of a sister."

"I know that," Cole laughed. "That's why I want to take advantage of every opportunity before they come to hunt me down. There's no telling which time might be the last."

"Well, I hope it won't be this one," Mollie said softly. "I guess it's not really such a terrible thing having you take advantage of me."

As soon as their lips met, Cole's hand closed over her breast with that particularly impatient passion of youth. Mollie drew a quick breath as she felt a wonderful hunger begin to rise within her.

"Every time we're together like this," Cole admitted, his lips drawing a few inches away from hers, "I keep thinking you're going to suddenly change your mind and run me off."

"Sometimes I think I should," Mollie said. "It hits me sometimes how many risks we're taking, but then I start to wonder if it isn't the risks that make it so exciting. If we were married and could bed down together without worrying about whether anybody found out, the idea probably wouldn't appeal to either one of us nearly as often."

"That sounds like the kind of notion that would come into your head, Mollie," Cole chuckled. "As for me, I don't know much about those kinds of things, but I do know about now."

He reached for her again, pulling her body against his as he touched his lips to hers. Judging by the way he held her, Mollie knew that if she was going to slow Cole down before things went too far, she'd better get busy.

"Are you going to sleep in the barn tonight?" she asked. Occasionally he did that rather than make the long ride home.

"I had planned to drop you and the buggy off and ride my horse on home," he said. "But with this rain coming on, maybe I should change my plans."

"I could slip out after everyone has gone to sleep," she suggested. "That is, if you think you could stay awake long enough for me to —" She paused as a strange, unexpectedly serious expression came onto Cole's face.

"I was only teasing you, Cole," Mollie tried to explain. "I just —"

"Hush!" Cole hissed at her. He cocked his head, as if straining to hear some distant noise borne toward them on the wind.

Then Mollie heard it too. It was the sound of voices and the easy *clop* of walking horses approaching from the north.

"Easy, Ned. Easy, Stony," Mollie whispered to the horses. They were beginning to shift nervously in their traces.

"Get down and keep the horses still," Cole whispered to Mollie as he stepped down and reached for his gun belt under the seat. He strapped the belt and holster around his waist, then drew his pistol and cocked the hammer. Mollie climbed down from the other side of the buggy and walked forward to take control of the two animals. Stroking their muzzles, she whispered reassurances into their ears to keep them from making any sound that might reveal their presence in the grove.

As the sound of the approaching strangers grew ever louder, Cole slipped away into the darkness in the direction of the road. Mollie could hear them quite plainly now, and even heard Jason's name mentioned. An anxious chill ran through her as she suddenly realized what was going on.

Though it was never mentioned in their home, she had known for months that her brother's name was on a list of targets compiled by the leaders of the abolitionist raiding parties. Now, it seemed that if they had their way, Jason would be made to pay tonight for the numerous forays he had led against them.

The strangers passed at last, and moments later Cole returned to where Mollie was waiting for him.

"It's four goddamned Jayhawkers," Cole spat as he went immediately to work on the harnesses that held the horses within the traces of the buggy. When Mollie realized what he was doing, she fell to work helping him unhitch the animals.

"I've got to get over there and warn your brother before they can slip up on him," Cole said urgently. "I heard enough of what they were saying to know that they aren't here just to try and throw a scare into him this time. They're out for blood."

"I'm going along," Mollie announced. "My rifle's under the seat, and if I peel off a few of these petticoats, I won't have any trouble riding Stony bareback."

"I'd be glad to have you with me when I open up on their backsides," Cole admitted, "but I've got something else in mind for you. I want you to ride in the other direction and spread the alarm. You can have all the help we'll need rounded up within half an hour, and with any luck, your brother and I can keep them busy for at least that long."

Mollie didn't argue. Although she would much rather be going with Cole, she knew he was right in sending her for help, and she also realized that even a moment wasted in discussion now might be paid for later with the blood of some member of her family.

The moment Ned was free, Cole leaped on his back. "Here, Cole, take this," Mollie said, handing her rifle and ammunition up to him. "You'll find more use for it than I would."

Cole accepted the rifle, then dug his heels into Ned's flanks and pointed the animal toward the trees. An instant later horse and rider were out of sight.

Within another minute, Mollie had Stony unhitched. It took her only a few seconds to strip off the layers of petticoats from beneath her full skirt, then she too quickly mounted and raced off into the night.

Jason was working late in the barn, shoring up a sag in the loft floor so it would be ready to bear the weight of hundreds of pounds of hay and feed when the fall harvesting began.

He judged that it was sometime past eleven. He seldom worked this late, but tonight he had needed a good excuse to get out of the house for a while, and the loft floor had been as good a one as any other. Things were worse than ever with Arethia, and he hoped to stay out long enough so that she would be in bed and asleep before he went in.

Earlier in the day Jason had revealed to his wife that he and his men would be leaving soon for another trip into Kansas. Before, when presented with such news, Arethia had usually begged and argued and sometimes even resorted to tears in her attempts to convince him not to go. This time had been different though. She had simply accepted his announcement. Her coldness had been more difficult to deal with than any previous reaction, and Jason was still reeling from the growing realization of how wide the chasm between them had become.

He had no idea how to narrow the distance between himself and his wife, nor was he even sure now what the future might hold for him. He had thought at times about simply packing his family up and moving back to Virginia, but he realized that if they did go back, they would simply be exchanging one sort of struggle for another. There was nothing for them back there. The future lay here. Life could be full, happy, and prosperous if only . . .

Jason reached instinctively for his rifle the instant he heard the shot outside. These days he was never more than a few feet from a weapon, and he had grown accustomed to performing such routine tasks as plowing and milking with a pistol belt strapped around his waist. It was a hell of a way to have to live, but situations such as this one proved the wisdom of his precautions.

He doused the lamp, then moved to one of the front windows of the barn and looked out cautiously. Even as he watched, the lamps in the house were quickly extinguished, but he could see no sign of whoever it was who had fired the shot.

He knew that at this moment his wife and children would be taking all the precautions that he had carefully laid out for them. John and Daniel would be guarding the front and back doors with loaded shotguns, and Arethia would be herding the younger ones toward the trapdoor that he had cut in the floor of one of the back bedrooms. If anyone set the house on fire, they could be through the opening and out into the side yard in a matter of seconds.

But still Jason knew that all these precautions would not be enough. Two half-grown youths could not be expected to hold off a determined attack by a party of grown men for long, and if Arethia and the younger children were forced to leave the house, they would be in the open and completely unable to defend themselves.

Another shot was fired, and somebody hidden in the hedgerow beyond the front yard yelped in pain. A fusillade of shots followed, and then the shooting stopped as quickly as it had started. But something about the gunfire didn't make sense, Jason thought. The boys both had shotguns, but the first shot he had heard, the one that had apparently struck somebody in the hedgerow, had come from a rifle.

He had to find out what was going on out there and, if possible, reach the house so he could defend his family.

Moving to the back of the barn, he eased a door open and slipped out. His eyes had not fully adjusted to the darkness yet, and every shadow around him seemed to contain a threat. He started moving along the back wall of the barn, thinking that he could use a nearby fence row for cover until he reached the back yard. From there he could make a break for the back door.

He had come to within a few feet of the corner of the barn when a slight sound ahead made him stop. He raised the rifle to his shoulder and waited. A second later a head peeked around the corner for an instant and, spotting him, disappeared once again. Jason swung the muzzle slightly to the right and pumped a quick shot into the weathered plank wall near the corner. The boards were thin, no match for a thumb-sized slug, and the bullet found its target. A man staggered forward into the open, swayed on rubbery legs for a moment, and toppled into the manure.

Pausing only long enough to check the man and reload his rifle, Jason eased around the corner and over to the fence that he planned to follow toward the house. The shooting had started over by the hedgerow again, but there was still no indication that a single shot had been fired at the house. None of the front windows had been shattered, as they surely would have been if someone was shooting inside, and all Jason could figure out was that he must have had a friend out there in the darkness, someone who was keeping the raiders so busy that there wasn't time to rush the house.

As if in response to his thoughts, a voice called out suddenly, "Jason! It's Cole! They've got me pinned down over by the big elm! One's between me and the house, and the other is coming at me from the north."

Of course, Jason thought. In all the confusion he had forgotten that Mollie and Cole would have been on their way back from the party just about the time all the trouble started. But where was Mollie now? She could be out there with Cole, or she could be . . . he was loath to even consider the idea . . . already dead.

Several more shots ripped through the night, and Cole called out desperately, "Jason, help me!"

Casting caution aside, Jason vaulted the fence and began running toward the voice. As he reached the front yard, he spotted a man lying on the ground behind a holly bush. He had his rifle pointed in the direction of the elm tree Cole had mentioned, but when he saw Jason racing toward him, he rolled over on his side and tried to swing the muzzle around.

Jason fired on the run, and an instant later his opponent's gun went off, but both shots went wild. Within another couple of seconds, Jason had closed the distance between them. The raider was trying to rise to his feet, but Jason, swinging his rifle like a club in one hand, struck him hard across the shoulder and knocked him back to the ground. Before the man had the chance to try to get up again, Jason's sheath knife was buried deep in his chest. The dying man's body arched in one final, agonized spasm and then went limp.

"I got this one, Cole," Jason called out. "How many more are there?"

"Just one," Cole replied. The two of them were in sight of one another now, Jason hunkered down behind the holly bush and Cole behind the elm. "I've lost sight of him, but their horses are off to your left. That's probably where he's headed."

"All right, let's get the bastard," Jason said as he pitched his rifle aside and pulled out his pistol. He raced to the thirty-foot hedgerow that separated the yard from the road, but then instead of plunging into the thick tangle of brush and saplings, he raced along its edge and around the end.

The man they were after had already mounted one of the horses and was pulling it around with one rein. Jason's and Cole's shots sounded at almost the same second, and the last raider toppled backward out of the saddle as his startled mount bounded forward. He was dragged along for several yards before Jason was able to grab the reins of the runaway animal and yank him to a stop.

As Cole approached, Jason saw that his head and chest were bloodied, but a wild grin was plastered across his face. "That's the last of them," he announced. "There was only four."

"Damn, Cole!" Jason exclaimed. "You're a mess!" He examined his friend closely. "Where'd they get you?"

"No place," Cole said. "After I dropped one of them from behind and they started shooting back at me, I dived into the bushes over yonder, and I hit my head on something. It was a rock I guess, but it's not so bad. It just bled a lot."

"What about Mollie?" Jason asked.

"She's all right. I sent her for help. By now she's probably got half the county out of bed and headed in this direction."

Jason heard a low moan and was surprised to see the last man they had shot moving, his foot still hanging in the stirrup.

"I thought that son of a bitch was dead," Jason growled. Without further comment, he raised his pistol to correct the oversight, but before he could fire, Cole reached out and stopped him.

"Hold off a minute, Jason," Cole said. "There'll be time for that, but why don't we see what we can find out from him first. I'd like to know who they were and if there's any more of them in the area."

"All right, talk to him if you want to," Jason said, sticking his pistol in its holster. "I'm going to check on my family and let them know it's all over."

As Cole began to free the wounded man's foot from the stirrup, Jason turned and started toward the house.

After he rounded the hedge and started across the yard toward the house, he called out, "Arethia! Boys! It's me. Everything's all right. We took care of them."

The first one to greet him at the door was Daniel. The boy's eyes were as big as silver dollars, and he still held the long double-barreled shotgun in his hands.

"We did like you said, Daddy. I was here all the time, and John was in the kitchen watching the back door. We wouldn't of let none of them get to Mama and the kids."

"That's fine, son, I'm proud of you," Jason said gently as he took the shotgun from the boy and leaned it against a wall. "But you don't need this anymore. It's all over now."

A moment later Arethia came into the front room from the back bedroom, and John appeared from the kitchen. Arethia crossed the room and put her arms around her husband, burying her head against his chest. Her body was trembling, and he could feel her hot tears wetting the fabric of his shirt as he gathered her into his strong arms.

"I was so afraid for you out there," she whispered from the haven of his arms. "We just kept hearing all this shooting and yelling. We didn't know what was going on, and I was afraid . . . I was afraid you were . . ."

"It's all right," Jason said, softly stroking her hair. "Cole jumped them from behind, and that gave me time enough to get ready."

At the mention of Cole's name, Arethia drew back from him with a start and stared up at his face. "Cole and Mollie! Oh, my God!"

"She's OK," Jason explained quickly. "Cole sent her for help, so she wasn't around when any of the shooting was going on. She's probably miles from here right now waking up our neighbors."

"Thank heavens!" Arethia exclaimed. "Oh, thank God you're all all right." Tears of relief flooded her eyes, but in a moment she began to compose herself again.

"How many of them was there, Daddy?" John asked, unable to curb his curiosity any longer.

"There were four, son. Just four."

"And you and Cole killed all four by yourselves?" the boy asked in amazement.

"We were lucky," Jason said quietly. He decided not to mention that one of the Jayhawkers outside still clung to life because he realized that, one way or another, the man surely would not survive the night.

"Daddy, can we . . . ," John asked. "Can Daniel and I . . ." Jason knew that the boys were anxious to go outside, eager to see the aftermath of battle, but Jason felt an odd sense of shame when he contemplated the sight of his sons gazing down at the men he had killed.

"I want everybody to stay inside until Cole and I . . . uh . . . until we take care of things outside," Jason announced. He could see that John was ready to protest, but he silenced the boy with a stern glance. Then turning to his wife, he began, "Arethia —"

"I'm all right," she assured him. "I'll take care of things in here while you do what you have to do out there."

Nodding, Jason turned and left the house, closing the front door behind him.

Without warning, a feeling of dizziness and nausea began to invade Jason's gut, and he was able to stagger forward only a few more steps before a sickening rush of bile spilled out of him.

How much more could any of them take? he wondered. How much longer could he and his family be expected to go on now that they had reached the point of fighting for survival on the very doorstep of their home? It wasn't their fight. It never had been. And yet now they were in the middle of it, as deeply involved as William or Charles or any of the dozens of other single-minded zealots on both sides who had lost all touch with reality in their blind drive to conquer.

Gazing across the yard at the dark form of the man he had killed only a quarter of an hour before, Jason wondered how much longer it would be before an attack such at this one succeeded, how many more days or weeks or months would pass before that was he lying in the dust with a knife or a bullet or a saber buried deep in his chest. And which of his family members would perish with him? Which of the people he loved most in this world would be the ones to be sacrificed on this great, bloody altar of insanity?

"Are you all right, old boy?" Cole asked. Jason looked around and saw his friend approaching from the direction of the hedgerow. He now wore a kerchief wrapped around the wound on his head. "I heard you heaving from clear up by the road."

"It just came on me all of a sudden," Jason answered. "But I'm all right now. What about your prisoner?"

"I think his back was broke or something. He couldn't hardly talk. He mumbled a couple of names, but finally I decided he was in so much pain that it would be better just to give him some peace."

Jason nodded. The brutal rules of war by which they fought made few allowances for prisoners, and few were ever tolerated. He would find out later what the man had said before Cole finished him, but there was more urgent business to be taken care of right now. "We've got to get these bodies cleaned up and figure out what to do with them," Jason said. "I don't want the kids to come out and see this mess."

"We can put them on the wagon, and I'll take them into town. I'll take their horses with me when I go too. I'll give the undertaker one for the price of four coffins and sell the others. We might as well make a few dollars from this business."

"I don't want any money, Cole. You do whatever you want with it. I just want to get these bastards out of here."

It took them only a short time to hitch two of the Jayhawker horses to a wagon and gather up the four corpses. Before covering the bodies up with a piece of canvas, Jason took a minute to stare at each of the lifeless faces. They were ordinary-looking men, each somewhere between twenty-five and forty, men not unlike Jason's own friends and neighbors in Clay County.

Now that the fighting was over and the four Jayhawkers were laid out like slabs of beef in the back of the wagon, on their way to anonymous graves, it seemed incredible that they were even here at all. What were all their high ideals and heartfelt beliefs worth to them now? It sounded fine and noble for a man to say he was willing to die for whatever cause he believed in, but what had the deaths of these men accomplished? And how many of them would have come at all if they could have known beyond any doubt that this was to be their fate? Nobody ever truly expected to die.

The approaching riders announced their presence from a long way off, wanting neither to be shot for Jayhawkers nor to ride into the middle of a fight without receiving some kind of warning. There were three of them, and as soon as Jason heard Judge Younger call out his own name, Jason assured them that it was all right to ride ahead.

Somehow he could tell that something was wrong as soon as the judge and the other men dismounted in the yard. None of them took the time to cast more than a casual glance at the bodies in the wagon, and Younger had a look on his face as solemn as any Jason had ever seen. He shook Jason's hand, then turned and did the same with his nephew.

"Jason, I've got bad news for you," the judge said uneasily. "I've just come from your brother William's house. He's been killed, he and his overseer, Milt Bailey. All the slaves are gone too, stolen or run off, I guess."

"William's dead?" Jason asked numbly. "He's dead?"

"I saw his body myself," Younger said. "There's no mistake."

"What about Mollie, Uncle Jim?" Cole asked anxiously. "Did you see Mollie Hartman anywhere about?"

"She's the one who found William," the judge said. "She must have arrived just after the raiders left. A number of us were out on patrol tonight and met her on the road just west of the Salem Church. She was half out of her mind, babbling about how everybody was going to be killed, but we finally calmed her down enough to learn what was going on. I sent some of my men off to spread the word and brought the rest of them here. Mollie told us you were under attack, but I see you've taken care of things."

"We've taken care of things," Jason mumbled.

William was dead. The painful realization of that fact was slowly beginning to sink in.

"Jason, I can't tell you how sorry I am," Thomas Younger said. "Your brother was a fine man, perhaps the best friend I ever had, and his loss will be felt deeply . . ."

But Jason was beyond hearing, staring dazedly into the darkness. How much more?

"But I swear to you, Jason, that this time they won't get away with it," Younger continued. "Riders are already on their way to alert the border patrols to the south and southwest, and word of this tragedy has also been sent to Senator Atchison. If we can just keep them from escaping back into Kansas tonight, by dawn we'll have two hundred men scouring the countryside for them."

"That's good," Jason said dully, his mind finally focusing on the words being spoken to him.

"We'll send word the minute we've caught them, Jason. Maybe that will at least provide you with some small consolation for William."

"You won't have to send word, Thomas. As soon as I take care of a few things here, I'll join the search. I want to be there when they die. I want to see their faces when the rope draws tight around their necks."

"No one could deny you that."

Jason had not noticed when Cole wandered away a minute earlier, but now the young man came toward him leading the saddled horse of one of the raiders.

"Uncle Tom, could you have one of your men get these bodies away from here?" Cole asked. "I have to ride over and see about Mollie. She'll need somebody with her."

"Yes, of course, Cole. I left a man at Williams with her, but I agree that you still need to go. You can join us later if you think it's all right to leave her."

"Tell her Arethia and I will be over soon," Jason said. His mind was beginning to function again, to concentrate on all the things that must now be done. The fact of William's death still lay like a stone in the hollow of his stomach, but the acceptance process had started.

As Cole rode away, Jason turned back to the house once more, dreading the next difficult task. His family had to be told of William's death, and the news could come from no lips but his.

Mollie was sitting on the wooden steps of William's front porch when Cole rode up. A lamp burned brightly in the parlor of the house, outlining her form against the light that spilled through the open front door. Nearby Stony grazed peacefully on the lush grass of the front yard. The place was eerily quiet. She looked up as Cole approached, an expression of absolute despair etched on her tear-streaked face.

"They're all right over at Jason's," Cole told her gently. "You don't have to worry. Everybody's OK."

Mollie nodded, unable to find her voice.

During those first moments with her, Cole could not seem to find the words to communicate the feelings that were in his heart, so he simply sat beside her on the step and put his arm around her trembling shoulders.

Finally, after what seemed a long time, Mollie turned her face to look up at her friend. Her eyes were clear and bright, and it seemed that finally the initial, devastating wave of grief had passed.

"I was just sitting here thinking about how many times in the past few years people here in Missouri, and people just across the line in Kansas, have had to suffer like I'm suffering now. It's terrible, Cole. It's like having some wild animal trapped inside you, gnawing away, and you know that there's nothing you can do about it. There's no way to let it out and no way to ease the pain even a little bit."

"I know, Mollie," Cole told her softly. "I've had that animal trapped in me, and I know what he can do, but it passes, Just like everything else in life passes."

"It passes," Mollie said. "I know that. But knowing it doesn't help with the way I feel now."

They sat in silence for a minute longer, then Cole asked, "Is there anything I should do around here? Anything about your brother?"

"He's inside on his bed," Mollie said. "I found him over there in the yard, about where your horse is standing, but some of the men who were here carried him inside. They took Milt Bailey around to the back porch instead of putting him inside because he ... because his head —"

"Well, if they're all right for now, then let's just sit

here," Cole said. "Jason and Arethia will be along after a while, and he can handle things. He'll take care of your brother and Milt." He waited a moment, unsure of whether to broach the other topic that was on his mind, then decided at last to go ahead. "Your brother and I fought it out with those men we heard on the road," he told her, "and I had a chance to try and talk to one of them before he died. He told me something I knew you would be interested in."

"What's that?" Mollie asked. She didn't seem interested, but Cole knew that would change when she heard what he was about to say.

"He was about gone, and I couldn't make much out of what he said, but he mentioned a name. Boone Septin. I'm not sure what he meant, but there was no mistaking it."

"Boone Septin," Mollie whispered, the name slipping past her lips like a curse. "He couldn't have been responsible for this, Cole. He was from the South. He thought the abolitionists were devils!"

"Well, he's been among the devils for two or three years now," Cole pointed out. "Maybe he's changed his mind. Maybe the coins that have fallen in his collection plate over there have convinced him that *we're* the devils."

"Is it possible?" Mollie asked incredulously.

"Mollie, with a man like that, anything is possible. But the main thing for us to think about is that he's back now. No matter where he's been or what he's been doing for these past years, now he's back within our reach. And if he did have any part in what happened here tonight, that's all the more reason for us to go after him."

"What did the others say when you told them?" Mollie asked.

"I haven't told anybody," Cole admitted. "I started to tell Jason, and later I almost mentioned it to my uncle, but both times something stopped me. I'm not sure what.

It was almost like Septin belonged to us and I didn't want anybody else to have any part in killing him."

"But if he killed Wiliam —"

"I doubt if he was the one who actually killed William or even led the raid," Cole interrupted. "My guess is, if he was here at all, it was probably more as a guide. Someone had to have shown those Jayhawkers where your brothers lived, and it could have been Septin."

"But you're still just guessing," Mollie reminded him. "All we've ever been able to do about Boone Septin is guess."

"But the man spoke his name, Mollie!" Cole said. "What else could it mean except that Septin had some part in what happened tonight? What other explanation is there?"

"None, I guess. But what difference does it make to us now? What can we do about it?"

"We can do what we planned to do all along," Cole said. "Unless he's caught, he'll certainly head straight back to Kansas, where he knows he'll be safe, and I'd be willing to bet that once he's there, he'll go for the safest haven in the territory. He'll head for John Brown's place, and with a coup like this one behind him, he'll certainly be welcome there."

"My God, Cole!" Mollie exclaimed. "How can you expect me to go with you now like I used to do? One of my brothers is lying dead in there, and the other has spent half the night fighting for his life. Jason's family has been attacked and scared half to death, and the whole countryside is about to explode into one big war. And in the middle of all that, you expect me to just drop everything and ride off into Kansas with you?"

"You're right, Mollie," Cole replied quietly. "It wasn't fair of me to ask. In fact, it probably wasn't fair of me to even mention it to you at all."

"I can't go," Mollie pleaded. "You understand, don't you? I just can't!"

"I understand," he assured her, "and it doesn't change a thing between us." He fell silent for a moment, then continued. "I guess it isn't fair of me to ask this either, but I'm going to need a few things. If I could get some food from your brother's pantry and maybe some ammunition for my pistol, if he has any here —"

"Take what you need, Cole. There's certainly nothing here that he'll need ever again."

Cole stood up and entered the house, but Mollie remained where she was. He wasn't familiar with William Hartman's house, so it took him a while to locate the cabinet in William's small office where the ammunition was kept. Taking what he needed, he went to the kitchen in back and loaded a few supplies into a flour sack.

As Cole was turning to leave the kitchen and start back to the front of the house, he saw Mollie standing in the kitchen doorway watching him. In the bright lamplight, he could clearly see the furrows that her tears had made in the dust on her face, but the expression that controlled her features now was not one of sorrow.

Cole had seen that look on her face many times before and knew what it meant.

"You might as well get enough for two," she told him.

"I already did," he said. "Just in case."

14

By dawn, Jason was riding south toward Independence
in the company of Bill Quantrill, whom Thomas Younger
had sent to get him. According to Quantrill, the Jayhawker
raiding party had been discovered a few hours earlier
in a wooded area southwest of town. It was a fairly large
group, about fifteen men, and they were soon entangled
in a desperate battle as they struggled to make it back
across the state line. Word had gone out as soon as the
raiders were located, and scores of angry Missourians
were flocking to the area. Quantrill seemed confident that
few, if any, of the abolitionists would escape.

Jason was exhausted and hungry, but eager to reach
the battle before it was over. He had left behind utter
chaos — an unburied brother and a family devastated
by sorrow and turmoil — but even those things did not
seem to matter quite as much as killing these men did.
If they could manage to annihilate every Jayhawker who
had taken part in the events of the previous night, he

thought, then not only would his brother's death be avenged but all of Kansas would realize that it was senseless, not to mention fatal, to attack the people of Missouri on their home soil.

As Jason and Quantrill neared the edge of Independence, they paused to talk with a teamster who carried more recent news.

The man reported that about two hours earlier the Jayhawkers, exhausted by the night's activities, had made their stand in the Rock Creek area a few miles southwest of town. Several had been killed on the spot, and some prisoners had been taken, although the man was unsure how many. A few of the raiders had somehow managed to break through the lines of the Missourians and were fleeing toward Kansas, but they were being hotly pursued by Atchison's forces.

"Well, I guess we missed the fight," Quantrill said as they rode on, "but maybe we'll get there in time for the hangings."

"I just hope they take the time to question their prisoners before they kill them," Jason said grimly. "If I can find out who was behind the raid against my home and my brother's, I won't rest until I've put a bullet in his head. Even if it's Old Brown himself, I swear to God I'll find some way to get to him this time and put an end to him forever."

"I have an idea that you won't want for help when you head out to do that," Quantrill told him. "I've already heard talk about how the time is right to cross the border and clean out that hornet's nest at Osawatomie. After what happened last night, David Atchison will have all the men he needs together in one place, and they'll be fired up enough to follow him anywhere and do whatever he says. What happens over the next couple of days could bring an end to this business once and for all."

If only that were true, Jason thought. All the fighting had taken a devastating toll on him. He was exhausted, physically and spiritually, and he wasn't sure he could go on much longer, no matter what the consequences. His family was being destroyed, and now, after the previous night's raid, he was starting to recognize the horrible fact that he was one of the major contributors to that destruction. It had to end. It had to.

When they reached Independence, they found the town full of armed men. Most of them had arrived too late to take part in the attack on the Jayhawkers, but all were ready for action and seemingly ready to follow the commands of anybody who took it upon himself to assume leadership.

Jason and Quantrill rode straight to the Jackson County Jail, where Atchison and Judge Younger had set up temporary headquarters. The senator had commandeered the sheriff's small office for his own use, and the place was a beehive of activity as plans were formulated for a retaliatory raid into Kansas.

Thomas Younger spotted Jason as soon as he walked in the door and quickly led him into the back office where Atchison was holding his council of war with a few selected lieutenants. The senator greeted him with a warm handshake.

"I'm sure I speak for every man here when I tell you how stricken we are over the death of your brother," Atchison said. "It will be a great loss to the community and, in fact, to the entire state of Missouri."

"Thank you, Senator," Jason mumbled. He was in no mood for amenities, but he knew that Atchison, always the politician, was compelled to say them anyway.

"If there is any comfort to be found in such a tragedy," the senator added, "then perhaps it can come from the knowledge that William Hartman was a brave man who died for a noble cause. He will serve as an inspiration to us all during the campaign which we are now planning to avenge his death."

"Then you are going after them?" Jason asked with rising enthusiasm. "You're planning to cross the border again?"

"It seems an ideal time. We have the motive, and we have the manpower, and equally important is the fact that we have hard evidence of who was behind this most recent atrocity."

"It was Brown, wasn't it?" Jason asked tersely.

"Without a doubt. Of course, there was little question all along that he had a hand in this, but a short time ago one of our prisoners confirmed the fact that it was Old Brown who sent them out two days ago to kill you, your brother, and another man here in Jackson County."

At that point, Thomas Younger moved to place a hand on Jason's shoulder. "Listen, Jason," he said gently. "I hesitate to bring this up because of all that you've been through in the last few hours, but you're bound to find out anyway. It's about the prisoners . . ."

Jason spun around, knowing immediately by the judge's tone of voice that he was in for another piece of bad news.

"Two of the men we're holding are named Joel and Herbert Hartman," Younger said quietly. "Apparently they are your nephews, sons of your brother Charles."

"No!" Jason exclaimed. "It must be some kind of a mistake! No matter how badly Charles and William might have disagreed, Charles would not have sent his sons out to kill his own brother! He doesn't have it in him to do such a thing!"

"They claim not to have known whose farm they were raiding until it was already too late," Younger explained, "but I doubt that there's any truth in that. It seems more likely that your brother and his sons simply feel more loyalty to their damned abolitionist cause than they do to the members of their own family."

Though he realized that it was pointless to argue, Jason refused to believe that such a thing was possible. "Where are these prisoners?" he asked abruptly. "I want to talk to them myself."

Younger and Atchison exchanged concerned glances before either of them replied. Finally the senator spoke up hesitantly. "That could be very awkward, Jason. You know what we do to Jayhawkers when we capture them alive, and there was never any discussion of treating these two any different from all the rest."

"I want to see them!" Jason was shouting now. "Damn it, it's my right! You can't hang them before you give me the chance to find out if what you claim is true!"

Atchison considered the matter a moment before finally giving his consent. "All right, Jason," he said, "but you must remember that they're likely to tell you anything you want to hear if they think it might save their lives."

"I'll know the minute I see them if they are my brother's sons," Jason said. "And if they are, when they find out who I am, I don't think they'll feel much like lying about anything else."

"All right, take him to the prisoners, Thomas," Atchison ordered.

Younger ushered Jason into a room containing four ten-foot cells and pointed to the last one in the line. "They're in that one," the judge said. He watched Jason walk toward it, then turned and left the room.

There were two men in the first cell Jason passed and one in the second. All of them glanced up with hate-filled eyes, but no one spoke to him. Jason moved on until he stood outside the door of the last cell.

Neither of the young men inside appeared to be much over twenty. Both sat listlessly against the back wall, their knees pulled up to their chests, their eyes vacant. Both had been badly treated by their captors. Their faces were bruised and swollen, and one of them, the smaller of the two, was cradling his right arm in front of him as if it were broken. Fear registered clearly on their battered features when they saw Jason stop outside their cells.

"Come here, you two," Jason ordered.

Neither moved for a moment, but his command visibly heightened the look of dread on their faces.

"Who are you?" the taller one asked at last. "What do you want?"

"I want to get a better look at you," Jason said. "Now get up and come over here."

The boys rose reluctantly and started across the cell. The taller one moved with a pronounced limp, and the other continued to cradle his injured arm as if it were a baby he was afraid of waking.

They had been so badly beaten that it was difficult to imagine what they might look like without the cuts and livid bruises, but there was something about their eyes . . . They could be his brother's eyes, Hartman eyes, Jason thought.

"I'm the brother of the man you killed last night," he said abruptly, "and if the two of you are telling the truth, then I'm your uncle as well. My name is Jason Hartman."

The announcement caught both young men off guard. They stared at him in surprise for a moment, then the taller of the pair replied slowly, "I'm Joel, and this is my brother Herbert. We have been telling the truth. Our father is Charles Hartman, your brother."

"What is your mother's name?" Jason asked.

"Gertrude," Joel said. "She was Gertrude Goebels before she married."

"And where did you live before you moved to Kansas?"

"We had a small farm in Pennsylvania, and our father ran a store there. We lived in York County, near the Susquehanna River."

Then it's true, Jason thought. They were his nephews,

Charles's sons. And because that was true, then it must also mean that Charles must have . . . He still found the thought so abhorrent that his mind balked at considering it.

"What are they going to do to us, Uncle Jason?" Herbert asked nervously.

"What have you always heard happens to Jayhawkers when they're caught in Missouri?" Jason retorted.

"But you won't let them hang us will you, Uncle Jason?" Herbert pleaded. Tears glistened in his eyes, but he struggled not to lose control.

"Why should I stop them?" Jason shot back. "If William's death didn't matter to you last night, why should yours matter to me now?"

"We didn't know it was his farm until it was too late," Joel insisted. "We wouldn't have had any part in it if we had known. We would have done something."

"Are you trying to tell me that you came all the way over into Missouri with a band of over twenty men and never knew who you were coming here to kill? Do you want me to believe that you never once heard William's name or mine mentioned in all that time?"

"It's not like that," Joel said. "There were three groups that started out at the same time, and everything was kept secret so if somebody from one group was caught, they wouldn't be able to tell who the others were after. We came after a man named Walt Eberhart, who lived right here in Jackson County, but we got lost in the dark and couldn't find his place. Finally our leader decided we should just go help one of the other groups get their man. We caught up with some of the others just before they got to Uncle William's house, and we never heard his name spoken until they started shouting for him to come out. And by then it was too late. Everybody was shooting, and there were bullets flying everywhere. We couldn't have stopped it if we tried."

It could have happened that way, Jason thought, or

it could be that Atchison's assumption was accurate. They could be lying simply to stay alive. Somehow he had believed that he would know the difference, but even he couldn't tell.

"Did your father know that two of the groups were coming to kill William and me?" he asked.

"I don't know," Joel replied. "I honestly don't. We've lived at Osawatomie for a year now, and Mr. Brown trusts our father. He sometimes consults father on things like this, but father seldom talks about it with us."

"Help us, please," Herbert begged. "This was my first time over here, and it was only Joel's second. I never even cocked the hammer on my rifle. I never shot at anybody, and I don't want to die." The tears were flowing freely down the youth's cheeks now, and despite himself, Jason found it difficult not to be affected.

"We've been talking about going to California, Herbert and I," Joel said. "Things are crazy where we live. All anybody ever talks of is raids and stealing slaves and killing proslavers. When we talked to our father about leaving, he forbade us to go, but we had decided to go anyway. Before summer's end."

"But you came here instead," Jason reminded him.

"Mr. Brown told us to, and our father told us to." Joel shrugged. "But we didn't kill anybody, not Uncle William or anybody, and we don't want to die. Please help us, Uncle Jason!"

"There's no use in me promising you anything," Jason said at last. "No matter what was in your mind, you came here and you got caught. Things have gone too far, and I don't see how I could help you even if I tried. I'm sorry." He tried to keep his voice hard, to keep his feelings locked away as he had so many times before to do what must be done.

Joel accepted his verdict with a simple nod, but Herbert leaped toward the bars and reached out to grasp Jason's clothing. It wasn't so much an attack as an attempt to cling to one last hope for life. "Please," he wailed. "Please!"

Jason knocked the youth's hand free, then stepped back and out of his reach. There was nothing more to say, nothing else to do. They had done what they had done, and now they would die for their acts. As Herbert collapsed to the floor and his brother bent to comfort him, Jason turned and hurried away. He passed through the crowded front room of the jail and out the front door without pausing to speak to anybody. He had to find a place to be alone for a while, if any such place existed.

The gallows was a simple affair, hastily constructed but adequate. Across the alley between two buildings, someone had nailed up a four-by-four plank about twelve feet off the ground. Three nooses hung from the plank, and a flat-bedded freight wagon sat beneath it.

Jason had seen men hanged before. There was something morbidly fascinating about watching a man perish this way, and the fact that the five men who were to die here today had in some way been responsible for William's death made the event something he felt compelled to witness.

And yet he still felt strange about it, different than he ever had before. His conversation with Joel and Herbert Hartman had affected him deeply, wrenching feelings from him that he had not expected ever to feel again. During the hour that had passed since he spoke with them, one thought kept running through his head. *What if they were telling the truth?*

What if they had come over here *only* at the insistence of their father and John Brown, and what if they had not been knowing participants in William's death? What if they truly did want to go to California to escape all this madness and start new lives for themselves?

They were just boys, after all, hardly older than his

own son John. What harm would it do to let them go?

He had fought against these notions, pushing them out of his head again and again. This was not a time for displays of sentiment or weakness. William was dead, and the men responsible must die for it, no matter who they were or what their ages. It was one of the rules of the war they fought.

And yet . . .

A crowd gathered quickly when word went out that the hangings were about to begin. Judge Younger and two of his assistants kept the alley clear so that the horses hitched to the wagon could be driven forward at the appropriate time, but the street at the alley entrance was soon packed with hundreds of onlookers, all shoving for a choice position. Jason scanned the crowd for Atchison but did not spot him anywhere. Probably, he thought, the senator was still back at the jail, unwilling to interrupt his tactical meeting long enough to witness the deaths of the five men.

Jason stood off to one side, jammed against the plank wall of a dry-goods store, no more than a dozen feet from the wagon, within easy view of the ominous hemp nooses. A strange apprehension clutched his gut as he recalled that he himself had once faced such a noose; but there was the accompanying sense of relief that today those coils of rope would claim someone else's life, not his.

The first three prisoners who were brought from the jail, their hands already tied tightly behind their backs, were strangers to Jason. Though they had been badly beaten and abused by their captors, their faces were set with a stony determination not to break down at the last moment and give the crowd the satisfaction of seeing them beg for their lives.

They were hoisted roughly up onto the wagon bed and the nooses were fitted around their necks, the knots placed strategically behind one ear. No man of the cloth was present to comfort them, and none was asked if he had anything to say. Once they were in position, the judge simply gave a signal to the wagon driver, and the driver slapped the reins across the backs of his team.

Two of the men were killed almost immediately as their feet slipped off the back of the wagon, the ropes drew taut, and their necks snapped. The third man, however, was not so fortunate. For a full minute his body arched and spiraled in the air as his feet and legs kicked and contorted wildly in a bizarre death dance. A low murmur rippled through the crowd as the last man died a slow, agonizing death.

When it was certain that the three were dead, the wagon was repositioned and half a dozen men leaped up onto the bed to remove the ropes from the dead men's necks. Then instead of lowering the corpses to the ground, they were simply pushed off to one side of the wagon bed.

A shudder ran through Jason's body when he heard Herbert Hartman howling. It was obvious that he was not going to die with dignity, so it was perhaps merciful that the men who brought him out had beaten him nearly senseless by the time they dragged him through the crowd to the wagon bed.

Joel was doing somewhat better. His face was ashen with terror, and his legs failed him more than once as he was led forward, but he did not struggle against the men who held him nor did he utter a single plea for his or his brother's life to be spared.

As the two brothers were hoisted up on the wagon bed, Herbert was limp in his captors' hands, unconscious, Jason suspected. Joel's knees buckled as his eyes settled on the three corpses, but strong hands caught his arms and refused to let him fall. He quickly averted his gaze from the bodies and was again able to stand on his own as the noose was fitted around his neck. In fact, his eyes seemed to be scanning the crowd as the rope was drawn tight and the knot was shifted into position.

"Damn it, Saul! Put the leather to that team this time so we get a good clean snap!" Judge Younger shouted.

Herbert was beginning to come to, and was able to stand unsupported by the time the other men climbed down from the wagon. The two brothers looked at one another and exchanged some parting words, then Joel turned his gaze back to the crowd. His eyes found Jason just as the wagon driver bellowed out a thunderous "Hee-yahhh!" and the reins stung the horses' rumps.

"Nooooo!" Jason screamed and pushed off the wall and fairly leaped across the backs of the men in front of him. He fought through the crowd like a madman, flinging startled men carelessly out of his way in his wild struggle to reach his two nephews before it was too late. Their legs were already dangling and twitching in the air by the time he got to them, but still be grabbed them in a desperate bearhug and tried to lift them up enough to relieve some of the strain, enough to keep them alive.

"Goddamn it, Jason!" Judge Younger thundered, shoving his way forward past several men. "What in the hell do you think —"

"Help me, Thomas!" Jason screamed frantically. "Help me save them! They don't have to die! I'll make sure they go to California!"

"Damn it, Jason, they're already dead!" Younger told him. He fought to loosen Jason's grasp from around the young men's legs, but Jason refused to let go. "Look at them, man! They're dead!"

Suddenly an army of hands seemed to be grabbing at him from all directions, pulling his arms loose and hauling him away from his nephews. He lashed out with his fists and caught Younger in the chest and then smashed the face of another man. Then someone hit him hard in the middle of his back, and something hard crashed against the side of his head. He fell, unconscious before he hit the ground.

When he came to, he was lying on a narrow bed, and it took him a moment to orient himself well enough to realize that he was now in the same jail cell that Joel and Herbert had occupied. The cell door stood open, and as soon as he felt up to it, he got to his feet and stumbled out. All the other cells were empty.

A lone deputy occupied the front room of the jail. After the throngs that had filled the place when he was last there, it seemed strange to see it so vacant and quiet.

"What's going on?" Jason mumbled. His tongue felt thick, and the words pounded in his head as he spoke them.

"Ah, I see you finally come around," the deputy said, turning his head and grinning at Jason. He was a portly man of late middle age with a friendly face and an easy manner. "The doc checked you out and said he thought you was OK, so we just decided to leave you like you was for a while."

"How long was I out?" Jason asked.

"Nearly eight hours," the man said. "You had quite a sleep."

"Where is everybody?"

"Gone home mostly."

"You mean the raid was canceled?" Jason asked in surprise. "Atchison decided not to go after Brown?"

"No, they're still going," the deputy told him. "The senator sent everybody home to get food and pack up whatever they want to take along. All them that decides to go along is supposed to meet back here at first light tomorrow morning."

It took Jason a moment to digest what he was hearing. Apparently Atchison had decided to invest a little more time in preparation rather than racing off in the heat of the moment at the head of an angry, unprovisioned rabble. Then as he began to think more clearly, he recalled the events which had caused him to be lying unconscious in the jail.

"The men who were hung, the Jayhawkers, where are they now?" Jason asked.

"I reckon they're still down at the undertaker's," the deputy answered. "Leastways, I doubt if ol' Potter's got them buried yet. If he has, it's the first thing in my re-collection he's ever been in a hurry about."

A germ of an idea sprang unbidden into Jason's mind. It seemed to be a crazy notion at first, perhaps the most reckless thing he had ever considered doing in his life. But if it worked . . .

"I'm much obliged for the information," Jason told the deputy, "and for the use of your cot. Now if you could just tell me how to find this man Potter . . ."

Rumbling along on the wide dirt road, steering the wagon team toward the setting sun, Jason realized that if any member of his family, or anyone else he knew for that matter, had been sitting on the seat beside him right now, they would be certain beyond reasonable doubt that he had completely lost his mind. And he had to admit that on the surface it did seem ridiculous, even suicidal, to be driving a wagon load of dead Jayhawkers back to Kansas.

But the more he thought about it, the smarter it seemed. In fact, the audacity of what he was doing might be the key to pulling it off. There was no denying that it was risky and riddled with uncertainties, but if it worked, it might earn him the peace he and his family so desired.

Before leaving Independence, he had sent a message to Arethia instructing her to go ahead with arrangements for William's funeral. This time of year, families could not afford to leave their dead unburied for long, and he knew that his wife would have all the assistance she needed in completing the necessary rituals. It bothered him to think that he would not be there to pay his last respects to his brother, but it could not be helped.

Explaining why he was not coming home was a more difficult task. He could not tell Arethia what he was up to, but she would know when all the other men in the community came home for supplies that he was not joining Atchison's invasion force either. Finally he settled on no explanation at all and asked that she try her best to trust him one more time. He knew it was probably a useless request. He had drawn too many times on her reserves of trust, but it was the best he could do. With some effort, he put his family out of his mind and began to concentrate on what lay ahead.

The realization that had inspired this trip had come to him during that fleeting second when his eyes had locked with those of Joel Hartman an instant before the young man's death.

Up until that instant he had believed, or thought he believed, that he was firmly on the side of right, that he was doing no more than any just man should do to protect his own life, the lives of his family, and the home they had worked so hard to build for themselves. And by standing firm in that belief, he had been able to commit terrible acts of bloodshed and brutality, justifying everything with the argument that for him to live, all those who stood against him must die. It was neat and convenient. It was a blanket under which every horrible act, every crime, could be hidden.

But there was a problem. The blanket he used to cloak his sins was the same one used by the opposition, and when one of them committed some dastardly act, such as the killing of William, they justified their deeds with the same arguments he himself used. William had to die so they could live. Right was on their side. Their cause was right and just, so anything they did in the name of that cause was also right and just.

But in that moment when he gazed at the face of a young man whose life was about to end, the truth came to him, stark, clear, and undeniable. There was no bastion of righteousness behind which any of them could hide. They were just a lot of people who were killing each other. The morality of the causes they had once fought for had long since been lost in a dense fog of hatred, deception, and passion for revenge.

He knew there was no point in trying to share this new revelation with anyone else. The combatants on both sides of the border would never listen to such logic. But that was no reason why he could not use his new-found understanding to salvage the ragged remains of his own life. Nearly everything he had worked to build in his life had been torn down during this last tragic year. But if he chose to do so, he could begin rebuilding right now, today — unless John Brown decided to kill him the minute he reached Osawatomie River.

He didn't stop when darkness fell, nor did he leave the road to avoid discovery. He pushed on even after he had crossed the border into Kansas and was well into abolitionist territory, believing that the bodies he was returning to their families for burial would guarantee his safe passage until he reached his destination.

It seemed strange to be passing through this disputed territory now without caution or fear of discovery, but then he realized that that in itself was a sign of how warped and corrupted the times had become. This was America, the land that a free people had carved from the wilderness, the land where a man was supposed to be able to go anywhere he wanted without fear because the soil he trod belonged to him as much as to anyone else.

By dawn he was far beyond the point that any prudent

Missourian would have ventured alone, and by the time he paused to munch on a hunk of meat and a piece of bread for his midday meal, he was well into the piece of the territory ruled by John Brown's iron will and deadly saber. Glancing back at the inert, canvas-covered forms, he muttered, "Almost home, boys. I'm sorry about California, but at least now you can rest in peace among the people who loved you." Then he added wryly, "I just hope I don't end up resting there with you."

Jason spotted the five horsemen while they were still a long way off across the rolling prairie. His rifle lay in back, unloaded and out of reach, and his pistol and gun belt were rolled up beside it. He made no attempt to retrieve either as he waited for the horsemen to arrive.

15

John Brown knelt in the small back room that he called his sanctuary, praying for the souls of his fallen brethren. The recent raid, which had been dispatched with such high hopes for freeing the enslaved and wreaking just retribution against the foe, had been utterly disastrous. This three-pronged attack was to have been one of his most notable achievements, a historic, telling blow against the powers of darkness, but instead it was a miserable failure. Of the twenty men who had ridden out four days before, only five had returned, and one of them was now dying.

The whole community had been shaken by the carnage. The countryside was full of grieving, widows and families, and Charles Hartman was nearly insane over the news that two of his sons had been captured near Independence. It had taken all of Brown's considerable persuasive powers to keep his friend from leaving immediately for a desperate rescue attempt, and finally Brown and two of his sons had been forced to immobilize Hartman with a huge dose of laudanum.

To bring some semblance of order to his people and to begin the process of putting the tragedy behind them, Brown had instructed that a memorial service be scheduled for early that evening. There would be no dead to bury, no graves to honor, but it would serve as the closest thing to a funeral service any of his fallen comrades was likely to have. The itinerant preacher Boone Septin was handling the arrangements for the service, and it was to be held right here in Brown's compound. Right now Septin was riding around the countryside spreading the word, and the people were already beginning to flock in for the ceremony.

Brown didn't care much for Septin, didn't fully trust him, and didn't think that most of what he said had any substance, but he did have to give the man credit for one thing. He knew how to stir people up, to wrench precisely the emotions that he was seeking from their hearts, and to unite them behind a common cause. People followed John Brown because of the fearsome force of his deeds, but they believed Septin because he convinced them that they should. Brown didn't trust the man, but he used him.

Morale was in such a state of disarray that John Brown doubted that he could have mustered half a dozen fighting men at the moment, but he was already beginning to look ahead and consider what his next stroke against his enemies in Missouri should be. His flock would eventually recover from this setback. New believers would be enlisted, and those already behind him would soon rediscover their courage and commitment to freedom. And when that happened, he would strike again, more firmly and decisively than ever before.

Of one thing he was certain, even now during this dark time. These deaths would be avenged, and the good fight would continue. No other alternative ever even occurred to him.

John Brown turned his head and scowled at the door of the room when he heard somebody tapping lightly on it. Everybody knew that he was not to be disturbed when he was in here with the Lord. It was a cardinal rule of the household that his conferences with the Almighty were not to be interrupted. But whoever it was seemed intent on disturbing him. The knock was repeated, and then a subdued male voice called out, "Papa, I have something important to tell you."

Rising on knees that had grown painfully stiff during their hour-long contact with the hard plank floor, Brown stood and unlocked the door. "This had better be as important as you say, Owen," he growled.

"It's very important," Brown's son assured him. "A patrol has just brought a man in, and he has the bodies of five of our people with him. He brought them all the way back from Missouri."

"Who is this man?" Brown asked. "Is he one of ours?"

"Not hardly," Owen replied. "It's Jason Hartman."

"Him? You mean he's still alive?" Brown exclaimed. "Damn!" The survivors of the raiding party had brought back confirmation that William Hartman had been killed, but none of the group sent to take care of Jason Hartman had been heard from. Brown had assumed that all of them must be dead, but he had hoped that they were able to carry out their assignment before they perished.

"And you said he's brought five bodies with him?" Brown asked. "Men from the raiding party?"

"That's right. Charles Hartman's two sons and three others. He says all five of them were hung yesterday in Independence."

Brushing impatiently past his son, Brown marched through the house and out the front door to sort out this bewildering situation. When he got outside, he saw a wagon sitting in the middle of the compound, and just as Owen had reported, Jason Hartman was standing casually beside it.

A sudden fierce elation filled him as he realized that now, by the grace of God, one of his most hateful enemies had finally fallen into his grasp!

It took a great effort on Jason's part to suppress a shudder when he saw John Brown appear suddenly in a doorway across the compound. After all these months of battle, the man had become a specter in his mind, larger than life and deadly beyond all imagining. Now to be confronted with the reality of the man made Jason's sphincter muscles tighten involuntarily.

A crowd was already beginning to assemble in a wide ring around Jason and his gory cargo as the abolitionist leader marched across the compound. As if by telepathy, everyone seemed to realize at the same instant that the stranger their leader was about to confront was not one of them and that something of great import was about to take place. John Brown stopped directly in front of Jason and glared at him, their faces no more than a foot apart.

"You must be out of your mind to come here!" Brown stormed.

"I probably am," Jason replied with all the calm he could summon.

"Then before I kill you, tell me why you've done it." Brown demanded. "What kind of devilish deception are you up to?"

"This is just what it looks like," Jason answered. "Two of my nephews were hung in Independence yesterday, and I've brought them home to be buried by their family. These others were killed at the same time, and I saw no harm in bringing them along as well."

John Brown found Jason's apparent lack of concern

for his predicament utterly infuriating. His body trembled with pent-up rage, but his curiosity about the situation was stronger than his anger. "Do you have any idea what you've done by placing yourself in our hands like this?" he cried. "Do you know that some of these very men were sent out to execute you only four days ago?"

"None of this lot was," Jason told him. "These men were all among the group that killed my brother William and his overseer."

John Brown could restrain himself no longer in the face of such insolence. He drew back a huge fist and struck Jason in the face with a blow that caused him to stagger back against the front wheel of the wagon. Jason straightened himself and raised a hand to dab at a trickle of blood at the corner of his mouth but made no move to fight back. Brown stepped forward and struck him again, knocking him to the ground this time.

"I would like to speak to my brother," Jason said. He tried to rise, but John Brown kicked him in the stomach, toppling him over sideways.

"My brother Charles," Jason groaned, fighting now to spit the words out past the pain. "I want to see him."

"Are you mad?" Brown screamed at the top of his lungs. "Has the Lord utterly robbed you of your senses? Don't you know that I'm going to kill you right here, right now?"

Jason tried to stand up, and this time Brown permitted him to struggle to his hands and knees and then to his feet. When he was finally erect, he looked the abolitionist straight in the eye. "I had hoped you wouldn't kill me," he replied. "Because of them, and because of what I have to tell you."

"Do you think that any words you could utter would dissuade me from taking my vengeance on you?" Brown scoffed. "To me, you are the vilest creature that ever inflicted his presence on the earth. You are the personification of evil in this land, and I consider it my sacred duty to crush the life from you."

"You still don't see it, do you?" Jason said. "You still don't understand the real reason why I'm here." The taste of blood was thick in his mouth and waves of pain were shooting through his side, but now these things were only minor annoyances, almost irrelevant. He was going to say what he came here to say unless Brown beat him senseless first.

"Tell me then, you son of Satan," Brown challenged. "Share the great light of your wisdom with all of us here."

"I came to tell you that I've quit," Jason told him. "For me, the war is over."

"And you think that simple pronouncement will save your life?" Brown asked incredulously. "After all you've done?"

"I don't know. That will be your decision. I came here knowing that there was a good chance you would kill me, but if you must, at least do it knowing that I'm just a man. Not a devil or any great personification of evil. Just a man. And do it knowing that the act you commit is nothing more than murder because whether I live or die no longer makes any difference to this ridiculous conflict. I'm through with it."

"These men must be avenged," Brown insisted, pointing toward the bodies in the wagon. "These and all the other brave men who have fallen at the hands of men like you."

"If you feel that way, then murder me," Jason challenged him.

The terrible emotions that distorted John Brown's features gave every indication that he was about to do just that, but Jason also saw that another force was coming into play as well. The crowd was murmuring now. Obviously, people were beginning to consider what he said and to wonder whether or not his death was justified. Brown seemed to realize this as well, and for the first time his determination to execute Jason on the spot began to waver.

"This is a trick," he growled. "If I let you go, I have no reason to believe you won't go back to persecuting us just as you always have."

"If that was my aim, then why would I be standing here now?" Jason asked. "I came because I knew this was the only way to end my involvement in this nightmare once and for all. I want my family to sleep safe at night without wondering whether they will live to see the morning. I want to watch my children grow up free from fear, and I want to quit fighting every day of my life simply to survive. I want to quit being a killer and go back to being a farmer and a husband and a father again."

As Brown was bracing himself to respond, a woman stepped forward from the crowd and touched the sleeve of his shirt. "Mr. Brown, she said, "my husband Robert is over there. He brought my husband back for me to bury, and the others as well."

As John Brown gazed down at her, for the first time ever Jason saw a look of compassion and sorrow cross the fierce abolitionist's features. Tears were flowing down the woman's cheeks, and Brown reached out a hand to comfort her. Then he raised his eyes to look first at the row of bodies in the wagon and then at Jason.

"You must stay here until your fate is decided," he declared. "We'll deal with you after we have buried our dead."

The verdict was less than Jason had hoped for, but for the time being, it would have to suffice. He still had not laid eyes on his brother Charles, and his demand to see him had been ignored, but the time was not right to ask again. Wherever his brother was, when he heard that Jason was here, he would certainly show up to talk to him.

On a sign from Brown, two men stepped forward and

took Jason by either arm. As they led him away toward a squat log building on the south side of the compound, several men went to the back of the wagon to begin unloading the bodies.

Cole drew his pistol and squatted low behind a tree when he heard the sound of a horse moving through the brush at the edge of the woods. He was pretty sure it was Mollie, but there was no sense in taking needless chances. A minute later he saw her riding through the trees toward the spot where he waited.

"Any luck?" he asked.

"Yes, finally," she smiled down at him. She stopped her horse near where his was grazing, dismounted, and dropped the reins to the ground. "The woman I talked to at the last little homestead said she fed him a meal just yesterday moring."

"Hallelujah!" Cole cried. "Did she say which way he went when he left?"

"West. Just like we thought."

For two days, Mollie and Cole had been working their way west across the Kansas countryside, trying to pick up the trail of Boone Septin. To avoid suspicion, Mollie had been the one to make most of the inquiries at the farms and homesteads they passed while Cole waited at a convenient location nearby. The story she used was that she was Septin's niece and that she had been searching for him to tell him that his brother in St. Louis was deathly ill. The lie brought her immediate sympathy at almost every place she stopped, but until now it had not produced any leads to the itinerant preacher's recent whereabouts. But now, late into the afternoon of the second day, she had finally turned up a fresh trail. The problem that still remained, though, was what to do about the lead now that they had it.

"I guess this practically confirms that he's headed back to John Brown's place," Mollie said. "But knowing that he's there and finding a way to get to him are two different matters entirely."

"I've been thinking about that," Cole told her, "and I think I have a way figured out that we can at least get inside."

"How could we possibly get past the sentries and across the walls?" Mollie asked. "The way you've described the place to me, it sounds more like a fortress than a farm."

"I've scounted the place twice," Cole said, "once on my own, and another time with Bill Anderson, and both times I came to the conclusion that there was no way for a man to get in there without being caught. But while you've been out asking questions, I've been going over the layout in my mind."

"Go on," Mollie prompted.

"Anybody that builds a place like that does it with the thought that eventually they might be put under siege," Cole reasoned. "And if you were under siege, what would be the three things you would not want to run out of?"

"Ammunition and food, I guess," she answered him. "And, of course, water."

"That's right. Water!"

"I guess if they were smart, they would probably have barrels of it stored somewhere inside."

"They might," Cole told her. "But there's also a creek that flows down through that valley. In fact, the place is named for it — Osawatomie River. And John Brown built his compound right at the very edge of it."

"Does it run *through* the compound?" Mollie asked.

"No, it passes just outside the walls. But I'll tell you what I was thinking. If I built that close to a source of water, I'd make damned sure I had a way to bring some of it in without ever going outside the wall. A cistern, maybe, or a pool, or even a small tunnel under the wall."

"Now this is beginning to make a little sense," Mollie smiled.

"Well you might as well like it," Cole told her, "because

it's probably our only chance. Now here's the way I see it. We'll have to enter the creek way up at the head of the valley because we'd never be able to cross any of the open country around without being seen. The creek cuts deep enough that we can use it for cover most of the way, and when we get down even with the wall, we'll try to find a way inside. If there's no other way, we could just climb the damned wall and hope for the best."

"Wonderful, Cole," Mollie complained. "That sounds about as safe as jumping off a cliff."

"Damn it, I didn't promise you safety, Mollie. I just promised you a chance at Septin. Besides, if we get down there and the whole thing looks too risky, we can just slip back out again and wait for another time."

"I have to admit that this is our best chance ever to get that damned preacher," Mollie said. "And there's no way to tell if it might be our last chance as well. I can't see Septin staying around John Brown for too long. It's too dangerous, and none of these dirt farmers around here can probably spare more than a few pennies a week to drop in a collection plate."

"So do we agree?" Cole asked. "Are you willing to give this a try?"

"I can't suggest anything better, so I guess this is it."

"All right then. We'll push on west for another hour or so, and then we'll hole up and rest somewhere until after dark."

As they mounted their horses and prepared to leave, Mollie had one final question. "In all the thinking that you've done," she asked, "have you considered how we'll go about locating where Septin is after we've made it inside?"

"I don't have the foggiest notion how to go about doing that," he admitted. "But considering the kind of preacher he's turned out to be, maybe the Lord will guide us to him!"

They traveled as far west as they dared ride in daylight, then hid in a small copse of trees about three miles east of John Brown's stronghold, taking turns sleeping in two-hour shifts until darkness had arrived and a sliver of moon had risen in the eastern sky. Then they mounted their horses once again and Cole led the way to a hill overlooking John Brown's valley from the west. He located a reasonably safe spot to leave the horses, and then they proceeded on foot to the crest of the hill. From there, Brown's compound was visible about a half mile away as a scattering of campfires and lighted windows.

"I'm scared, Cole." Mollie shivered as they lay gazing down at the flickering lights.

"How scared?" he asked. "Too scared to go through with it?"

"I don't know. I've got this bad feeling inside, like maybe this is the time when our luck is going to run out."

"I never put much stock in those feelings, but I know some folks do," Cole said. He found her hand with his in the darkness and gave it a reassuring squeeze. Then he asked, "So what do you think?"

Mollie thought for a moment, then leaned over and kissed him on the cheek. "I think after we get started I'll be OK. And I think that if we let this chance get by and there never is another, I'll hate myself for the rest of my life. Let's go get him!"

"We'll get him, Mollie, don't you worry. We'll find a way, and we'll live to tell the tale too." With that, he dug his heels into the prairie soil and began to crawl down the hillside through the thick grass. Mollie followed, remaining close behind as Cole had instructed her to do. On a brightly moonlit night they would probably not have been able to cross the open hillside so boldly, but it was so dark tonight that one of Brown's guards would have had to stumble across them before he could have seen them.

It took them nearly half an hour of careful maneuvering before they reached the creek, which entered the shallow valley from the southwest and then took a sharp turn eastward as it passed Brown's stronghold. Cole led the way over the rim of the bank and into the ten-foot trough that the running water had cut for itself over the centuries. For the first time since they had left the hillside, Mollie felt reasonably concealed and safe.

Cole slid over close beside her and whispered, "How are your knees?"

"They're a little bruised, but the pads have taken most of the abuse," she answered. At their last rest stop, Cole had cut his chaps up and fashioned knee pads for both of them to wear over their trousers. To protect their hands, they both had the heavy leather gloves that they usually wore during long rides.

"All right, from here on, I think we can risk walking instead of crawling, but I want you to stay farther back," Cole said. "Here, you take one end of this cord, and I'll have the other. We can put about fifteen feet between us, and if we keep it taut, we can use it to talk to each other. One jerk means stop, two means go."

"And how many jerks means run like hell because they've spotted us?" Mollie teased.

"I don't think you'll need any help to know when that time comes," Cole replied. "You'll get the idea when the lead starts flying."

The Osawatomie meandered through the valley. At times they were able to walk along the stones and occasional patches of sand at the edge of the water, but more often they found themselves wading in the foot-deep currents, struggling almost constantly for good footing in the muck that lined the creek bottom. Cole paused frequently to listen to the night sounds and to attempt to penetrate the darkness with his gaze, alert for any indication of danger, and twice he climbed up the edge of the bank to determine how much progress they had made. After the second check he doubled back to meet Mollie and reported that they were almost there.

Drawing up close to her, he whispered in her ear, "Still sure? It's not too late to turn around and get out of here."

"I'm all right," Mollie whispered. "I want to go on."

"OK. The creek makes a wide curve to the right, and then about ten yards further is the wall. Once we get there, we'll know more about what we have to do to get inside."

"Lead away then," Mollie said.

Cole kept them tight against the left bank, moving with extreme caution to avoid making any sound that might give them away. Every muscle in Mollie's body tensed as they drew closer to their destination, and her eyes continually swept the banks ahead, expecting at any moment to see men with guns appear and begin blasting away at them.

Finally, Mollie felt two short tugs on the cord, and then the line went slack. Cole had stopped and was signaling for her to come ahead. She moved forward until she was close beside him, both of them huddled tight against the left bank.

"The wall is right above us," Cole whispered. "You wait here while I check and see if there's any way to get inside. If there isn't, then we'll decide whether to climb the wall."

Mollie nodded, hoping with all her might that he would find something. The thought of crawling up out of this ditch at John Brown's doorstep and then trying to scale his defenses seemed almost suicidal at this point, and she was not sure she had the reserves of courage left that the act would require.

Cole eased away from her so slowly and quietly that his shadowy form seemed to dissolve in the darkness. Above her from somewhere within the compound, Mollie could hear the faint sound of two men talking, but they were too far away for her to understand what they were discussing. A moment later a pair of crickets began a chorus from the opposite bank, and away to the south a mockingbird demonstrated its medley of imitations.

It seemed that Cole was gone for hours before he finally returned. He eased up close to her and put his lips close to her ear. The news he delivered filled Mollie with relief. "Come on," he whispered. "I found a place that leads right under the wall." Then he turned and started away and Mollie hurried to follow.

The place Cole discovered was so cleverly concealed that Mollie was not sure she could have spotted it on her own. A small, stone-lined tunnel had been cut in the creek bank just above water level, with a thick holly bush planted directly in front of the entrance. As Cole led her into the tunnel, she discovered that it was built just big enough for a person to sit up inside without hitting his head.

"There's a reservoir or a cistern or something about ten feet farther along," Cole muttered. "It's so dark in here I almost fell in the damned thing before I realized it was there. And there's a ladder and a trapdoor down at the far end too, but I didn't open it to see where it leads."

"Well, we can't sit here all night," Mollie said. "Let's find out."

Cole led the way to a spot where the ceiling seemed to open into a vertical passageway. Mollie could never remember having experienced such absolute darkness in her life, but it was easy to feel her way along the smoothly mortared stones, and she was reassured by Cole's nearness and by his unwavering confidence. If they had made it this far along without being caught, she thought, surely they were meant to succeed. In another few hours they would be on their way home, their mission completed and their years of searching for Anson's murderer finally over.

Cole climbed the short ladder and pushed against the trapdoor above. At first he could not seem to get it open, and Mollie's heart sank as she thought that it might be barred or blocked from above. But then Cole put his shoulder to it, and Mollie heard what sounded like the trapdoor scraping open. A long, tense moment passed as Cole waited to see if there would be any response to the noise. Then when nothing happened, he opened the door further and stepped up another rung on the ladder.

"It's a room," he called down to her in a voice that was little more than a whisper. "Some kind of storage room, I think." He climbed another rung and moved the trapdoor back out of the way, then said, "Come on up. It's safe."

The room was about fifteen feet square, with log walls and an earthen floor. A door to their right led to the center of the compound, and two small windows on the same side gave them a view of the very heart of John Brown's stronghold. Mollie guessed that it was past midnight now, and most of the fires they had seen from the hilltop had died down to beds of glowing coals.

Spotting the clusters of sleeping people under the tarpaulins, Mollie said, "I had no idea there would be so many people here. I wonder who they are and why they're here?"

"They probably live around here," Cole guessed. "They might have come here for safety, or Old Brown might have called them in for some kind of meeting."

As Mollie continued to study the layout of the place through the small, dirty pane of glass, Cole examined the contents of the room. In a couple of minutes he was at Mollie's side. "Do you know what's along that back wall? Kegs of powder, lead bars, and bags of shot. And there's a case of rifles back there too. Damned if we haven't stumbled into Old Brown's armory. Why, one fuse lit in the right place and we could blow half his fortress right off the map."

"Yes, but that's not what we came to do," Mollie reminded him. "We're here to kill Boone Septin — and to get out of here alive. Let's leave the demolition to somebody else."

"I know," Cole chuckled. "So do you have any ideas?"

"I was just wondering," Mollie began, "how many people do you think are here right now?"

"I don't know. Fifty or sixty from the looks of things. Maybe even more."

"A lot anyway," Mollie agreed. "And I bet not everybody out there knows everybody else. And as dark as it is, it's hard to make out faces —"

"Are you thinking that we could just walk right out there and look around for him?" Cole asked.

"Not we. The guards would probably challenge any man they didn't recognize, but I doubt if they'd think twice about a woman they didn't know. By myself, I bet I could go almost anywhere I wanted."

"I hate that idea, Mollie." Cole's voice was hard.

"Then come up with a better one," she challenged. "Maybe we could just wait here by the windows with our guns cocked and hope he walks by so we can shoot him."

"Damn it, Mollie —"

"It's our best chance, Cole," Mollie insisted. "We haven't got all night, you know. We've got to be back down that tunnel and out of here before daylight or we'll be in a mess for sure."

"I still hate the idea, but I guess you're right," Cole conceded. "You'll have to leave your rifle here, but you can hide my pistol under your shirt."

"OK, and I want to take your knife too," Mollie said. "If he's asleep when I find him . . ."

Cole passed the weapons to her without waiting for her to finish. It was clear that he was upset about her going out alone, but there was little he could do about it. From this point on, the success of their enterprise was in Mollie's hands. After concealing the weapons inside her clothing, she gave him a final hug and was out the door before he could come up with any last-minute objections.

There were still enough people moving around the compound that nobody paid Mollie much attention as she crossed to one of the bonfires. A few of the people who were still awake at this late hour had gathered to share one another's company, and two of the armed guards had just come over from their positions at the wall to drink a cup of coffee. A couple of conversations were going on nearby, so Mollie decided just to listen for a while before she tried to speak to anybody.

The two guards were talking about some sort of memorial service that had apparently taken place earlier that evening, and Mollie soon discovered that Boone Septin had been in charge of the service. Any lingering doubts in her mind about whether Septin was still here were extinguished.

"The man's got a way with words, I'll give you that," one of the guards said. He was a tall fellow with a full beard covering the bottom half of his face. He held a Sharps rifle tucked up casually under one arm. "But I still say there's some things about him I just don't trust. Like how did he know where all them proslavers lived? And was it just a coincidence that so many of our fellows got killed when he was the one that led them over there? Something about the man sticks in my gut like a handful of green apples."

"Hell, you don't trust nobody anyway, Carl," his companion chided him. "I'd be surprised if you *wasn't* suspicious of this Reverend Septin, but in my book he's still an all right fellow. Any man that gets as fired up about slavery as he does just has to be against it right down to his soul."

Mollie almost laughed out loud as she recalled the many fiery sermons she had heard Boone Septin preach against the evils of abolitionism. It was possible that he had experienced a change of heart since leaving Missouri, she thought, but more likely he had just turned his bread over once he got into Kansas so he could get the other side buttered. His stock in trade, it seemed, was in telling people exactly what they wanted to hear.

But hearing about Septin's deceptions wasn't putting her any closer to finding out where he was, so Mollie decided it was time to get a little bolder with her search. She sidled around the edge of the fire to where the guards stood and said, "I heard you talking about Reverend Septin, and I was wondering if either of you knew where he is right now. I have something I need to talk to him about."

Both of the guards looked at her closely enough to make her feel uncomfortable, but neither asked any questions.

"Up until a day or so ago," one of the men responded, "he was bedding down in that little storm cellar over there." He pointed as he spoke to a small structure on the east side of the compound. It appeared to be half buried in the ground, with a berm of dirt across the top to serve as insulation from both summer sun and winter cold. Such cellars were common in this part of the country, serving double duty as storm shelters and root cellars for food storage. "But now that we got that prisoner locked up in there, I don't know where he's sleeping."

"Seems like I seen him go into Mr. Brown's house

a couple of hours ago. They're meeting late over there tonight, and I expect he's sitting in."

"Then I guess I'd better not disturb him if that's where he is," Mollie replied.

"Prob'ly not," the man agreed.

Mollie was curious about the prisoner the first guard had mentioned but decided not to press her luck by asking any more questions. She had enough problems just trying to figure out what to do about getting to Septin without taking on any others. Whoever the poor devil in the storm cellar was, he would just have to fend for himself.

The guards took a few more sips of their coffee, then poured the dregs onto the fire and wandered back to their posts. Mollie remained where she was, no longer certain about where to go or what she should do. She certainly couldn't march right into John Brown's house in search of her quarry, but she was beginning to feel vulnerable about remaining out in the open. Eventually somebody was bound to get curious and start asking her some very difficult questions. It would have been nice to go back and talk the situation over with Cole, but she didn't want to risk being seen going and coming from the armory too often.

Finally she decided to let some time pass and see if anything encouraging happened. It was late now, and the meeting Septin was in, if indeed he was in a meeting, was bound to break up soon. If that happened, he might come out. There was always a chance that things might still turn in her favor. With that in mind, she moved over under the tarpaulin shelter closest to Brown's front door and sat down with her back against one of the thick support poles.

A long, tense hour passed. The last few holdouts eventually drifted away to bed, and then the only movement inside the quiet compound came from the wandering guards who patrolled the walls. Once in a while a man came in from his guard post on the hillside and another went out to take his place, but Mollie paid them little attention, knowing that a man like Septin would religiously avoid any chore as dangerous as guard duty around this place was likely to be.

She decided at last that she would have to abandon her vigil soon if she and Cole were to make it away safely before daylight. It was disappointing to have come so far only to be thwarted at the last minute, but leaving for the night didn't mean they would have to go all the way home to Missouri. There was always tomorrow night, and the next night, and the next . . . As long as Boone Septin remained here and their entry remained undetected, there was no reason why she couldn't keep trying until she got the opportunity she wanted. It amused her to consider that she might even become acquainted with enough of the people inside the compound that she could move around freely among them.

She was so caught up in her own thoughts that it took her a moment to pick up the sound of pounding hoofbeats on the hillside. At about the same time that she started paying attention, the rest of the compound began to come alive. As he neared, the rider shouted out his name, and the guards at the main entrance, apparently recognizing him, swung the gates open.

People on all sides of Mollie were beginning to stir and rise in alarm as the man thundered right up to the steps of John Brown's house, leaped to the ground, and began shouting for Brown to come out.

An instant later a man appeared at the door, rifle in hand. Mollie had seen John Brown only once before, on the night he had visited Jason's farm and terrified his family, but she recognized him immediately. As he stepped out into the open, three other men followed onto the porch. Mollie's gaze narrowed, and her hand went instinctively toward her hidden weapons as she recognized the spindly form of Boone Septin standing behind and slightly to the left of Brown.

"They're coming!" the rider announced breathlessly to Old Brown. "Hundreds of them! A whole damn army of them!"

Nobody bothered to ask *who* was coming. Everybody knew. Instead, Brown marched down the steps to where the messenger stood and said, "All right, just stay calm now, boy. The first thing I want to know is how far away they are."

"No more than three miles west of here," the man announced. "We jumped their outriders just down the road from the Mathis place, and before we knew what was happening, it seemed like the sky started raining bullets. They killed Mike Perry and Gil Simpson right off, and the rest of us scooted right out of there."

"So where are the others?" Brown asked.

"One of them cut off toward Lawrence to spread the word, and the other two fell back to see if they could pick off a few of their lead men. I rode straight here to warn you."

"And you say there's hundreds?" Brown asked. "You *saw* hundreds?"

"I don't know how many I saw, Mr. Brown," the man said excitedly. "When the shooting started, they spread out on a skirmish line that seemed half a mile wide. They were all over the place, like hornets pouring out of a hive, and they're headed straight here!"

"All right, there's two things we're not going to do," Brown announced to the people who were quickly assembling around him. "We're not going to panic, and we're not going to fall at their feet like sheep the way Lawrence did last year. If they think they're going to take this place away from us, then I hope they came prepared to pay the price!"

As Brown continued speaking, Mollie edged forward

so she could hear what was going on and keep a close eye on Septin. She had an idea that if serious trouble was heading in this direction, Boone Septin would make an effort to get away as soon as he had the chance. What he had no way of knowing, of course, was that as soon as he separated himself from the rest of Brown's forces, she and Cole Younger would be on him like two starving wolves. He wouldn't get away from them this time.

Brown's first order was to send some of his forces out to create a delaying action against the invaders. Then he began to organize an effort to evacuate as many women and children from the compound as possible before the attack came. He speculated, and rightly so, Mollie thought, that the Missourians would avoid harming the families of Brown's supporters if they could, so the idea was simply to get them out of the compound and into the surrounding countryside, where they could make their way to their homes on their own.

Brown's people fell to their various tasks with surprising speed and discipline. Within a few short minutes after the arrival of the messenger, a party of about a dozen men were riding out to harass the Missourians and the first wagonloads of women and children were starting out the gate.

When Mollie saw Boone Septin slip away into the crowd, she started after him, knowing he was probably ready to make his escape. If there was a chance, she thought, she would go get Cole and tell him what was going on, but if not, she would do what must be done by herself.

She was so intent on keeping her eye on Septin that she passed through the crowd only a few feet from where John Brown stood issuing a stream of orders. But none of that made any difference to her now. All that mattered was not losing sight of her prey until the moment came when he was alone and she could take out the gun she carried . . .

"Kill the prisoner. I know he must have played some part in this treachery. I want you to kill Jason Hartman before he slips through our grasp again!" The words, spoken by Brown to one of the men near him, stopped Mollie dead in her tracks. For a moment she found it difficult to believe what she had just heard. How could it be? How could Jason possibly be a captive here?

In the next instant, though, Mollie realized that this was no time to try and figure things out. It was a time for action, and she would have to do something fast if she hoped to save her brother's life.

"All right, Papa. I'll just go in the house and get my shotgun, and then I'll take care of it."

Mollie turned in time to see the man who was charged with the duty of killing her brother disappear inside the front door of John Brown's house. She didn't wait for him to come back out. Instead she turned and hurried away to the building where, she hoped Cole Younger was still waiting for her to return.

Her heart sank as she approached the door of the armory. Men were moving steadily in and out the door, distributing arms and ammunition in preparation for the assault.

"Mollie! Over here!" a dark form stirred in the shadows between two buildings.

Mollie hurried over and threw her arms around the neck of her friend. Tears welled in her eyes as she sobbed, "Oh, Cole! For a minute I thought you must have . . . I didn't know what to think . . ."

"It's all right, girl," Cole told her. "When I heard what was going on, I knew I'd better get out of there fast, so I slipped out here. But what about Septin? Right now is the perfect time to get him, but we're going to have to get it done and get out fast before all hell breaks loose —"

"Forget him, Cole," Mollie said urgently. "I just found out that Jason's here! Don't ask me why or how, because I don't know. But he's locked up over there, and I just heard John Brown order one of his sons to kill him!"

"Come on then. Let's find him and get him out of here. After they've gotten what they need from that storage room," Cole said, "we can probably slip back down through that tunnel and leave the same way we came in."

As they hurried across the compound toward the storm cellar where Jason was imprisoned, they heard the rattle of gunfire. Apparently, Brown's front-line troops had met the Missourians, and the battle had begun.

16

Jason stood with his ear pressed against the plank door of the storm cellar, trying to hear what he could.

It didn't take a genius to figure out what was happening. The flurry of late-night activity inside the compound, the the chatter of distant gunfire that had started only minutes earlier, could only mean one thing. David Atchison's army was near, and the forces that John Brown had under his command were preparing to make a final, desperate challenge.

This battle had been inevitable, but he had hoped to be far away from here before it started. Now, though, looking at the situation with cold-eyed clarity, he realized that his own chances of survival were slim indeed. He had gambled his life for the sake of his family's future safety, and he had lost the bet.

He stepped back toward the center of the small, damp chamber when he heard the sound of somebody working with the chain and padlock that secured the door. In a moment the door scraped open, and he saw the outline of a man standing in the opening, straining to peer into the darkness. By the light of a fire that blazed brightly several dozen feet away, Jason could see that his unwelcome visitor held a rifle or shotgun at the ready.

Every instinct told Jason to attack immediately, while he still had the darkness working for him. There was always a chance that he could get his hands on the man's gun and wrestle it out of his grasp, and then he could . . . But what could he do? Go outside and die instead of dying here? There was the remote chance that he could take this fellow and then perhaps kill one or two more of Brown's supporters as well, but what would it accomplish?

"Don't think I can't see you back there, Hartman, because I can," the man in the doorway warned. "Are you going to take this like a man?"

"What choice do I have?" Jason asked.

"No more than our friends had when you bastards hung them in Independence."

Jason knew that there was no use arguing at this point. And in a way, he thought, he had taken part in the executions in Independence simply by the fact that he had not stepped forward to oppose them. It was all so maddeningly confusing, and all so pointless.

The man raised the weapon to his shoulder and aimed it at Jason. As his intentions became immediately obvious, Jason struggled against the sudden impulse to plead for his life. In the past, when it was he holding the gun and threatening another man with death, he had always felt a deep revulsion when his victim began to beg and whimper, babbling desperate promises and supplications, but now he thoroughly understood the impulse. Perhaps if he vowed one last time never to oppose the forces of abolitionism or told the man how desperately his wife and children needed him —

"You got anything to say, Hartman?"

Outside in the compound the men stationed around the walls were beginning to open fire. Apparently, Atchison's forces must have reached the surrounding hillsides, and the final showdown was about to begin. But the man in the doorway was so intent upon his mission that even that did not distract him.

"Nothing that would make any difference," Jason answered, hating the obstruction in his throat that made his voice thick with emotion.

Jason saw only a brief flutter of movement in the doorway behind his executioner before the shotgun exploded.

"Noooooo!" Mollie wailed, her voice filled with pain and despair.

Cole's charge had carried him and the man in the doorway into the storm cellar, and they lay now in a heap on the floor, locked in a furious, deadly contest for control of the shotgun. Mollie leaped over them, nearly falling on top of their tangled bodies, mindless of everything except the need to get to her brother. If only they had reached the cellar a second earlier, she thought. If only they had not been quite so cautious in making their way across the compound from the armory, they might have got here before the murderous shotgun blast was fired.

Out of the darkness a stout arm flung her roughly aside, and a form plunged past her. For a moment it was impossible to tell what was happening in the melee by the door, but then, suddenly, the fight was over as quickly as it had started. A shape rose from the heap, and then another. A third body lay unmoving between them.

"Cole? Is that really you? Then the one I knocked out of the way must be —"

"Jason! You're alive!" Mollie squealed. She leaped forward, locking her arms around her brother's neck and smothering him with tearful kisses. "I thought we were too late," she sobbed. "When I heard that gun go off —"

"What is it with you two?" Jason asked in utter amazement. "Do you just go anywhere you want any time you want?"

"We'll be glad to explain the whole thing," Cole told him hurriedly. "But not now, and not here. Come on!"

With Cole in the lead, the three of them made their way cautiously back out into the open. Guns were blasting away from all four walls now, and the attackers on the hillsides were responding with one furious fusillade after another.

The trio paused for an instant to take stock of the situation, but nobody seemed to have noticed the single shotgun blast in the storm cellar. Looking around, Jason saw that several fires on the hillsides nearby illuminated the figures of the mounted men, making them clear targets for the defensive fire from with the compound. Apparently, Brown had ordered that his own crops of wheat and corn be put to the torch to provide light for the battle.

"This way," Cole ordered, rushing off across the compound toward a log building on the south side. Although Jason could not imagine how they planned to get away, he followed without question, understanding that they must already have an escape route in mind. Bullets peppered the interior of the compound like hailstones, but it was no time for caution. Despite the battle somebody was bound to discover them soon if they didn't get out of sight and out of this place as quickly as possible.

When they reached the log building, Cole plunged through the open doorway, with Mollie and Jason close on his heels. Cole entered with his pistol ready, but the place was empty. A lamp burned dimly on a nearby bench, providing just enough light to illuminate the interior. Cole moved immediately to the center of the room, flung a trapdoor open, and started into the darkened hole below.

"Hold it!" an angry voice demanded from the doorway. "Just stop where you are!"

Jason glanced up and was shocked to see his brother Charles standing there. The rifle he held in his hand was levelled at the three fugitives, and his finger was on the trigger.

"Don't shoot, Charles!" Jason exclaimed. "It's me. It's your brother Jason. And this woman here is Mollie, your sister." Out of the corner of his eye he saw that Cole was about to raise his revolver for a shot, but Jason stopped him with a slight shake of his head.

"I know who you are," Charles replied. "You killed my boys!"

"I didn't kill them, Charles," Jason cried. "It was me that brought them home so they could be buried near their family."

"It's all lies," Charles snarled. "Everything you've said since you came here was a lie!" His face, illuminated in the lamplight, was a mask of anger and madness. "He corrupted you. I saw that he was leading you down his devilish, infernal path, and I hoped to stop him before he ruined you, but we got to him too late."

"Then you knew about it?" Jason asked. "You knew that those raiding parties were going to kill William and me? How could you let that happen, Charles? How could you live with yourself knowing that?"

"He had to die," Charles explained. "And because of what you had become, the same was true for you. It was an issue more important than any accident of birth. And now my task is to complete what so many others have failed to do."

"But what about Mollie, Charles? What about your sister? Will your insane hatred and grief bring you to the point of killing your own sister as well?"

No trace of feeling crossed Charles's features as his gaze shifted to the young woman who stood beside Jason. She was nothing to him and certainly not a person whose life should be spared for the sake of family ties. That look said more than words ever could about how far beyond the realm of reason and sanity their brother had journeyed.

Jason leaned slightly to one side and in one swift movement caught up the lamp and hurled it at his brother. Charles was able to duck to avoid being hit, but his clothes were splashed with oil as the lamp crashed against the wooden door frame. In an instant he was engulfed in flames.

The rifle dropped, forgotten, from Charles's hands as he clawed at his flaming garments, roaring out his agony as he turned and staggered off across the compound.

"Help him, Jason!" Mollie cried. "Do something! He's still our brother!"

Wordlessly, Jason went to the doorway and picked up the rifle his brother had dropped only a moment before. Charles was more than thirty feet away now, his head and body consumed with yellow flames. He was still on his feet, stumbling along like a living torch, his arms waving wildly in the air as his legs and feet propelled him senselessly forward. The sounds that came from him scarcely resembled anything human.

Jason drew a careful bead on his brother's back and squeezed the trigger.

A thick carpet of grass covered the smooth mound of earth beneath which William Hartman lay buried. The fresh flowers piled around the headstone marked a recent visit by Mollie. Jason stared down at the grave, lost in thought. Now, though more than a month had passed since William's death, he still found it difficult to believe that his brother rested beneath that pile of dirt.

A hand slid softly into Jason's, and suddenly Arethia was beside him. He and his family had been on their way home from town when he decided to stop and visit his brother's grave. Glancing over, he saw that she was staring not at the grave but at him. Tears glistened in her eyes and she shared his pain.

"I guess the letter has reached Daddy by now," Jason said.

"It's been five weeks," Arethia said softly. "I'm sure he knows now."

That letter had been without doubt the most difficult composition Jason had ever undertaken. With every line he put down, he ached with the knowledge of how devastating it would be to his father to learn, in one blow, that two of his sons had died. But equally as painful as the words that Jason put down were the ones he left out. He had written simply that his two brothers had died in the recent fighting. In his heart, Jason hoped their father would go to his own grave without ever having to hear the full truth about the manner in which William and Charles had died.

"I'm still not sure how I'm going to go about living with all this," Jason admitted quietly to his wife. "Sometimes I almost wish I was there in the ground with them. It would be so much easier than carrying around the knowledge of what I did for the rest of my life."

"You'll learn to handle it as time goes by," Arethia assured him. "You'll understand it better, and some day you'll know in your heart that you had no choice. You didn't just save your own life over there, you know. You also saved Mollie's and probably Cole's as well."

Arethia was one of the few people in the world who knew exactly what had taken place that night in John Brown's fortress. Both Mollie and Cole had sworn never to tell anybody about the way Charles died, but there was never any question in Jason's mind that he must tell his wife everything. He would have to draw on her strength and love to survive.

But some things were starting to get better, Jason had

to admit. Even the assault on John Brown's compound had not turned into as severe a bloodbath as it might have been, and the entire episode had provided the impetus for what could become a breakthrough in the tragic border war.

Somehow, Brown's forces had managed to hold out even against the heavy assault by such overwhelming numbers of Missourians. After the first heavy charge, and then a less determined second, David Atchison had realized that his casualties were much greater than he or any of his subordinates had anticipated. Watching so many of their fellows fall, his men had become dispirited and had refused to take part in a third ride down the bloody hillsides.

After dispatching their dead and wounded on the long journey back to Missouri, they had bivouacked for the night out of range of Brown's deadly Sharps rifles, and a relative calm overtook the area. Desertions were rampant that night, and by morning Atchison found himself in command of scarcely enough men to carry out a proper siege. By then, further attacks were out of the question, and it was becoming evident that the entire expedition was turning into a fiasco.

By the time a contingent of troops arrived from Fort Leavenworth the following day, Atchison and his remaining supporters were more than willing to comply with the military commander's order to return home.

Jason had heard all of this only secondhand. After escaping that night, he, Mollie, and Cole had slipped through the lines of the Missourians and headed straight for home.

Days later the abolitionist raid into Missouri and the invasion by Atchison finally brought action from the federal, state, and territorial authorities. Soldiers with orders to shoot to kill now patrolled the most hotly contested border areas, and the Missouri legislature had hurriedly passed a bill outlawing all private militias, such as the one Atchison, William, and Younger had led.

And in Kansas, the territorial authorities made it clear to men such as John Brown that their lawless activities could no longer be condoned under the umbrella of the abolitionist cause. The most sensible leaders among them were beginning to realize that, with Kansas now firmly in antislavery hands, it was only a matter of time until the territory was admitted to the Union as a free state and that further bloodshed would only damage their cause.

Those four days of lawlessness and slaughter had finally made it clear to the leadership on both sides of the border that things had simply got out of hand.

After several days at home, Jason finally started going through the motions of living again. He began to catch up on all the work around his farm that had been so sadly neglected throughout the summer, and together he and Arethia also started the long process of restoring the bonds of love and commitment that had once held his family together. Soon the crops would be ready for harvesting, and he was actually anticipating the long hours of relentless labor as an escape from the mental torment that had plagued him so often since his return from Kansas.

Mollie was talking about leaving. Jason and Arethia had hoped that soon she and Cole might start talking about marriage, but for some unexplained reason the two young people didn't seem interested in steering their lives in that direction. Mollie had it in mind to begin working as a seamstress in some nearby town, perhaps Independence or Kansas City, and Cole was talking about making a trip to Texas to buy a herd of horses.

Now, looking down at his brother's grave, Jason could not help but wonder what the future might hold for all of them. A truce of sorts had been forced upon the combatants on both sides of the border, but nothing had been done to resolve the conflicts that lay behind the four-year border war. He prayed each night that after all the losses they had suffered, at least his family's part in the struggle was ended, but there was no reassurance even of that. The hatred was still there, festering like an open wound, and as long as men like John Brown and David Atchison were allowed to hold sway, there would be no real refuge from the danger.

"Come on, Jason," Arethia urged him quietly. "The children are waiting in the wagon, and it's getting toward supper time." She tugged gently at his sleeve, pulling him, in her wonderful way, out of the past and into the present. "It's time to go home."

HERE IS YOUR CHANCE TO ORDER SOME OF OUR BEST

HISTORICAL ROMANCES

BY SOME OF YOUR FAVORITE AUTHORS

WESTERNS

JOHN BALL
AUTHOR OF **IN THE HEAT OF THE NIGHT** INTRODUCING, **POLICE CHIEF JACK TALLON** IN THESE EXCITING, FAST-PACED MYSTERIES.

FREE!!
BOOKS BY MAIL
CATALOGUE

BOOKS BY MAIL will share with you our current bestselling books as well as hard to find specialty titles in areas that will match your interests. You will be updated on what's new in books at no cost to you. Just fill in the coupon below and discover the convenience of having books delivered to your home.

PLEASE ADD $1.00 TO COVER THE COST OF POSTAGE & HANDLING.

BOOKS BY MAIL

320 Steelcase Road E.,
Markham, Ontario L3R 2M1

210 5th Ave., 7th Floor
New York, N.Y., 10010

Please send Books By Mail catalogue to:

Name _____
(please print)

Address _____

City _____

Prov./State _____ P.C./Zip _____

(BBM1)